The Road of Fathers

By Steven R. Barron

Acknowledgements

The author would like to thank the following for their support:

Special thanks to my editor, Lisa Clausen for amazing guidance and wisdom

Timothy W. Farrell

Holly Candage

Tricia Barrett

Jen Renee Paulson

Brian Kennemer

Bud Lee

James Van Damme

Jennifer Jack Kinsey

Sho Shana

Celia Townsend

Amber Seyler

Linda Ode

John O'Reilly

Albert Cook

Cover Illustration: Taylor Barron

Cover text/design: Theresa Domingo

Map Design and Illustration: Timothy Farrell

And a very special thank you for support to John O'Reilly and Brian Albright

eBook Conversion and paperback layout: Bill Raymond at www.opticalauthoring.com

Copyright

Map of the Kazhan Empire

Cast of Characters

The Great River Forest

- Tyrian Fellhawk
- Wolf
- Cabatic Fellhawk, Tyrian's father
- Petter Fellhawk, Tyrian's uncle, the second eldest Fellhawk and the patriarch
- Alshanna Fellhawk, Petter's wife
- Oskar Fellhawk, Tyrian's uncle
- Jeshon Fellhawk, Tyrian's uncle
- Didrik Fellhawk, Tyrian's uncle
- Sverre Fellhawk, Tyrian's uncle
- Vegard Fellhawk, Tyrian's uncle
- Djuri Fellhawk, Tyrian's cousin
- Ol' Kragin Ullnik, shopkeeper in Battgadl Square
- Clans of the Great River Forest
- Fellhawk
- Grock
- Ustin
- Ullnik

Coteville

- Heir Gabriel Theobald, Governor of Coteville and 121st in line to the Azjik Throne
- Océane Theobald, Gabriel's wife
- Anjelain Theobald, Gabriel's eldest daughter
- Beatrice Theobald, Gabriel's daughter
- Nicitania Theobald, Gabriel's daughter
- Gabriel Theobald II, Gabriel's son
- Andoni, Cote Militia Soldier
- Leonce, Cote Militia Scout
- Dechaume, Cote Militia Officer
- Nicodème, Cote Militia Officer
- Croucien, Cote Militia Officer
- Déodat, Cote Militia Officer
- Placide, Cote Militia Officer
- Theirn, Cote Militia Officer

Fulldalr

- Heir Kreistle Volkummen, Governor of Fulladlr, and 120th in line to the Azjik Throne
- Greit Schultheis, Volkummen's first lieutenant
- Roserie Argaune, ex-counselor of King Azjik and wizard

The Three Riders

- Gorka Osa, Anarchist leader of a band of mercenaries
- Babbel, mercenary from the foothills of the Jotun Peaks
- Dò bbeldam, mercenary from the Grytician Valley

Castle Azjik

- King Konik Azjik, King of the known world, descendant of The Kazhan Dynasty
- Farafah Fruz, trusted counselor of King Azjik and secret partner of Argaune
- Margda, slave woman
- Serena, slave girl
- Enut, governor of the Vilczyyz Tents, home of the Desert Pirates

Chapter One

"There, in the dawn, the hero found his King, like an animal finds its food…"

- From the Book of Tribes

The Fellhawk Road began at the gates of the clan's compound and led into the depths of the Great River Forest. The first several strides along the road were lined with pale green cabbage shrubs and crimson hyacinths, serving more as a welcome home than a warm send-off; the Fellhawks enjoyed returning home far more than beginning a journey.

At sixteen years, Tyrian Fellhawk knew this road better than any of his clan: he travelled it every day for work; he spent his leisure time wandering its many subsidiary pathways, clearing and maintaining all of it. He recognized every dip and gash. The bulky wagons that carried split wood, and the heavy brunblakk dray horses that pulled them, chipped away at the smooth surface he took so much pride in. He made a mental note of every hole to fill later. And he would always take a moment to clear the fallen leaves to the side, if only for appearance.

Indeed, the well-cared-for soil of the Fellhawk Road felt comforting and familiar beneath his feet. The dirt smelled sweet, unlike the musty forest soil beyond. It was *his* road more than anyone else's, he thought. But for the boy the road leading away from the Fellhawk compound was exactly that—a road away; it was his garden, a living thing to cultivate that provided peace and solitude for him. In other ways, with his clan having no structured faith, the road served as an altar for him where he could physically kneel and pray. The moist soil absorbed the boy's nomadic anger.

It seemed at times to Tyrian that besides the wiry dog, Wolf, the road was his only friend. It guided him through the forest, protected him as if he was born of the road itself. It was also an escape from the taunts of his cousins or the whispers of sympathy from his aunts. Being motherless, he was seen as an orphan. And although his father still lived, Cabatic Fellhawk's self-imposed exile painted the boy as fatherless. Because of this, Tyrian bore the angry mark of a boy too soon become a man.

Tyrian stood a full head taller than other boys his age. He carried on his back a well-cared-for wood-cutting axe. Although the handle was worn and faded, the blade itself was sharp and clean. The axe was heavy, clumsy, and, like nearly everything that made up his life, was made simply for splitting wood.

In the commerce of the Great River Forest, the Fellhawk clan ran the wood trade. The older uncles felled the trees, the young men split the wood, and the youngest boys stacked it. Tyrian was a splitter, and he was probably the hardest worker of all of the boys his age. Where most boys worked in teams, he was more comfortable by himself, accompanied of course by his counterpart, Wolf.

Midway through this day, as on every other day, boy and dog were hungry. Tyrian dropped to the grassy floor, tired, as Wolf snatched up a small bundle from their pack. The grey beast dropped it into Tyrian's lap, then, as was their ritual, licked the boy's calloused hands clean. Tyrian laid out a pile of meat scraps and vegetables that Wolf slowly and methodically lapped up. The boy, meanwhile, devoured his meat pastry quickly. He snuck a slice of meat from Wolf, then leaned back against a rotted stump, one of a thousand round pillars of remembrance; they had a certain sorrow about them.

Tyrian looked over at the two pensive, strapping horses that stood a short distance away, bound to the cart of split wood. They could have been twins, with their chestnut-colored, coats, save for the creamy white mane on one, and the darker brown on the other. Both stared soberly into the gaping chasm of the never-ending forest, gnawing at hay from buckets set at their feet.

Tyrian dozed off, losing his battle with fatigue. Sleep, and the familiar green canopy, closed in on him as his eyes fell shut. His thoughts turned toward the road beyond the forest. The great road, the Road of Fathers. He could see the mysterious Zanagar Dragon that patrolled the stark mountain skies. The poisonous desert serpents that burrowed through the vast dry desert. The gray-skinned, mountain people he was told of, like ghost stories, in his youth. The lost tribe of High Elves, dead for four generations. And beyond, the Serpents Grave Desert, near the gates of King Azjik's capital, where someday he swore he would stand guard as a proud soldier.

This was his time for heroic, adventurous dreams; the nighttime brought dark, uncontrolled images of a marauding clan burning his homestead, the screams of his mother, his father's eyes, red with anger. Or were they actually memories?

During the day, with Wolf lying protective at his side, he let his mind relax. The cool air on his cheek and the dank scents of moss and maple calmed him. He absent-mindedly stroked the back of Wolf's neck and the dog's tongue dangled in a smile. He knew that the Fellhawk Road eventually led to the Road of Fathers, but he had never travelled it. It was the grand highway commissioned by ten kings. For several decades it was named after the first King Darciux, who was the original monarch to envision it and mandate its construction. But, during a reign of populist fervor, King Darciux IV renamed it The Road of Fathers, in honor of every generation of man who had helped clear it. It seemed it had been under construction for so long that everyone's father and their father's father had worked on it.

Tyrian imagined what the Road of Fathers must be like. Green, lush grass, perfectly cut to feel soft on one's bare feet, lined with foreign flowers of unimaginable colors. The sweetest dream for him was simply walking its length and never stopping.

The Road of Fathers began at the gates of the king's castle and wound through his territory until it hauntingly vanished within the dank rainforest mud of The Great River Forest. The Great River Forest was a vast swath of canopied land that covered almost the entire northeastern quarter of the known world.

The Great River itself ran directly through the forest, cutting it almost in half diagonally from the northeast to the southwest. It was a wide and raging river at its heart and yielded countless varieties of fish. On Tyrian's birthdays his Uncle Petter would take him to the Great River to fish its rushing waters, and on these anniversaries the boy let go of his resentments. And Petter treated him as if he were his own son.

And so Tyrian spent the remainder of his lunch break in dreams of the lands beyond his clan's reach. Lately he had been thinking about the Lost Tribe of High Elves. His father, in their secret lessons, taught him of the Elf Wars, generations before. When men were a minority race in the civilized lands, and the three tribes of Elves ruled the lands. There were the Yellow Elves, distant and cold, known for their strange night rituals, singing to the moon. Daylight saw little of them, and heard even less. They were also known as the Quiet Elves. They uttered few words and their language was made up mostly of hand signs, intricate facial expressions and head movements. They were by no means mute, for they had beautiful singing voices.

Then there were the Red Elves, vicious and violent. They were constantly testing the borders of their Desert kingdom. They were skilled at the Elf weapon of bow and arrow. But they also excelled at sword play. They were solely carnivores and hunted beasts for food. They hunted humans for sport.

Lastly, there were the High Elves. They were the proudest, the brightest and most civilized. Their kingdom was well-protected. They had a successful flow of trade with the Yellow Elves to the West, the tribes of men in the north, and the mountain villages of dwarves. They had an intricate court system, commerce and order of laws.

Tyrian's father described the ten-year war in which all three tribes fought each other for rule over the known lands. The High Elves held the upper hand and legend has it they destroyed all of the Red Elves and most of the Yellow or Silent Elves. But they had disappeared. None of the three tribes had left much evidence of their existence. King Azjik's agents had scoured the lands and found coins, jewelry, weapons and tools, but there was scant evidence of their lost society.

In his daytime dreams, Tyrian fantasized about leading an expedition to uncover the remnants of their cities. The beautiful jewelry, art, weapons. He pictured himself riding through the golden gates of Azjik, leading a caravan of Elven riches. And his slumber carried him off.

# # #

Hours later, after loading all of his split wood into the cart, as the bleak daylight waned, he swatted the dray horses into action. The short trek was made longer by their slow, but determined, pace. Tyrian and Wolf walked a short distance ahead.

Halfway to the gates of the compound, always against his uncle's wishes, Tyrian wandered off the trail to his exiled father's secluded cabin. Uncle Petter never reprimanded the boy—he was careful not to tread on that bond—but on occasion firmly expressed his displeasure, for Cabatic had chosen his solitude.

Tyrian unloaded an armful of logs as his father greeted him with a wide toothless grin and a firm embrace. Wolf took his place on a matted bear rug outside the front door.

Tyrian threw a few logs on the fire as his father set out two bowls of soup and a pot of warm mushroom tea. It was his secret delicacy, a drink made from slices of a giant forest mushroom, cut in thin layers then soaked for days in Arabythian vodka, dried, then shredded and mixed with forest moss from the Great River and pine needles. It all came together in a smoky, earthy flavor that warmed the boy for the remaining trek home.

"Are you well, father?" the boy asked.

"As well as my years will allow, Tyrian. And how are you?"

"Tired. It seems as though the trees multiply overnight. For every one I cut down there are two more in their place the next day."

"Your hard work serves the clan well, boy."

Tyrian scanned the cluttered chaos of his father's abode.

"Father, how can you spend so much time alone?"

"My boy," his father replied, "we are born alone, we pass alone. And our afterlife is spent in complete solitude. We mistake companionship in our living age as being necessary—when in reality it is merely a luxury. We learn about others in company. But we learn the most vital truths about ourselves when we are alone."

There was a long pause, while Tyrian took in his father's words.

"I wish I was in the militia, father. I would rather be a soldier spreading justice, enforcing the King's word! Someday they will come and recruit me, will they not?" he asked, as he finished his soup and moved closer to the fire. He looked up at the books on his shelf. So many books. His father followed his gaze, then drew him back.

"Justice is never given, boy," his father replied.

"That is what the soldiers do. They set forth justice."

"True justice, boy, is earned."

"Man cannot be trusted to serve his own justice. That is what Uncle Petter says."

"I will not contradict the head of our clan, although I may respectfully disagree."

"But Father, you are the eldest."

"Petter is your father now. And I may be the eldest, but I gave up that post in mourning."

"Father, I feel as though I have no family."

"Tyrian, Petter is your father now. You must not confuse your feelings of hope with your feelings of loss. You must carry on as if this is the way it has always been."

"You are not even sorry for me, are you?"

"My sorrow does you no good."

"I would be in line to lead the clan someday, if you had not gone into mourning and exile."

"That is not reason for me to usurp my brother. We are a peaceful clan and I have chosen this life. You are better off with Petter. He will guide you now."

"Father, will you not give me the details of my mother's death and why you went into mourning?"

"Perhaps on your seventeeth year, Tyrian."

"Last year it was 'perhaps on my sixteenth year.'"

Tyrian's attention drifted back to the books against the wall. His father smiled proudly, observing his son's curiosity, a rare gift among the forest people.

"Did you finish the book I gave you, boy?"

"Almost, Father."

"You are not concentrating on what you read."

"I am, Father. That is why I read it slowly. For fear of missing something, I read each sentence twice."

Cabatic let out a loud laugh, filling the small room.

"I want to read your father's journals. I want to know about the battles in the desert and the battles in the mountains. I want to know of his time in the militia."

"You must finish what I gave you first. Adventure stories will mean nothing without knowledge of the land and philosophy and politics. All in good time, boy."

"I wish I would have known my grandfather," Tyrian sighed.

"Take heart in the family that you have. Not the family that you do not have."

"Uncle Petter teaches me nothing. He is no father."

# # #

As Tyrian approached the gates to the homestead, several herding dogs approached but were rebuffed by a snarling Wolf. The dog was far gentler with the young boys who ran to meet them at the gate.

The homestead sat in a distinct clearing and was made up of a vast compound of houses and stone shelters used to store the split wood and keep it dry. A low wooden fence marked the borders of the Fellhawk property. The decrepit barrier reached around the clearing and met at the gate, which arched high into the dank air, tall and crudely carved with the Fellhawk insignia, a regalia reserved for a respected forest clan. Its simple majesty was painted modestly with the green mold of the rain forest. Just beyond the gate lay a dirt field with patches of gardens for flowers, herbs, vegetables. Apple and plum trees leaned along the borders of the yard.

The main house sat at the very center of the compound and was larger than the other houses. In the traditional hierarchy of the clans in the Great River Forest, it was the one luxury afforded the family of the head—usually the eldest brother—but it also had the only kitchen and dining quarters for the entire clan.

Tyrian had barely reached the woodhouse when his cart was surrounded by the younger cousins, who unloaded his bounty. Other carts were now starting to approach, and the tired older cousins seemed to vanish into their houses, only to be replaced by the younger ones, still full of energy, like tiny worker ants.

As Tyrian made his way to the main house he was suddenly struck by the full weight of a stout six-year-old boy, his cousin Djuri. The boy held out a long wooden stick as threateningly as he was able to, but his clenched jaw and vicious snarl were betrayed by the mischievous gleam in his eye. The young boy lunged forward, but Tyrian swung his hip round and brought the butt of his axe backwards, blocking the blow. Djuri laughed and then stepped back, ready to spar.

"Not tonight, Djuri," Tyrian said, disappointing the boy. "I'm too tired to fight."

"Did you see your father, today?" Djuri asked.

"Shhhh," Tyrian hushed the boy. "You know I am not to see him." But then Tyrian smiled and winked at him, "Yes, I saw him."

"When will you take me to see him, Tyrian?"

"Someday, when you are older. And you can keep a secret. But for now you must finish your chores and clean up for supper." He spun the boy around and shoved him off. Without looking back, Djuri ran towards the main house, swinging his wooden sword as he went.

After washing, Tyrian crept up to the long, wooden dining table and took his place between his uncles Oskar and Jeshon. At the head of the table sat Petter Fellhawk, a man crouched over from long years of labor, the same work that was all that Tyrian had ever known—woodcutting. Before Petter sat the entire Fellhawk clan, the youngest ones at smaller tables off to the side.

This night the women had prepared a feast of roasted deer and potatoes with mushrooms and herbs. The harvest of fruits was nearly beyond ripe so, to the children's delight, the women had prepared a season-ending surprise; Tyrian could smell the warm apple and plum pies cooling in the kitchen.

"Uncle Petter," Tyrian said, quieting the adults at the table, for few bothered the elder during his meal.

"Yes, son," Petter looked up from his plate.

"Why have there been no Fellhawks in the Great River Forest Militia since my grandfather?"

"My father was a good man, but foolhardy in his thirst for adventure. Our clan has learned the wisdom of peace and hard work. We are here to provide fuel for fire and lumber for house-building. It is true that most of the clans in the Great River Forest are violent, unreasoning beings. But we pride ourselves in being better."

"But can one not fight for peace?"

"War and peace do not co-exist, Tyrian. One can either be for peace or for war, not for both."

"What if one were to choose a life of war so that the ones he loved could live a life of peace?"

Oskar gently, but firmly, gripped Tyrian's wrist. "Finish your food, nephew. Leave your uncle to his roast. Tomorrow you will go with me into Battgadl Square to sell."

"Your Uncle Didrik has felled a few trees just south of the August Pike," Petter said. "You will start on that first thing when you return. You should probably get an early start to bed tonight. There is plenty of work to be done."

Oskar continued, "And I trust you will leave Cabatic to his mourning tomorrow."

"My father no longer mourns," Tyrian snapped.

Tyrian pushed his plate aside, suddenly losing his appetite, then rose, bowing clumsily to his uncles.

"He chose to stay in exile for the peace of the clan. His mourning ended years ago," Tyrian declared as he left the room.

Tyrian rose early the next morning. He pulled his cousin Djuri from his sleep to help him ready the horses and their loads before his Uncle Oskar had risen. Djuri was all too happy to be with his cousin. An anxious Wolf met him in the main yard. The dog knew by the clean scent of Tyrian's trousers and blouse that he was not working and the dog would be on his own. They played a quick game of tug before Tyrian bid him farewell for the day. Tyrian sent Djuri back to bed and Wolf out into the forest.

"Stay out of trouble, Wolf. Go into the forest and leave the pups alone." The beast growled his discontent, then disappeared into the forest.

Oskar and Tyrian strolled alongside the horses and their carts. They both wore their trousers tucked into heavy leather boots, and dress scarves wrapped in a quick knot atop their blouse, their best merchant clothes. Oskar topped it off with a long leather cloak and a hat against the rain that was sure to come. There was a heavy stillness in the air, and although they could not see the clouds gathering above the tree canopy, it was darker than usual that day .

Every now and then Tyrian heard Wolf's panting in the distance and caught his image in the trees. He motioned the dog away, only to see him return, defiantly in the shadows.

"A nice break from your work today, eh boy?" Oskar said.

"Yes. I may buy a new axe, Uncle," Tyrian replied. "If ol' Kragin has anything worth more for cutting trees than for show!"

They both laughed.

"I respect the choice your father has made, Tyrian," Oskar said, after a distance passed in silence. Tyrian at first did not respond.

"We are all like your fathers now, my brothers and I," he tried again.

"And I really only want one father and many uncles."

Tyrian's head was down, watching his footsteps. He read the sorrow in his uncle's silence and reached over, grabbing his hand tightly for a brief moment.

"Thank you, Uncle."

The pressure in the air eased a bit as they could finally hear the light drumbeat of the rain high above their heads.

"Uncle Oskar," Tyrian's voice rose above the pattering of rain, "I want to know how my mother died."

"Your father has never told you?" Oskar was surprised.

"He puts it off every year. Am I not man enough to hear it? Is it such a horrible story to hear?"

"It may just be too horrible a story to tell."

Tyrian fell silent again. He had never considered his father's feelings in the matter.

"You were barely three years old, Tyrian," Oskar began. "Your father was the proudest man in the forest. He held you in his lap every free moment that he had. He fashioned a tiny wooden sword, blunt blade-edge, and put it in your hand, wrapping his own hand over yours to close the grip. It was a majestic image, as if he were a king raising an heir. Your father fancied you a warrior from the beginning."

Tyrian drank up his uncle's words, intoxicated by the description of a father he did not recognize.

"One evening, there was a rape in the forest. The youngest son of Fortis Grock, Small Vandor Grock, who was not so small at all, had broken into their neighbor's compound and attacked and raped a young girl. As Fellhawk Elder, and Magistrate of the Western Ridge, your father heard a grievance from the poor girl's father. It was a clear case and your father sent the youngest Grock into exile.

"Now the Grocks, as you know, are a violent clan, blood-thirsty, vicious. Although they honored his word by sending the boy into exile, they also exacted their own penalty in answer to your father's law. Fortis Grock and his clan rode into our compound one night, shouting the words, 'There is a price for your judgment,' into the darkness.

"They burned down one of the woodsheds and the horse barn, sending our steeds out into the panic of the night. And Fortis broke into your own house, into the very compound that now houses my brother, Petter. Fortis, with all his bulk, forced his way into your mother's room, and..."—he looked away from the boy, as if in shame—"...forced himself on your mother, and in his rage, squeezed the breath out of her. He would have smothered you, as well, had your father not broken free and cut Fortis down. But there lay his wife, your mother, sweet Maralla, still and vacant, as he held you close, crying and kicking. For those moments he held you as if you, too, were going to leave him.

"The sorrow and guilt were too much for him, and he wandered off into the forest that very night, Tyrian. Not to abandon you, but to save you an upbringing under the shadow of his pain."

"His sorrow has waned, though, Uncle Oskar," Tyrian said.

"It has merely burrowed itself deeper. Sorrow outlives our own material lives, boy."

"I need my father, though."

"Do not blame him, boy. He made a choice he thought was best for you. Whether that be true or not, only your manhood will answer. But, always know, he made a choice for your well-being alone."

Tyrian was quiet. He looked out at the green, brown foliage. He saw Wolf dart behind a line of shrubs. For once, he thought of the sorrow his father must have felt all these years.

Oskar stopped and turned to the boy, taking his shoulders firmly in his grip. "Those are the details of your mother's death, Tyrian. You must let your father reveal his own story in his own time. The facts are like rocks firmly planted in the dirt, they will never vanish. But you must let him give you the rest of it; he must give you his feelings and sorrow at his own pace."

The journey into town was not long—the road wound westward from the Great River towards a wide clearing along which all of the compounds bordered. All of the family roads intersected at Battgadl Square.

The storm above the forest canopy had closed in on the market-place. The rain had been pressuring the treetops for hours and had only now begun breaking through in inordinate patterns of rushes—like miniature waterfalls. The merchants and townspeople ran for cover or huddled under leather tarps. The dirt floor of the town square had quickly become muddied and slick.

As they entered the square, Oskar went directly to Kenzil Ustin's store to bargain the price of seven chugs of split wood and twenty jars of maple sap. It was a routine they went through each time, and the asking price never changed. It gave them a chance to share a small glass of birch brandy. Oskar and Kenzil Ustin had known each other since childhood and, in the ensuing years, found very little new to talk about. Their mutual stories had become as familiar a routine as their negotiations. Theirs were two of the only three "civilized" clans of the Great River Forest.

The first stop for Tyrian was the horse barn. He left the horses to be fed, washed and brushed, then he wandered the streets, hoping to run into a familiar face. He browsed a cobbler's shop first, then a horse stable and finally a blade shop. The walls were lined with long, beautiful broadswords and rounded shields.

"Tyrian Fellhawk," the swordsmith called out with a smile on his round face.

"Kragin," Tyrian answered, "what do you have to show me this week? I could use a new axe."

The stout swordtrader winked his one good eye and motioned the boy to come over. Opening a creaky cabinet door, he pulled out a long dirty cloth that was wrapped loosely around a mysterious, heavy object. He paused dramatically to make sure they were alone, then pulled a lantern closer. He carefully unwrapped the cloth and let it drop to the floor. In his hands he held a long, curved blade. Tyrian had never seen a weapon as strange and feminine as this. Kragin gently offered it to the boy, hilt first, and Tyrian took it in his hands. He gripped the rough handle, still tethered with fraying golden rope. He held it out before him and his eyes moved along its widening, curved blade all the way to its pointed end, which replicated a silver crescent moon. The reflective, almost mirror-like shine of the blade reflected the lantern's flame into his eyes.

"I've never seen a weapon such as this, Old Kragin. Is it a woman's sword?"

Kragin threw his head back in laughter. "This is the weapon of the desert people, boy. This is what the royals of the great dry ocean fight with."

"But how?"

"Only they could know. It was found in the booty of a band of slain Mountain Pirates. I took it off of a hungry trader not two nights ago."

"You'll not sell this then, Kragin! You must keep this!"

"I'm a merchant! I've no need for things. Things are to be sold."

The bell on the front door clanked violently as the door was suddenly thrown open. Tyrian and Kragin turned their attention to the front of the store as the door crashed against a shelf, sending goblets and bowls shattering on the floor.

Two young figures entered—thin, wiry and dirty. The shorter one found a bare strip of wall and leaned against it while the other boy approached Kragin, who quickly took the blade back from Tyrian and wrapped it up again.

"Whuddya have 'are, Old Kragin," the boy asked.

"Nothing. I've nothing here. You get out of here, Uller. You are not welcome in my shop."

Both boys laughed, obviously undeterred. Uller stepped into the light of the lantern and finally recognized Tyrian.

"Agger, look who we have 'ere," Uller called out to the shorter boy against the wall.

"'Oo do we have 'ere?" Agger asked.

"'dis Tyrian—the woodcuttah rat from the Fellhawk compound."

"I 'dought they never let'm leave da compound, Uller. I heard he had brain leprosy and was given to fits!"

Tyrian stepped forward and said, "If Old Kragin asks you boys to leave, you should leave."

"Not until I see what he has 'ere. He always has the nicest gifts for me. Let's see it, old man. Let's see your latest treasure."

"I have nothing," Kragin cried out, putting the blade away in the cabinet and slamming the door shut.

"Let's have a see what y're hiding," Uller shoved the old man to one side. Tyrian stepped forward, directly in front of Uller, blocking his way.

"Get away, dog," the lanky boy snarled. Tyrian could see the other boy, Agger creeping up from his perch against the wall. Kragin had backed himself into a corner, unconsciously grabbing a small dagger from a shelf.

"You'll leave this man be. Go back to your games in the street and leave this man to feed his family."

"We needa feed our family as well," Agger said, as he pushed another clay bowl to the ground, breaking it.

"Your family can eat out of the gutter, the same as you!" Tyrian shouted, lunging forward. He grabbed Uller's ears in pincher grips, and butted him in the nose with his forehead. Uller stumbled backwards, stunned, as Agger charged ahead, long rusty dagger in hand.

"No!" Kragin cried as Agger thrust his dagger forward, barely missing Tyrian's abdomen. Tyrian brought his arm down, pinning the boy's hand on a nearby table, then brought his other fist down onto Agger's out-stretched arm, snapping the bones in two. The boy screamed in pain, clumsily pawing at his smashed arm. Tyrian turned to Uller, who was now rising to his full height, fists trembling with anger.

Uller stepped past Agger and threw his full weight at Tyrian, knocking him to the ground. He grabbed Tyrian by the shirt and brought down a succession of punches. Tyrian was stunned and dizzied; he tried to move away but was held down by the other boy's fury.

Tyrian felt himself being suffocated by the other boy's hand around his neck. His muscles pulsed, and he saw only the thin, dark eyes of Uller before him. Everything else faded from focus. Uller was stronger than his slight build suggested. The grip he held on Tyrian's throat tightened. Uller seemed to gain pleasure by holding him down. Sweat formed on his narrowed brow and it dropped onto Tyrian's face. Tyrian felt his chest fill with anger and his arms tighten.

For a brief moment Tyrian remembered the story told to him by his uncle: Fortis Grock trying to suffocate the infant Tyrian. He pictured his mother being held down and raped. He could take it no more. He felt his breathing becoming more difficult; restraint felt like death.

Tyrian suddenly jutted his head forward, sinking his teeth into the cheek of the surprised boy. Uller's grip on Tyrian's throat loosened as he tried to pull away, screaming in pain. Kragin looked on in shock.

Agger, moaning and holding his useless arm, moved backwards out of the shop. Uller tried to shake Tyrian from him, but Tyrian was caught up in a spell of rage. Finally, as old Kragin's horrified wail penetrated the boy's consciousness, he let go his grip and shoved Uller out the door. Uller fell to the mud at the foot of the stairs, holding onto his gashed cheek in shock. He looked up at Tyrian, towering at the top of the stairs, breathing heavily, a mixture of sweat, blood and saliva streaming down his chin and neck. Uller followed Agger down the street.

Tyrian looked out at the crowd that had gathered and saw his Uncle Oskar pushing towards the front. He could sense the disappointment before he could see it; Uncle Oskar's brow curled, not in anger, but in sorrow.

Tyrian wiped his face quickly and stepped down into the muddy street. He met his uncle in the midst of the crowd and followed him through the throng quietly to the horses. The load had been emptied and the horses were washed and fed. Oskar paid the horse tenders and led his nephew back onto the Fellhawk trail.

Silent.

The storm had subsided and the last few strains of daylight were breaking through just as the shrouded sun was beginning to set. Tyrian finally spoke.

"Is there no one to protect our people, Uncle Oskar? Those boys threatened Kragin freely, with no fear of recourse. Is that how it should be?"

"If it is true that there is no law, boy," Oskar replied, "we cannot take on that role. We are one of the civilized clans. That means we do not fight without cause."

"But we had cause. Old Kragin was helpless. They planned to steal from him and do him harm. Is that not reason enough?"

"It is not our place to enforce the King's law. I will not bring this up with my brother Petter."

"Then it is true that we are ruthless barbarians," Tyrian lowered his head, "victims of our lowest instincts." He continued on through the gates of the compound, leaving his uncle behind.

Tyrian passed by the main house and went straight to his bedroom, where Wolf awaited him. The boy lay hungry in the darkness of his room, Wolf's steady breath the only sound. Hunger seemed an easier burden than shame. Soon he passed into sleep.

His slumber was penetrated now and then by hunger pangs and dream images of Agger and Uller. And the look of shame in his uncle's eyes. He mumbled illegible curses to the forest militia, wherever they may be.

Tyrian woke several hours later in the breathing blackness of the night. There was a low, but constant, rumbling beneath him. He crept to the window, only to find Wolf already there, sniffing at the air outside. They exchanged looks of confusion. The faint, rolling waves were more of a feeling than a sound; like thunder turned upside down. It had a movement about it that Tyrian could not recognize.

Boy and dog sat for hours, staring into the void, unable to decipher the strange moving code beneath them. Eventually the rustling outside signaled the coming daybreak. To Wolf's dismay, Tyrian dressed and started his day early.

They took their dray horses and empty wagon on the nearly hour-long hike to the August Pike, where several tall trees lay flat against the moist morning ground.

Tyrian dropped his pouch next to a large boulder and took the axe from its strap on his back, wasting no time getting to work.

It was mid-morning. He was lining up stumps to piece out when he felt the dirt beneath his feet vibrating. He stopped and looked over to Wolf, who was looking back at him. It was the same sensation as the night before, only deeper and wider. Whatever it was, it was getting closer.

Instinctively, Tyrian ushered the dray horses and carts into the brush, hidden from view. Then he sheathed his axe against his back and climbed up into a tree to get a better look. He moved up the bark quickly, and steadied himself on a low, sturdy branch. He could hear a low growl coming from Wolf. Looking down he could see the wild dog's hair standing on end. He moved up still higher until he could see further into the distance.

Finally, Tyrian caught sight of it—a dark blur of movement inching towards him. The boy whistled down to his friend and motioned him to hide. The dog did not move at first, but quickly sensed the urgency. Wolf ran into the brush, wedging himself in shrubbery, safe from view. Tyrian could now make out shapes—a group of horses with helmeted men on their backs, swords drawn and charging forward. There was an eerie lack of sound, even as they approached closer. Finally, as the tremors in the ground became audible, as if rising above the fog of silence, he heard a deep voice, "Ride! Ride! Ride!"

Tyrian could now make out two distinct groups of riders. The first numbered about twenty, with almost all of the riders' heads down, hunched forward in fear, both hands on the reins. The larger group, numbering about a hundred, fanned out, and from Tyrian's vantage, seemed to envelop the smaller group like a cloud. These riders rode with one hand on the reins and one hand held out, blade piercing through the morning mist. Tyrian marveled at the disproportion between the two militias. He sensed the fear in the prey as the short gap of retreat was quickly closing.

Suddenly, almost directly below the boy, he could see the horseman who led the smaller group; he wore a full helmet that covered his face and a drab auburn-colored cloak beneath his armor. The armor itself was simple chainmail and bore no markings; a breast plate and shoulder coverings. The men he rode with simply wore leather, and their helmets covered only the tops of their heads, leaving naked their gaunt looks of fear. The lead rider finally turned his horse to face the predators and yelled to his followers, "Now, men, it is time to fight or die!"

The lead rider faced his attackers directly. He rode an animal that was distinct from those of his fellow warriors. Whereas his was a stark black, muscles perfectly sinewed through its shiny coat, the others rode jennets that were stocky and more used to rocky, mountain terrain. These poor beasts were unsure in the muddy, soft forest floor and terrified of the oncoming assault.

The lead rider swung wide but precise arcs as first one attacking rider, then another, passed by him.

Tyrian saw a few of the fearful riders dismount and draw their swords. In an instant, their leader cried out, "Do not dismount, you fools!"

It was too late, though. They swung their blades, only to be cut down by an enemy blade or trampled by a horse.

The leader's horse stood nearly still, seemingly free of fear. No doubt this proud steed had held this position countless times.

Suddenly, fending off one attack, the lead rider was blind to an attack from his rear. He was knocked from his horse, sent tumbling to the ground. Quickly, the soldier regained his feet and planted himself in his battle stance. He motioned his horse away; then, in one swift move, swung his blade out at the first enemy rider to approach him, knocking him to the ground and sending his rider-less steed into the chaos of battle.

The lead rider had already taken down four more men, while the others behind him stumbled and faltered—it was obvious to Tyrian that they were far less skilled than their captain and were void of bravery. A few of them simply tripped over each other, attempting to flee. Every few moments, the leader shouted at his riders. Tyrian was unsure if the commander intended to inspire or chastise his men. His voice was deep and penetrated the air around them, "Fight! Stand up and fight!" The men would have sudden flashes of courage, only to succumb to terror once again. The leader again called out, "By the God-twin that fights beside you, stand up like men!"

The lead rider fought with a grace and style that was distinct among these warriors: his left foot leading, his knees slightly bent as he lowered his hips or raised them, dodging and lunging. He seemed to exert very little energy. When an aggressor attacked from what seemed a blind angle, he would pivot on his rear foot and within seconds deflect, dodge and lunge, then pivot back to his first position.

Tyrian's eyes were fixated on him, mesmerized by his elegant and potent motion. It was as if this man alone was fighting and all the others were doing something grotesque and without purpose. But no matter his skill and strength, for each man he cut down, three more were taking up the fallen man's place. Tyrian saw the leader look out amid a sea of attackers still charging forth; the captain's shoulders slumped a bit with fatigue.

The battle seemed to go on for hours. Tyrian grew cramped on his perch and his mind travelled to the borders beyond the Great River Forest. He tried to trace the path these two militias traveled. Were they from King Azjik's army? Were they from some unknown desert kingdoms? He began to imagine himself in battle armor, in the middle of the fight, taking down two men at a time.

Tyrian was alerted to reality again by the simple snorting of a horse. And that was it. As he opened his eyes, he realized he no longer heard the clanking of metal on metal. No more screams of pain or squeals of fallen horses. Just the abrupt exhalation of a steed.

Tyrian had just witnessed a massacre.

And as he looked out over the small patch of land, he saw fallen men and horses everywhere.

On a rise in the distance stood a horse with a rider. It was this horse that had snorted. The lone rider held his helmet at his side, exposing his long red hair and beard.

Tyrian was puzzled by the size of the horse. It was as short as a pony, but its wide forehead, stout, muscular legs and broad shoulder gave it the strength of an adult. It was a beautiful gray color, if that color ever were to convey beauty! He soon realized that all of the attacking warriors rode similarly short horses. This was a militia from a strange land, he thought.

The red-haired knight sat erect as he watched his soldiers rifle through the fallen. It was obvious they were looking for something specific and he had the patience to wait.

Finally, word was passed from one to another and up the line to an officer who approached the red-haired knight. The messenger bowed his head and waited until he was summoned to speak. Officer and General exchanged quiet words, then the red-haired knight turned his horse and rode off, without a word.

The others quickly mounted and followed. And as suddenly as they had arrived, they were gone. Tyrian waited for some time, then dropped down to the ground. Wolf was already inspecting the bodies with his nose, growling at the sour scent of death. All about them were bloodied, cold bodies. There were dismembered limbs, torsos and heads, muddied and painted with blood. Horses stumbled confused through the trees, seemingly in shock. There was no sight of the lead rider and Tyrian wondered if he had escaped in the chaos. Or perhaps his disfigured body was lying somewhere in front of him, unrecognizeable.

As if in answer he heard a haggard cough. He turned and saw the warrior behind him, hunched over beside a large boulder, head down, unable to look at the carnage.

Chapter Two

Tyrian approached the lone survivor cautiously, a tight grip on his axe. Wolf hunched a few paces back—growling, head low, muscles tight.

As Tyrian drew closer he noticed the weariness on the knight's face—his eyes half-moons of fatigue, his square jaw hanging low as he tried to fill his lungs. Tyrian loosened his hold on his axe as Wolf crouched lower to the ground. The stranger wiped his hand clean and held it out for the wolf-dog to smell, but the beast planted its feet firmly and growled more deeply.

"It is the blood," the knight finally spoke.

"Excuse me," Tyrian asked?

"The smell of blood agitates him."

"He is not used to seeing this much... death." Tyrian paused for a moment before adding, "Nor am I."

"Maybe you could tell him I am not capable of a good fight at the moment."

"Wolf, move back," Tyrian said, grabbing his friend by the nape of the neck as he sheathed his axe on his back.

"My name is Gabriel Theobald."

"I am Tyrian Fellhawk. And this is Wolf." After a moment he noticed, "You are injured badly."

"Yes. I am not sure where the blood comes from, but I have a few guesses. I am in need of a day's rest before I continue on. Do you live nearby?"

"I can take you to my father's cabin."

Tyrian helped the knight into the back of the still-empty cart. The fallen trees remained untouched while the forest was growing cold and dark. The stench of mass death overwhelmed the usual mossy smells of the forest. Critters and birds had started closing in on the corpses.

The ride was bumpy and Gabriel gripped the side of the cart to keep as still as he could, but with each jolt he stiffened in pain. The cold air preyed upon his weakened body. As Gabriel pulled his cloak tighter, he felt Wolf clumsily dropped on top of him to warm him. Gabriel fought to squirm his body out from under the dog but, after a few tries, settled back in defeat and soon enough was warmed into slumber.

As they approached his father's cabin, Tyrian could see the faint glow of a fire. Wolf sat up, waking Gabriel. The boy guided the horses close to the front door and helped Gabriel down from the cart. The stairs were unstable and the boy and the knight ascended slowly. Cabatic Fellhawk met his son at the door as usual, but was taken aback with the injured stranger at his side.

"Tyrian!" his father said, low and grave.

"Please father, this man needs help."

"Come in."

As the two figures disappeared into the cabin Wolf took his spot on the bear rug at the edge of the threshold.

Tyrian helped Gabriel into a chair close to the hearth and the knight collapsed in exhaustion. After a few moments Cabatic returned with a tray of warm tea.

Tyrian threw a fresh log on the waning fire and stoked it back to life as his father retreated into the kitchen to prepare tea.

"Father," the boy offered, "this is Gabriel Theobald."

"Welcome to my home," Cabatic Fellhawk gripped Gabriel's hand.

"He survived a horrible battle out by the August Pike," Tyrian continued.

"Sit back. Rest your legs. Let us get you cleaned up."

"Thank you, kind sir."

Tyrian helped him off with his boots as Cabatic poured three cups of tea.

"For whom do you fight, young man?" Cabatic asked.

"I fight for your king and your country. I come from beyond the great Kyggian Desert. I was escorting some merchants with a load of spices for the King's commerce."

Tyrian was excited to be in the presence of an agent of the king. The monarch that ruled his life seemed so far away as to not even exist. But here was a reminder that his reach, did, in fact, exist. Beneath Gabriel's tattered cloak, Tyrian spied the delicate patterns of his chainmail, something only soldiers wore. And, even through the bloodstains of battle, it was a symbol of order and justice.

"You must eat before you rest, Gabriel Theobald," Cabatic said. "And we will tend to your wounds. Tyrian, get me some heated water and a cloth and my trunk."

As Tyrian followed his father's orders, the elder man helped Gabriel out of his cloak and chain-mail. The wounds could not be seen at first, hidden by dirt and matted blood. By the time Tyrian returned, his father had brushed off the surface mud, then carefully and methodically cleansed the skin. Cabatic finally found the source of Gabriel's pain—deep, thick gashes. Tyrian moved a lantern closer as Cabatic opened the thick wooden chest—it was filled to the top with packets of herbs, leaves, bark, dirt, dried mushrooms, and other exotic bundles. He pulled out packets of leaves and roots in twine, held each up close to his face to examine, then closed his eyes as he pressed them to his nose and breathed in deeply.

When Cabatic was satisfied that he had the exact combination of leaves, roots and bark required, he gathered them in a clean cloth and dabbed the concoction in hot water. This produced a syrup that he squeezed into the length of the first gash, releasing its healing fluids into the injury. Next he took a needle, threaded it with a long blade of thin vine and stitched the slit closed. He repeated this procedure for each wound.

"You must let your wounds breathe now. The fire will keep you warm, but you must not cover them just yet."

"Thank you..." Gabriel breathed in slowly.

"I am Cabatic Fellhawk. You were lucky this boy came along. I live in seclusion and have few visitors."

Tyrian, hungry for details, pressed Gabriel, asking quickly, "Who did you fight by the August Pike?"

Gabriel turned to Tyrian and lifted himself up slightly. His voice dropped low to a whisper, a softness below the crackles of the now healthy fire: "This is dangerous business, boy."

Tyrian nodded and then looked up at his father, following Gabriel's watchful gaze. "With all respect in your home, sir," Gabriel said to Cabatic, "this is dangerous business for you both to hear."

"You can trust us," Tyrian said.

Cabatic nodded his head slowly in agreement. Gabriel's attention was pulled to the warmth of the flames that danced before him. He finally looked up at Cabatic, who was leaning in towards him as he said, "We may be your only friends in this God-forgotten forest."

"The men who attacked us were from the hills of Fulldalr, led by their Heir, Volkummen."

"Do you not fight for the same king as this heir?" Cabatic asked.

"Yes, I do. But the men I led do not."

"Who were they? And why were you escorting them?"

"They were Mountain Pirates with no home. They bore gifts for the King. I was guiding them along a safe passage when Heir Volkummen and his men attacked us at the upper boundary of the great meadow. They followed us into your lush forest. I finally convinced my men to turn and fight, at the spot where your boy found me."

"Sir," Tyrian interjected, "it was a horrible battle. I witnessed the whole thing. Heir Volkummen's men were cruel and your men were badly outnumbered. Were you attacked simply for these gifts?"

Gabriel looked the boy directly in the eye, as if searching for any hint of deceit.

The crackling of the fire had a soothing rhythm, interrupted now and again by the abrupt pop of a soaring ember.

Gabriel watched the crackling tongues of the fire and thought of the battle and the frantic chase into the forest. He now realized he had no idea how deep into the forest he was. Normally he could find his way across the King's land with ease, but the terrain under the vast Great River Forest canopy all looked the same. And in this barbaric land, he would not be safe. Bearing the insignia of an heir meant nothing to these mad peoples. Gabriel needed the guidance of a local to the edge of the forest.

"I wish for you to do me a favor," Gabriel said.

"Of course," Tyrian replied.

"In the morning, I would like you to go out to where you found me. When you reach the point of battle, you will walk west in the direction of the Great River until you find a giant rock with one single sword marking on it. There will be a fallen rider lying dead. You must have a strong stomach, my boy. You will cut open this dead boy's stomach and there you will find a pouch. Do not bother yourself with its contents. Bring it to me."

"Cut the boy open?"

"Yes. You will find our offering to the King there." Gabriel noticed the discomfort in Tyrian's gaze as he sat back and stole a glance at his father. "The boy foresaw his death," Gabriel continued. "He sacrificed himself for this task and he is celebrating in his heaven as we speak."

"Do you truly believe he is celebrating?"

"Tyrian, everyone has their own after-life. You must discover what yours will be before you pass. For there is no turning back then and the conscious mind no longer matters. Your heaven in the after-life is what you see it to be in the living world. That boy chose to sacrifice himself for the many and so he now celebrates in the heaven that is his alone."

Cabatic reached over and gripped his son's hand, signaling him to end the conversation. Tyrian absentmindedly pulled his hand away and leaned in towards Gabriel.

"What will your heaven be, sir?"

"My God-twin has yet to reveal my paradise. My religion tells me that one must get closer and closer to his God-twin. The closer one gets, the more is revealed of the path forward. Until that final moment, the last breath, when the final message is the revelation of how your soul will return to that of your God-twin, and where you will spend eternity. A beach-front. A cabin in the woods. A mountain-top. Under a blade of grass. Time stands still as that final message is laid out in the greatest of detail."

Cabatic cleared his throat, "It is time for you to go home, Tyrian. You will no doubt be getting an early start tomorrow."

"Perhaps I should stay here with Gabriel Theobald."

"No, you must go be with your family."

Tyrian suddenly realized that he had cut not one log of wood that day and he would return with an empty cart. He bowed to Gabriel and then to his father, then turned toward the door.

Before he crossed the threshold he stopped and turned to his father. "Father, I wish to stay with you tonight. I have no memory of sleeping in the same house as you. All my life I have slumbered with the sounds of my uncle's breathing. For one night, I would like to sleep in your house."

"No, my boy," Cabatic replied, "your home is at the compound. With my brothers. I am sorry."

Tyrian gripped Cabatic's arms tightly and looked him square in the eye. Cabatic was suddenly taken aback by his son's penetrating gaze.

"Father, please take care of Mister Theobald."

"I will."

"You are the only family that I have," Tyrian added, "whether you accept that or not."

Without waiting for a reply, Tyrian darted out into the cool dark night. Cabatic stood frozen in the doorway; the love he felt for his son and the sorrow for the boy's inability to understand were beyond explanation. He could only watch the boy's figure disappear into the darkness, confident that understanding would blossom with the sun of maturity.

Tyrian started the long walk home, Wolf at his side, and the tired horses and cart in tow. The tree-filtered sunlight had long since vanished, and so he relied on the feel of the soil to guide him back along the Fellhawk road and towards the compound. The forest was now completely black, and Wolf brushed against Tyrian every few steps so as to not get separated.

After tying up his horses and setting out their food and water, he left the empty cart outside the shed and crept into the dining room of the main house. There he found an empty hall, bare tables spread out in the darkness. He lit a nearby candle and held it out before him. Shuffling through drawers, as quiet as he could be, he finally found what he was looking for, a wide, curved carving knife. He wrapped it in a thick cloth rag he found nearby and shoved it under his shirt. Then he went to bed, hungry.

#

Gabriel Theobald woke with a start; the healing of his wounds had given way to a fever. He was covered in heavy blankets and the fire still crackled beside him. His brow was wet with sweat. He peeled off a layer of blanket, catching his breath. He looked up and saw the old man, Cabatic Fellhawk sitting across from him, with lowered brow and a grave look in his eyes.

The depth of his sleep had taken his conscious mind far from the Great River Forest and far from the battle. His mind had been swimming in the cool waters of the shores of his home state of Coteville.

"The sweat is good, Master Theobald," Cabatic's low, whispered voice soothed him. "It means the fever has spiked. The evil spirits are on their way out. I've made you some more tea. Drink. Drink."

Cabatic moved the thick mug closer to the knight. Gabriel brought it to his lips, feeling the warm steam against his face before taking a sip. It tasted good, spiced with unfamiliar flavors. He sat back, closed his eyes and let his mouth relax into a smile.

"Thank you. I will always remember this. Your son, he is a good boy."

"That boy was a man the day he was born. He lives with the hounds of doubt nipping at his every step. But it has made him honest and strong."

"How did it come to be that you live alone in this secluded cabin, while the boy lives among your people?"

"This forest is cruel, sir. Some say the people make it cruel. Others say something in the foliage and darkness drives us crazy. The answer to the riddle is meaningless. The fact is, violence, cruelty, and dishonor live here. My clan is but one of the three civilized clans. For generations we have been the clan that hands out justice. As elder, I was the arbitrator and mediator of disputes. The justice I laid down on one especially brutal dispute led to revenge and my clan's compound burning, my wife dead and my son motherless. The guilt and sorrow were too much for me. So I went into exile, leaving the elder's duties to my brother Petter. Tyrian has a better life with my brothers and sisters than with one broken man."

"Perhaps," Gabriel said. "One never knows what choices will make the boy a man, eh?"

"I have had doubts over the years, but to change course now might cause confusion in his soul. He is a good boy, Master Theobald. He is honorable and strong. Born in another land, to another bloodline, he would be a great warrior or even king."

"It is true, the cruel fate of life is that we are victims to the wombs we are born from."

"I beg of you, good Theobald, take this boy with you," Cabatic pleaded. "He is nearly a man. His dream is to be a knight. He has no chance in this forest. The Great River Forest Militia is distant. They do not venture this far north. He will never be taken with them. He is meant for things other than cutting wood. He is meant for greater deeds. If you could see the fire in his eyes, the strength of his heart..."

"The Great River Forest Militia, you say?"

"They must fear their own people, for they do not visit us. They do not recruit our boys. They do not bring us justice. We must fend for ourselves."

"Perhaps if your son can bring me what I requested, he can join me. I will at the least need a guide out of this forest."

"He has a fear of disappointing his clan. Mostly his Uncle Petter. Please take him."

Gabriel swallowed the last cold sip of his tea and set the cup on the small table next to him. The clipped, muffled echo of cup on table punctuated the ending of the discussion. His fever had waned and he rested back into his chair, closing his eyes. He did not remember Cabatic leaving him, as his fatigue overtook him and he soon fell fast asleep.

# # #

The next morning Tyrian rose early, having barely slept. He laced his boots and crept into the silence of the main kitchen. Wolf was already at his side.

Tyrian took a loaf of bread and some cheese, tucked them into his cloak and crept out to the shed to retrieve his cart and horses. He moved them quietly out of the compound, fearful of waking anyone. Wolf trotted ahead.

After retracing their steps back to the August Pike, Tyrian found nothing but the same dirt, fallen trees, brush and rocks present the day before. There was nothing else. It was as if the battle the day before had happened in his dreams. No bodies. No armor. Nothing. Wolf was confused as well. The poor dog could smell the stench of death but could not find it. He howled his confusion into the air. Tyrian paced the area in wide circles, investigating the ground more and more closely. There was absolutely no visible evidence of a battle.

Had the bodies come to life and retreated in the night? Had they already passed into the netherworld?

Tyrian took the knife from his jacket and followed Gabriel's instructions. There, just as he had said, was a large boulder. There was one single sword scraping along the side. And just behind it lay a still, pale body.

The corpse was hidden and curled up as if asleep. How brave this boy must have been, Tyrian thought, to sacrifice himself. Tyrian gazed at the peaceful, serene expression on the boy's face.

Tyrian gripped the boy's shoulder and moved him over onto his back. With the crude butcher's knife he cut open the jacket and shirt. Wolf growled at him.

"Quiet! I do not like it either."

The dog whimpered and crouched back a few steps.

Tyrian poked at the skin a few times. It was tougher than he had expected. He closed his eyes and stabbed into the leathery flesh. With all of his weight, he pushed down and then along the torso towards the head, cutting open a long slit. He opened his eyes and expected the face to have changed to pain and horror, but it held its mask of serenity. He dropped the knife to the side and reached into the corpse. It was cold. And it smelled like nothing he had ever smelled before.

His hand searched blindly inside the hardened abdome, until he felt a tattered cloth wrapping, a texture foreign in a human body. He pulled it out and held up to his face—a small pouch of leather tied tightly shut. He quickly wrapped it in a cloth and tucked it away in his cloak.

"Wolf!" he called to the dog, as he pulled the horses and wagon from their spot and began the hike back to his father's cabin.

# # #

Gabriel sat up suddenly as Tyrian entered his father's cabin clumsily and hurriedly, as if on the run from a ghost. The boy took the pouch from beneath his cloak and held it out to Gabriel, proudly, his first official mission completed. The knight took the pouch from his hand and disappeared into the kitchen.

Gabriel pulled a bucket of cold water from a vat nearby. He knelt down and emptied the pouch into it. He let the contents sink to the bottom, then rise up again to the surface. He swished the water around a few times then pulled the contents out, and held them in his hand: long, thick spikes that looked like porcelain which he knew were the teeth of the long dead Green Kaditz Dragon. He closed his other palm against them, rubbing his hands slowly but firmly together.

When Gabriel opened his hands again, the teeth began to change hue—from drab ivory to crimson, then darker, an almost purple-black, and then finally green. They radiated heat in his hand and seemed to glow.

Gabriel dried them with his blouse and wrapped them again in a fresh cloth, hiding them in the pouch.

The front room was dark, despite the lateness of the morning. Gabriel returned and sat again, quiet and serious.

"Sir, how are you feeling?" Tyrian asked.

"Better," Gabriel answered. "On the mend, thanks to your father's mysterious leaves."

"Yes, my father knows everything in this forest."

"Only as much as this thick head can remember," Cabatic smiled.

"And are you passing these secrets down, Cabatic?"

"Only to this boy here." As his father nodded to him, Tyrian blushed. "Our clan believes in nothing but cutting wood and eating. Their lives are good and wholesome, spent providing for others. But they dare not veer away from that course."

"Sometimes it is better that way," Gabriel said. "In battle, the first ones to be struck down are the ones who least want to be there. Without the heart for adventure, adventure becomes folly."

Tyrian watched the knight closely: the way he considered each word before speaking; the way he studied the room in constant movement; his slow, graceful gestures as he spoke.

Finally, with the day's full light beginning to raise awkward shadows in his cluttered study, Cabatic excused himself to his bedroom to nap. Tyrian moved closer to Gabriel and spoke in a low whisper.

"Can I ask you a question, sir?"

"Of course, my boy."

"When I retrieved the pouch for you, there was no sign of the battle. There were no bodies or armor, no blood. Nothing."

"Of course not."

"But where could it have all gone? Overnight! Where did the bodies go?"

"For all of his faults, the King is a tidy man. He likes to leave no imprint of his militias, no trace of his fighting men. Just beyond every battlefront is the Burial March. They wait patiently, sometimes days, sometimes weeks. Ear to the ground, they wait to hear the silencing end of the clash. And at that point, under cover of night, they gather up the dead. The weapons and horses, and whatever riches may remain, are sent back to the King. The food is taken to the nearest village, to be given to the poor. The Burial priest goes from man to man and separates the ones with wedding bands and the ones without. The ones without are immediately married off to the Night Widows."

"The Night Widows? Who are they?"

"They are the women who offer up their lives to save the souls of soldiers. They are married under moonlight to fallen soldiers so that, in the eternal kingdom, these brave young men will have partners to join them in their rest someday. Once the girls are married they are sent back to the Kingdom's many nunneries and spend the rest of their days serving the King in honor of his God. They are maidens and nurses and seamstresses. It is a life of service spent waiting for the day they will pass on and meet their husbands in death."

"What a cold existence they live. Is it right for the King to burden these young women so?"

"It is not ours to question the right or wrong. With peace and order comes good and bad. No kingdom has ever had pure black or pure white."

Tyrian noticed the shifting light and realized he would come home with an empty cart again, if he did not leave soon.

"Mr. Theobald, pardon me, but I must get to the forest to cut some wood. My uncle will not be pleased with two days' loss of cutting."

"Of course, my boy. You go."

# # #

Tyrian was able to gather enough wood to barely disguise his lack of progress. As soon as he entered the compound he quickly unloaded the wood into the shed himself, shooing away the younger boys. Then he washed and entered the dining room with no words. He had no questions for his uncle this night. He kept his gaze down and tried to disappear into the gathering.

But halfway through the meal, his Uncle Petter set down his spoon and quieted the table.

"Tyrian," his uncle spoke low.

"Yes, Uncle Petter."

"There was a battle out near the August Pike yesterday, I'm told. Did you happen to see anything while you were working?"

Tyrian looked down at his plate. He simply shook his head in the negative.

"Strange," Petter continued. "It was by some accounts a spectacle. Fifty men or so, and few survivors. Well-trained swordsmen from beyond the forest's edge."

"I saw nothing, Uncle Petter."

# # #

Hours later, when the darkness of Tyrian's room was complete, he lay in bed with his hand over the side, gently stroking Wolf's head as he thought about the battle. He knew he was wrong to have lied. It was a seemingly innocent thing to deny, witnessing a battle. But the grace of Gabriel's fighting, the power of his battle call—these were things he did not want to share. He felt compelled to keep what he witnessed as his own.

The deep, soft-speaking voice. The slow, deliberate movements of his hands. The grace with which he carried himself. The realization of Tyrian's ideal—a knight in the King's Army—was there in flesh and blood. He was not quite ready to share it, for fear his family's intrusion may just well prove his vision false.

Tyrian woke from a night of half-sleep. His every groggy movement was amplified against the awkward silence of the early morning. He motioned for Wolf to follow him.

Tyrian entered the yard and crossed directly to the main house. Wolf nipped at his steps, wide awake. Still drunken from sleep and serious, the boy shooed him away.

Tyrian was greeted by Petter's wife, Alshanna, who led him into a side room, just off the main receiving chamber.

The small room was dark despite the several candles that bubbled up a flickering orange glow. His uncle filled almost the entire room as he sat at his writing desk. There was only an open doorway, no windows. Inside was one chair with a desk and a short bench, where Tyrian perched himself. His uncle sat at the desk making sporadic notes on a parchment ledger and sipping his tea.

Tyrian did not speak; he watched the dancing of the candle glare against the deep, dark stain of the wood beams. Finally, finishing his thought, Petter set down his feathered pen and turned his entire body to face his nephew. Tyrian saw what passed for a smile on his hardened uncle. The position of the mouth did not change, but the eyes softened.

"Good morning, Tyrian. You are off to an early start."

"Good morning, Uncle Petter. I came to apologize to you. I could not begin my day under the weight of a lie." Petter's body lurched forward as if he were going to engulf the boy.

"You are a good and honest boy, Tyrian. And a hard worker. Now, tell me, what did you lie about?"

"I saw the battle yesterday. I was there for the whole thing; well-hidden, but I witnessed the whole battle."

"Why did you lie to me, my boy?"

Tyrian looked down. "There is one survivor from the fallen side. He rests at my father's house. He led the vanquished militia," Tyrian paused. "I was afraid you would send him out of the forest before he is well."

Petter's brow lowered ever so slightly, "If you withheld the truth just yesterday, why do you bring it to me now?"

"You may not believe in the life of a soldier, uncle. But I do. And a soldier does not lie to his elders. It is what my father has taught me. I was ashamed. I wish to be a soldier."

"You are correct, my boy. I do disagree with your reason. But I do appreciate your honesty and respect your heart."

Petter sat back again and considered the situation, and then his posture once again stiffened. "He must leave! He must leave now. We cannot bring this into our peaceful corner of the Great River Forest."

"No, Uncle Petter, let him heal first! He means no harm. He is hidden and no one knows he has survived. Please, I beg of you, let him stay."

Then, as if to punctuate the end of discussion, Petter rose to his full height and closed his ledger book. "Your load was light yesterday, Tyrian. I hope today you will resume your usual productivity."

Tyrian bolted out the door and threw open the compound gates.

He knew the brothers of the Fellhawk clan would soon be on their way. The cold morning dew wet his face, but he kept up his sprint. Out of nowhere, Wolf again was at his feet. The boy took comfort in the fact that his friend always had his eyes on him. Even when the beast was unseen, he still watched the boy.

Tyrian found his father's cabin in darkness. He took the four steps of the porch in one leap and entered the dwelling. Wolf stopped short at the bottom of the stairs, barking anxiously and biting at the still, cold air.

Tyrian found Gabriel in his chair, smoking his pipe.

"Father!" Tyrian called out as Cabatic appeared in the front room. "Uncle Petter is coming with his brothers to force Mr. Theobald from the forest!"

Gabriel did not stir. He breathed in deeply and then exhaled a narrow plume of smoke.

"You must leave, Mr. Theobald, before my uncles arrive," Tyrian pleaded.

"It is true," Cabatic grumbled. "They will force you to leave."

"If they are reasonable men, we will reason," Gabriel spoke steady. "If they are not reasonable, then they will cut me down with ease. Either way, my God-twin will guide me. But, I shall get dressed for visitors, at the least."

At once, Gabriel's calm seemed to permeate the room. Tyrian sat next to the glowing fire and his breathing slowed. Cabatic retreated to his bedroom to dress. Gabriel gathered up his belongings in a bundle and laced his boots and blouse. He pulled his sword from its sheath on the floor and set it back against a wall, in sight, but not in hand.

"Tyrian, you must leave," Cabatic said, returning into the front room, the daylight now beginning to fill the entire room.

"No, Father, I will stay. My words are bringing Uncle Petter here. I will wait and answer for that."

"I agree with your father," Gabriel said. "You should go. There is no reason for you to receive the wrath of your clan."

Tyrian's stillness answered both men.

Finally, a heavy knock pounded on the door. Cabatic opened it, unsurprised to find Petter, Didrik, Sverre, Oskar, and the youngest brother, Vegard, filling up the small porch, standing close together with axes and hoes.

"What do you want at this hour?" Cabatic barked.

"You have a stranger in your house, Cabatic," Petter spoke slowly. "You know full well my feelings on bringing that into our homestead. He must leave now."

Petter nudged his way into the cramped living room and two of the other brothers followed, leaving those who could not fit craning their necks to see inside the house. Petter's gaze fell on the knight who sat next to the fire, and he was surprised to find Gabriel serenely holding a cup of tea. "Are you the knight who brings violence into our homestead?"

"I am Gabriel Theobald, dear sir. I bring nothing of the sort. I am delivering a gift to his highness, your King, and am simply resting at the insistence of your dear, gentle brother. I mean you no harm."

"You will leave us to our quiet ways this morning," Petter growled.

"I daresay," Gabriel dropped his voice to almost a whisper, "there is no need for such a confrontation. Thanks to the healing secrets your brother keeps, I am well on my road to recovery and can leave you this day. I will not threaten your homestead any further."

"No," Tyrian pleaded, "Uncle Petter, please let him stay another day. He is injured and must have more time to recover."

"He can recover beyond our borders, with his own people," Petter declared. "And you, dear boy, should be working."

"No, brother," Cabatic offered, "let Tyrian escort him away from our homestead and point him to where the trees end."

Petter considered, then shrugged and conceded; he nodded quietly. Tyrian was grateful for this mission. Gabriel gathered up his cloak and sword. Cabatic stopped him, though, and shoved another small purse into his hands. "Tea for the cold nights. And the pine-woven leaves... chew on them during the day. They'll ease the discomfort."

"Thank you, my friend." Gabriel pushed his way gently through the crowd and onto the front yard. From there Tyrian and Wolf led him back onto the main path and towards the August Pike, where they had met just two days before.

Chapter Three

The heavy darkness of the desert night was slowly surrenduring to a liquid blue. Impatient with the gradual crawl of the sun's rise, Heir Kriestle Volkummen summoned his top lieutenant, Greit Schultheis, to his tent. Greit's movements betrayed the contortions of countless battles. The cold air of the desert morning caused his calloused skin to ache.

As Greit crossed the short distance between tents, he looked up to see the first few brushes of the morning's pinkish hue scattered across the Serpent Grave Plains. The morning's light was now spreading quickly; the sky seemed to be as impatient as Heir Volkummen.

The fire-pits from the night before still burned. Greit could now make out the outlines of the forty scattered tents of Volkummen's militia. Zombie-like figures were now emerging, half-asleep or still drunk. One tent stood majestically taller, albeit drab from exposure to the harsh desert wind. Along one edge of the tent stood a wooden pole with a tattered flag of gold and green, the figure of a horse sewn on it. This was the flag of The House of Volkummen.

Greit took a bucket of hay and vegetables from the main supply tent and emptied it at the feet of the short gray horse that waited patiently outside of Heir Volkummen's tent. The general entered quietly and lit a lamp next to the opening. He marveled at the crude majesty of the interior. Quickly put together, with a sleeping mat, several pillows and a reading chair in the corner, it conveyed the simplicity of Heir Volkummen. Greit pulled over a stump of a stool and set it next to Volkummen's bed.

"Your Honor," Greit spoke softly. Volkummen stirred, then sat up, brushing his thick red mane aside.

"Speak."

"There were no survivors. A good distance from the battle the body of a boy was found."

"And why should I take note of this, Greit? What distinguishes this dead soldier from the others?"

"There were no marks of battle. His abdomen was opened up and he lay a ways apart from the battle."

"Apart from the others?

"A good distance."

"And where is the body?"

"We have it kept under cover of tent, sir."

Heir Volkummen abruptly stood and dressed. As he laced his boots he growled, to no one in particular, "It seems our prize was gone even as we were battling for it. It was not Mountain Pirates who deceived us. They are good thieves, but not worth much beyond that. No! Someone with reason and cunning deceived us."

"But who, my lord?"

"That is yet to be revealed. And I pray we will receive guidance to unravel that mystery."

Greit rose as Heir Volkummen gathered up his sword and helmet. Uneasy, and sensing his heir's urgency, he followed Volkummen out.

Heir Volkummen marched directly to the east fire and motioned for a young scout rider, who stumbled over himself to reach the heir.

"Yes, your Honor," the scout bowed.

"By sundown you will have reached all of my lieutenants and instructed them to meet at the Green Cliffs encampment on the day-break."

"Yes, sir," and with that the scout hurried to his steed and departed.

"But Heir Volkummen," Greit asked, "why retreat all of our men now, when we have come this far?"

"Because we are no longer chasing a militia. We chase only one man and it takes strategy now, not manpower."

Volkummen turned and strode into another tent, far off from the others. There he found his counselor, Roserie Argaune, alone at a small table, writing in a giant leather journal. Next to him sat a chest of books, which were crudely stacked in no apparent order. These were the only things inside the tent, save a blanket and pillow on the floor.

Roserie was a nomadic rogue from an obscure order of priests that lived high up in the Balles Mountains, beyond the Coteville border. Although they rooted their lives in the God-twin beliefs of the coastal tribes, their order was far darker. They were a tight band of disciples who, over a century's time, had left the order and devoted themselves to finding the limits, if any, of the more sinister nature of their orthodoxy. They kept their perverse theology well hidden from the outer world.

As a child, Roserie was orphaned by a violent earthquake in the Low Balles Hills. A good quarter of his village was killed, including his mother and father. With no other relatives to care for him, he was taken in by the church. As the memories of his parents faded, so did his memories of happiness and security.

Meditation and reading became his refuge from the laborious tasks that made up most of his waking hours in the orphanage. The priests were strict, and his childhood was an unhappy one: meals were meager; human contact was brief and cold, and the boy was left mostly to himself. His awkward height and sullen demeanor made him the target of many pranks and jokes by the few other children who lived there. He was an outcast among outcasts.

In his ninth year, Roserie Aragaune fell under the tutelage of a rebellious priest named Itzal Gaizka, who continuously argued with the other priests. Their arguments centered on Gaizka's desire to expand the defined set of principles within which they had always worshipped. To him, nothing was sacred; belief was always fluid and worship always evolving.

Itzal Gaizka found the young Roserie always alone. With empathy for the boy's solitude and sorrow, he would sneak him extra food in the mornings, read to him at night, find him less laborious jobs. Where the other priests saw anger, Itzal Gaizka saw passion. He nurtured the boy's curiosity.

One morning Roserie woke to a loud argument outside his room. Putting his ear to the door he could make out two or three voices angrily shouting at a lone defendant, whose voice he recognized as Itzal Gaizka. After the voices quieted, Roserie rushed to the window, where he saw his mentor walking alone from the rectory complex. He quickly grabbed some clothes and a few books and ran after him, stopping him just as he was crossing the threshold of the courtyard.

"Take me with you," he pleaded.

Itzal Gaizka took the boy away forever. Neither looked back. In exile, mentor and student hiked into the High Balles Mountains and joined a handful of other outcasts, all stretching the boundaries of their religion. Together, the small band cooked, ate and meditated.

The young Roserie Argaune was treated with much more attention than he was used to. With the elder priest's help he began to find the black magic uncovered through their dark prayers. He was encouraged to look inward at his anger and not shut it away. He was emboldened to let fly his independent spirit.

As Roserie Argaune grew into a young man, Itzal Gaizka led him on long journeys into the desert. They had become equals, and equally thirsty for knowledge. Together they learned the languages and customs of the desert tribes.

It was in the desert where Roserie Argaune eventually brought his one-time mentor to die, in his most novemberest days. It was the one time the young man gave himself up to emotion, collapsing to the ground in tears. He was forced to leave the only father, the only warm embrace he had ever known. On that day, the young wizard had learned the value against which a person's life would forever be measured. He now knew the value of life. And he felt the void left behind at its ending.

Years later, Roserie Argaune had maneuvered his way into the inner circle of young King Azjik's council. Argaune had become an advisor. He was a teacher to the king's three sons, as well as confidant to the monarch. But he was pushed out by a faction of advisors that mistrusted his black magic. Argaune never forgot this and, in his exile, he still retained a single contact within the King's council.

In his time in the King's court he made a handful of allies, most of whom had died or gone into exile since. But there was one in particular who had managed to stay in the good graces of Azjik. Farafah Fruz and Roserie Argaune had managed to keep their alliance secret over the years. They met covertly only once or twice a year, to exchange information and corroborate the status of their many schemes and plots. They became invaluable to each other. Farafah Fruz needed an agent outside of the kingdom with the power to move tribes and influence the criminal bands. Roserie Argaune needed an agent in the good graces of King Azjik to keep him informed of the decisions of the state.

Argaune took great comfort in his relationship to Farafah Fruz; it was his last tie to the arena of court politics. The King did not make one decision without consulting Fruz.

The wizard was suddenlly pulled away from these memories by the bellowing voice of the red-haired general, "Argaune!"

Argaune looked up and read his notes aloud.

"Upon the jagged cliffs of Sprighten Long

I gently spoke the thing I'd heard,

A curiously fragrant song,

From a wicked unwinged bird."

"I've no time for this!" barked Heir Volkummen.

Argaune cleared his throat, "How can I be of service then, your Honor?"

"The Mountain Pirates we chased were all cut down, yet still we found nothing."

"Can you be sure that they had our prize in their possession?"

Heir Volkummen looked over his shoulder and leaned forward, reminding Argaune of the secrecy. "They were weak and feeble. They stood their ground and fought only because of what they were protecting, Argaune. A corpse was found a distance from the battle. I believe it may hold a clue."

For a long moment the sorcerer stared down into the dirt of his tent. Then he shook his head and grumbled, "No, no, I've no skills at this. I can tell the lineage or age, but nothing further. I've no skills for such things. Your task requires a true sorcerer; I'm only a reader of books."

As was their routine, Heir Volkummen proceeded to coax it out of the old man. The red-haired knight gently gripped the sorcerer's shoulder and implored him, "My dear sir, wise magician that you are, I'm sure if left alone you'd find the correct book that would guide you. This is most important to us. Must I remind you that once we have retrieved the sacred dragon's teeth, and have redirected their passage from the King's hands to our own, you, too, will feast upon the fruits of their magic? It is only through your counsel that we can make use of their powers."

The old man rubbed his weary brow. He shook his head slowly and then finally nodded approval. "I think I may have remembered just which book may help me investigate your dead boy. It's just here in my chest of books. Bring me the body."

Heir Volkummen exited without a word.

# # #

Tyrian carried Gabriel's pack over his shoulder and pointed out the various trees and vegetation.

"Your father has taught you well, Tyrian," Gabriel said.

"My father knows every plant and tree in this forest. I only hope to know half as much as him at his age."

Gabriel could sense something was stirring in Tyrian; the boy was silent and his gaze was lost in the distance. "Your father is a good man, Tyrian," Gabriel prompted the boy.

"I am sorry for how my uncles treated you, sir."

"It is not your place to apologize for their actions, boy."

"My Uncle Petter desires no disturbance on our homestead. He calls us the anchor of peace in this violent sea. He seeks out nothing but peace."

"It is true one can live a peaceful life, but there will always be conflict, and one must be ready for that."

"That's what my father tells me," Tyrian agreed.

"Sometimes you must welcome the perception of danger; it may well unlock the mystery of actual danger."

"And which of those are you, Mister Theobald?"

"A stranger is always perceived as a danger. But sometimes it is a distraction from the true danger. One must learn to trust one's instincts. Tyrian, you have the heart of a knight. Your destiny is not the same as your family's. Cutting wood will not fulfill that destiny. This path that we walk on now will lead you there if, you so wish."

Tyrian came upon a small bush with needled leaves that was tucked close to a larger tree. He pulled a small leaf from the bush and plucked a small seed-nut from the base of the leaf, then held it up close to Gabriel.

"You see this seed here? This seed is poison, but a good poison. If you boil this in water it makes the inside soft like syrup. And if you cut a tiny hole in it and squeeze it out it will numb your skin. My father uses it when he is caring for Wolf after a fight. He cleans the wound and then rubs the syrup along the wound to numb it before he sews the wound up." He pulled a handful from the bush and put them in the pack he carried for Gabriel.

"Has your father also taught you to fight?"

"Yes, sir. He has given me my grandfather's sword at times and showed me the little bit he learned as a boy."

Gabriel fell silent and slowed his pace. After a few moments Tyrian turned, noticing that his companion had stopped completely.

"What is it?" Tyrian asked.

Gabriel approached the boy, laid both hands on his shoulders and looked him deeply in the eye.

"Tyrian, I must tell you something—a knowledge that puts you at great danger—but I trust you can care for yourself."

"I can."

"Tyrian, I am Gabriel Theobald, Heir of Coteville, one hundred and twentieth in line to the throne and a general in the King's Regular Stand Army."

Tyrian paused, and then clumsily dropped to one knee, bowing his head.

"Forgive me, your Honor. I did not know. Forgive any informalities I may have..."

"Rise, boy. I tell you this not for your apologies. I tell you this because our meeting is not by chance. And I must be honest with you from this point on." Gabriel studied the boy's face. It hardened, his eyes narrowed and his jaw tightened. As if understanding the gravity in Gabriel's voice, even Wolf sat on at attention.

"I carry with me a secret treasure for the King. A treasure that is also being hunted by other men, other heirs. I was sent in disguise to escort the pirates back to the King's gates. But we were attacked by Heir Volkummen's militia. I fear Heir Volkummen's allegiance to our king is quite fragile. I fear there are more heirs whose allegiance is... questionable."

"What is this treasure that you carry?"

"Tyrian, this prize," Gabriel said, holding up the pouch in front of him, "will eventually drive armies to war. In the wrong hands, it could divide the kingdom. It is what will bring to surface the good or the evil that lives at the heart of every man."

"What is it?" Tyrian leaned in, meeting Gabriel's gaze.

"In this pouch are the remnants of a long dead beast which, when ground to powder and consumed in the right concoction, will cure man of his natural journey towards death. The teeth of the

Green Kaditz Dragon. The legend is that even a small dose will add a hundred years to a man's life and give him the strength of one hundred men. Your dear King will lead an army stronger than any that's ever walked this earth."

Tyrian's eyes devoured the pouch in Gabriel's hand. It seemed unthinkable to him that such power could be encapsulated in such a small thing.

"How is all of that possible from just those teeth?"

"Strength is not something that can be measured. It is not something that can be seen with one's eyes. I have seen an army of ten men beat down an army of fifty. Because the strength in each man's heart emboldens the group. And the opposite is true; the weakness in the hearts of fifty weakens the whole."

Tyrian considered this for a long moment. Finally he turned back to the road ahead.

"You are an heir to the King. Why do you need my escort? No one will touch an heir to the King."

"Despite the reach of his law, there is plenty of land that is unruled and unruly. And this dark forest land is a maze to me. I need a guide and protector against the barbarians here. I am never truly out of danger until I am within the King's gates. Tyrian, if you come with me, I can train you as a knight."

"Can you train me to fight as you did in the forest?"

"I could teach you the Five Formations of Oro Tsaun. I could teach you the footwork of the Guardian of the Green Cliffs. I could teach you what I teach my students in the Coteville Academy."

Tyrian was quiet. He did not respond to the knight. He weighed an uncertain future of adventure against the comfort of his work and life in the Great River Forest. The journey hung before him, like an apple from a tree.

He knew what his Uncle Petter would say; disgrace would be brought upon the clan.

Tyrian continued onward, no words coming to him. The path was vanishing, a signal of how deep into the forest they were reaching. Gabriel left him to his silence.

# # #

Two soldiers entered Roserie Argaune's tent with a stiff form wrapped in a dusty blanket. In the corner sat Heir Volkummen and the wizard. Greit Schultheis, who stood at one side of the tent, motioned the soldiers to lay the corpse gently on the ground. After they exited, Greit took up a post at the tent opening, his back to his heir.

Argaune knelt down slowly. He motioned for Heir Volkummen to bring a candle closer, and then pulled out a round reading-glass. With a small, finely carved stick he pushed aside the blanket. Heir

Volkummen leaned in closely as the old man poked at the rubbery skin and traced the opening of the wound with the top of the wand.

Argaune opened the mouth with the stick and dug around. He bent down closer and inserted his index finger into the cold mouth, making little circles, and then held the tip of his finger up to his face to examine. He nodded to Heir Volkummen to look.

"You see these tiny black flakes?" he asked. "They are remnants of a poisonous leaf, which leads me to believe the boy willfully expired himself—a sacrifice. And here," he pointed at the open gash, "the incision is crude. It goes off to the side and then back. You see how it is uneven? This tells me that whoever cut the boy did so after his death and was unskilled in this art. He used a simple maiden's knife and was as clumsy as a butcher's apprentice. Look inside the wound," he implored the heir, holding a lamp closer to the open abdomen. "You see how everything is severed and tangled? The thief was uneasy and worked quickly. This is where your secret prize was hidden."

"But what does all of this tell me, Arguane?" Heir Volkummen was getting impatient.

"It tells you first, my dear general, that whoever was responsible for this was a man of reason and authority, enough to induce this boy to poison himself, knowing full well he would be carved up after death. Secondly, it tells us that this same diplomat instructed our apprentice butcher as to where to find the prize. So you are looking for a seasoned and experienced lord and his young protégé."

Heir Volkummen pulled at his long red beard as he considered this. "But who?" he finally asked.

"That is the greater riddle."

"I want no more riddles! I want answers! Look closer and decipher who the mentor and protégé are."

"My dear Heir, I am no magician. I cannot conjure up your phantom out of thin air. I can, however, give you clues that will lead you there."

"Can you not use your black magic or some crystal ball to find my prey? Can you not conjure up your blasphemous God-twin to hunt down my prey?"

"This God-twin you speak of is no blaspheme! You believe in your foolhardy religion just as I believe in mine. But... perhaps I can put my God-twin to use after all."

"Very well! I will leave you to your devil's work in private!" Heir Volkummen strode out into the cool morning air.

Heir Volkummen squatted by the east fire. A young soldier brought him a cup of steaming tea and some meat on a bone wrapped in a rag. The boy sat at Volkummen's side in silence as the red-haired knight methodically ate his breakfast.

Heir Volkummen watched as the boy's attention was drawn to Argaune's tent. The slight breeze had blown open the tent flaps and the Heir could see the figure of old Roserie Argaune kneeling, with his head arched back to the sky, his palms open and exposed to the tent ceiling. Argaune seemed to be in a trance.

The young soldier noticed a large hawk swoop into the opening and he worried briefly that the bird would interrupt Argaune's trance. But strangely, the boy could swear he saw another figure, a symmetrical image of Argaune. Just for a brief few seconds and then it was gone. And as it disappeared, a brown-feathered hawk escaped the tent and was off into the sky above.

The boy watched as the hawk turned northward into the ever-brightening sky, the day now making its presence known across the horizon. He was pulled to attention by the sound of Heir Volkummen's tin cup hitting the ground. The boy dropped to his knees to recover the vessel, just as Heir Volkummen marched off to an open field, several yards from the encampment.

There Heir Volkummen removed his cape and blouse and drew his long broadsword from his back. The heavy, burnt air felt like a blanket over his shoulders as he went through his morning formations.

Other men spent the silent morning hours in prayer or vomiting the grog of the night before, but Heir Volkummen spent these sacred hours communing with the open sky through his muscles and brawn. No one dared bother him during this time. No one knew if he worshipped the one god and one disciple decreed by the King or if he believed in the God-twin religion of so many—although it was a dying belief—or if there was an even more ancient deity he followed. All they knew was that these mornings, against the changing of the sky's color he could be seen facing west, swinging his mighty sword in mysterious formations, breathing heavily and grunting madly. Always to the west. As if he was fighting off the past. Always to the west, and no man dared break his concentration.

Heir Volkummen spent the entire day cutting his sword through the stillness of the open air. His footwork was as linear as Heir Theobald's was circular. His feet moved in straight lines forward and back, never in circles. He practiced lunging offensively and retreating defensively, although in battle this giant of a man hardly ever used the defensive. He was a man of forward motion and offense. Fighting was his prayer to the god of war.

# # #

Tyrian, Wolf and Gabriel had been hiking most of the day. The filtered daylight was dissipating and Gabriel was tiring, not fully recovered. He gripped Tyrian's arm tightly to signal it was time to rest. He found a rock and sat down.

"Are you tired, your Honor?" Tyrian asked.

"It's a long journey, boy, and I'm not healed as of yet. I think we should rest here for the night."

Tyrian began gathering wood for a fire. Gabriel was amazed to see Wolf find an open space and began digging a small pit with his front paws. This dog was truly an exceptional animal, he thought. This was obviously a routine they had played out several times in the past.

Tyrian returned with an armful of logs and sticks and set about building a fire. Gabriel was surprised again to see Wolf gather up the bags and packs and dragged them close by. Once Gabriel saw the flames jumping into the air, he hobbled over and sat close to the heat. He let the boy prepare the meal and lay it out. He watched the boy eat his food as he tore into his own. Crisp and blackened on the outside, but still gray and raw on the inside.

"One of the first lessons I would teach you as a knight," Gabriel said, "is how to cook."

Tyrian laughed and then nodded at Wolf, "My friend never complains."

"I doubt that he complains much in the way of food."

Wolf looked over his shoulder, wondering what the two were laughing at, but lost interest and went back to his pile of meat scraps.

"Your Honor, if you deliver the dragon's teeth to the King and he gets his inhuman army, he will use such a force for good, will he not?" Tyrian asked.

"He will use it for whatever he sees fit."

"And is it right to have such power in one man's hands?"

Gabriel paused, stoked the fire, and then looked up at the boy. "No man can answer that question. That is for the Fates to settle in heaven."

"Is it right for us to gamble on it then? Perhaps the fates wish you not to deliver."

"I follow the guidance of my God-twin. That is all I can do. And my God-twin has always led me towards order. There must be order. There must be a king with a strong hand to keep the order. Good does not always come from order; indeed, evil slips through on occasion. But that is a sacrifice we have to make for order. For without order, Tyrian, the resulting chaos would be unbearable for man."

Tyrian had more questions, but saw the heaviness in Gabriel's eyes. Gabriel dug a small hole and buried the remains of his meal, then tossed his plate to the ground. Just as he was rising he looked down at the boy and said, "Tyrian, your help is needed in returning this gift to the King."

Tyrian kept silent as he watched Gabriel limp over to a clearing, where he sat down cross-legged. Gabriel was partially hidden, but the boy could see an outline of his figure: he sat with his back arched slightly and his eyes closed, facing the sky. His hands were open, palms upward.

Tyrian could hear a low moan of song coming from the heir. He marveled at the stillness the knight kept. His eyes burned as they struggled to keep hold of the figure, as the darkness of night came quicker now. But just as he was losing sight of the praying form he saw a hazy, shining figure that soon became a mirror to the heir. It was as if a ghost figure—identical to Gabriel—had risen from the mist of the cool night air. Both figures sang their low moan to each other. Tyrian could not make out the words, but they sang to each other in what sounded like foreign dialect. Wolf growled at the ghost. Tyrian clasped the dog's mouth shut with one hand.

After a few moments the song ended and the ghost-Gabriel rose and took to the air, floating high above them all; the knight was completely still. The glowing figure ascended high up into the trees until it found an opening above tree cover. There, it reached its arms out, as if to hold itself there. It took a few slow revolutions, surveying the canopy of trees. Then it caught sight of something and froze; there was a hawk flying northward. This was no ordinary bird. Tyrian saw the hawk lock its gaze onto the image of the glowing ghost-Gabriel and circled it with a wide berth. The ghost figure circled as well; each was taking stock of the other. The hawk made another round and turned back towards the direction from where it had come. The ghost-figure lifted its transparent arms and lowered itself back down to its original position, sitting across from Gabriel. Then, abruptly, as the ghost-Gabriel evaporated into the darkness, Gabriel opened his eyes and ran back to the fire pit.

"Tyrian, we cannot rest tonight. We have to move."

"Your Honor, I do not understand. Why do we have to leave?"

"My presence is known. You must lead me through the night. We can make good time tonight. They will come to this spot in the morning and we must be far from here by then."

"How do you know this?"

Gabriel's answer was silence as he began gathering his belongings. Tyrian did the same and before long they were back on the trail, with just a small torch from the now dead fire to light their way through the blackness of the forest night.

Chapter Four

Against the white glow of the near full moon, a single hawk shot across the night sky. The arc of its path sharpened as it descended into Roserie Argaune's tent. After a moment, a replicate silhouette of the wizard, sitting cross-legged, appeared before him. Both figures sat in complete stillness. Finally, as the last embers of the fading fire disappeared into the air, the second figure was gone. Argaune let out a deep breath as his body sank into itself. He took a moment to regain his composure, then went to the tent-opening and rang a signal-bell.

Heir Volkummen exited his own tent and crossed the short distance to the wizard's shelter.

"What have you discovered?" Volkummen asked.

"I believe it may be one of my own countrymen that you seek. His God-twin was clumsy and revealed his identity in the Great River Forest."

Argaune fell silent. Volkummen tried to pierce the silence with his jagged stare. Finally, the wizard looked up from the ground, as if breaking a sudden trance, and stated, "It is the Heir of Coteville that you seek out, dear Volkummen."

"Heir Gabriel Theobald is the thief I hunt?"

"It would appear so."

"And where would I find him?"

"At the southern-most edge of the Great River Forest, although his God-twin saw my hawk. He is most certainly on the move by now. But I must go to see a friend who may provide me confirmation."

"Do what you must. But make haste. I am growing more impatient."

Heir Volkummen rose and exited. Argaune closed his eyes and gave himself up once more to his trance.

# # #

Tyrian led Gabriel on a slow, winding trail through the forest night. The path had been descending at a gradual rate, but was now dropping faster. Tyrian's breathing had become easier.

Wolf lagged a ways behind, but every few moments sprinted to catch up and then fell behind once again. They had been walking for several hours when Gabriel called for them to rest. They dropped to the wet mossy floor and Tyrian dug into his pack for food.

"Heir Gabriel," Tyrian finally spoke. "It looked as if you were speaking to a ghost back there."

"A ghost is the spirit of the dead, Tyrian. What you saw was a spirit of the living."

"I do not understand."

"What you saw was my God-twin. It is our belief, Tyrian, that one's true god lives within us. My religion tells me that at birth our souls are split into two. One becomes your guide, if you listen to it. Most men go their entire lives deaf and blind to their God-twin. But those who are able to hear its voice excel. And, more importantly, when one can communicate with their God-twin, a far richer existence is available to you."

"But I thought that the King had decreed belief in only one god."

"King Azjik believes there is one god and that we must worship his One Disciple. The Disciple is the gatekeeper to his heaven and that is who we must bow to."

"And yet you defy him in your heart with your own belief?"

"How does a monarch decree a man's belief? Our great king is wise and honorable, but he is still only a man. A god is something greater still."

"I've heard of this religion, but I never knew that you could actually see your God-twin."

"Not at first. It takes practice and study. Some men hear a voice. Others hear a voice and see a vision. Still others, men with dark ambitions and stronger God-twins, have the ability to place theirs in a physical vessel and see through another beast's eyes."

"Can one place their God-twin in another man?"

"No. It has never been done. Men are made of complicated matter."

"So you defy the King's Law with your religion?"

"Tyrian, to be an honorable knight means more than just fighting well and serving your king. A knight must have principles that he stands by and beliefs based on his own experience, not another's."

Tyrian nodded in the darkness. Wolf slept, panting and twitching next to Gabriel.

"With some work you will find your God-twin. Go on. Practice in the stillness of the night, boy. Sit as still as you can and clear your mind of all visions and sounds. Imagine your face before you, as if looking looking into a mirror. And listen. Do not bother with what you should see, or want to see. Concentrate on what you do see. Listen to what is audible, not what you wish to hear. Do this every night and have patience. There will be long nights of nothing. Like this dark forest tonight; if we rely on our eyes and ears alone, we appear to make no progress. But come sunlight, we'll see a different landscape. That is the same as reaching your God-twin."

Uncle Petter had raised their clan with no religion. They prayed to neither a God-twin or to the King's One Disciple, nor to the Mountain and Sea Gods that others believed in. Petter believed in rising early, working long hours, and going late to bed. This seemed to be the extent of his spirituality.

"Will you teach me to see my God-twin?" Tyrian asked.

"It is a matter of concentration and nothing more. Close your eyes, Tyrian."

As the boy closed his eyes, Gabriel sat back and watched him. "Now slow your breathing. Be aware of your breath. You must block everything out of your mind, even my voice. There must be no sound and nothing to envision. It is just your breathing and the blackness of your mind."

Gabriel watched the boy. After a few moments, Tyrian began absent-mindedly tapping his finger. Gabriel reached over and steadied his hand. The boy became restless again. Gabriel reached over and steadied him. Then, finally, Tyrian opened his eyes altogether and pleaded with his mentor, "Your Honor, there is nothing happening!"

Gabriel laughed as he sat back. "Of course not. It does not come at once. Sometimes the hardest work takes no physical action at all. Patience, I see, will be your first lesson. But for now we must move on."

Gabriel rose, waking a groggy Wolf, as Tyrian pulled their packs together. "Whoever sent their God-twin to find me is now on our trail. We must put as much distance as possible between us."

"We are very close to the edge of the Great River Forest, your Honor. I will leave you there."

"Consider escorting me further, Tyrian. I am not completely healed and I need healthy legs to lead me out of the forest. You have the strength of ten men and the heart of a leader. If you were born of another womb, you would be trained as a knight and put in line to lead a militia someday."

The tree cover was becoming lighter—they were nearing the edge of the forest and this was the farthest Tyrian and Wolf had ever been from the Fellhawk Compound. The vegetation was becoming foreign to them. The sounds were different, as well as the smells. Tyrian noticed there were wider patterns in the tree canopy, more open spaces.

They could hear the faintest roar of the Great River far off in the distance. An excitement and nervousness came over Tyrian. He had never seen open sky. He had never felt anything other than mossy floor beneath his feet.

"I've heard stories about the desert beyond the forest," Tyrian said.

"Some people call it the Serpent's Grave. Some call it the end of the earth. Some call it Hell," Gabriel replied.

Tyrian was silent as he continued to push forward. Wolf brought up the rear, right on Gabriel's heels.

# # #

Even though bright sky could be seen above, and the yellow orb of the sun shown behind the steep columns beyond, Roserie Argaune sat in darkness. Below the berth of a wide bridge, which led across the lake to the rear entrance of King Azjik's castle, the wizard Argaune remained completely still, in meditation. A cold, damp chill from the lake pricked at his skin.

Eventually he heard someone approaching: slow, light and deliberate footsteps that moved cautiously. They stopped just short of where Argaune sat. The old man opened his eyes and saw a figure even older than himself. Thin and tall. Dressed in a long, dark cloak and hood. Just beneath the hood he could see the dangling black point of Farafah Fruz's cap, part of the uniform of the people of the Eastern plains.

"Good afternoon, old friend," Fruz said.

"I despise the shadows, Farafah Fruz," Argaune said. "How I miss the open wind and sun of the Balles Mountains. Even the sun-baked blanket of the Serpent Grave Plains is better than all of this darkness and hiding."

"You know very well that if our union were to be discovered, all of our plans would be destroyed. I cannot abide by the darkness any more than you can. But let us get to business."

Argaune moved closer to Farafah Fruz and handed him a small leather flask. The old man threw his hood back and took a long drink of the sweet wine. He smacked his lips, smiled and handed it back.

"There will never be a sweeter wine than the stuff that you dark priests concoct. Thank you."

Farafah Fruz took a step back then bowed, a strange bit of etiquette that Argaune had never understood.

"Now, what news do you bring, good Argaune?"

"We are as close to prize as we have ever been. The dragon's teeth have been found. I have a good notion of who may be escorting them to our young king. Perhaps you can confirm it in council; the hundred and twentieth in line to the throne."

"Heir Theobald, of Coteville?"

"Indeed. I will set in motion three armies to disrupt their passage through the Witches' Bend. One to stop them, a second to engage them, and a third to retrieve the booty and return it to me."

"Hmmm. Well done, Master Argaune. You are truly a magician."

"And what news do you have?"

"Our young king has grown impatient for his gift. He has held counsel on exactly how to put it to use. He has a legion of young men awaiting their potion. He is being pulled in different directions on how best to use his new army. Some say unleash them in the Cretian Islands to secure the Cretian Passage. Some say push deeper into the south. Still other advisors would have him expand east beyond the mountains."

48

"And your counsel?"

"My counsel is always to engage... fight. Take over as many new lands as possible in the shortest amount of time. Expand his reach. Be the god on earth that his father never could be."

"That is quite an aggressive position for you to take. I am a bit taken aback."

"Roserie, you must understand that the young man who wears the crown fancies himself a resolute leader, a strong warrior, and a grand strategist. And, you and I both know, a country at war is always vulnerable. My goal is to seduce the imagined warrior within the young monarch, thereby sealing his trust in me. All the while I am sending him down a dangerous path."

"Indeed. You are as wise as I am deceitful, Farafah Fruz," Argaune laughed heartily. The wizard then looked up toward the length of the bridge, which led to the gates of Azjik's castle, and sighed, "Oh how I am saddened by my exile. I miss the gamesmanship of the Council. Reading men's thoughts, changing them, upending the power in any advisor's hand at will. But, no one has mastered this sport as well as you. I am humbled that you choose me to be in league with."

"You are the one who had the best plan. I admire your gifts as much as you admire mine."

Argaune bowed low. He gathered his cloak and pack. He handed the leather flask once more to Farafah Fruz. The counselor took another long drink, stepping back and bowing again. But before Argaune could take his leave, Farafah Fruz gently grasped his arm.

"My friend, there is something more."

"Yes?" Argaune stepped closer, matching Farafah Fruz's whisper.

"There are rumours of a long-believed dead tribe of elders awakening."

"Awakening?"

"They have sent an emissary down to our lands to gather information. This agent is to report back to them on our advancement, our nature."

"How could the elves have escaped our notice? How could my God-twin not have perceived their energy? This is troubling."

"It may be troubling. It may not. This is all yet to be understood."

"And who is their emissary?"

"All I know is what I've told you, Argaune. There is much more to learn. Just be cautious."

"Thank you."

Both men slipped out of the darkness, but in separate directions: Farafah Fruz, towards the bridge and the castle; Roserie Argaune to his horse, grazing nearby.

# # #

Tyrian noticed that Gabriel had suddenly grown quiet. Wolf growled intermittently at the brush that surrounded them.

Tyrian's tired eyes were playing tricks on him; ghosts were passing by in his peripheral vision. Gabriel had taken the lead and was pushing harder, directly forward. Tyrian heard a series of branches snapping off to his left. Wolf was crouched low, growling, hair standing on end. Gabriel grabbed Tyrian's arm.

"Tyrian, keep moving," Gabriel whispered. He had drawn his sword.

Tyrian reached over his shoulder for the worn tree-cutting axe on his back.

"Desert Pirates, boy. Keep moving!"

A chill ran up the boy's spine. Desert Pirates were nomadic wanderers, born of generations of inter-breeding between dwarves, red elves, humans, and other unknown creatures. Few people had seen their faces, since they covered their heads in dirty cloth masks to protect themselves from the sun. Their clothing was an absurd array of robes, scarves and thick cloaks.

They were nothing like their mountain namesakes, the Mountain Pirates. Whereas the Mountain Pirates were furtive night thieves, the Desert Pirates were surly, cruel devils who made their living kidnapping young boys and girls to sell as slaves and prostitutes in desert markets.

Wolf was agitated by the new odor that permeated the air.

Tyrian's hand was wet with sweat on the handle of his axe. He heard the snort of a horse and scanned the area. Gabriel gripped his forearm tightly as the boy turned back and saw three figures standing before him, their face and arms covered with stained and tattered rags. Their crude, simple blades were drawn.

Another two figures appeared beyond them, from behind thick tree trunks. Then another four appeared in a nearby clearing. Their faces hidden behind crude canvas sun-masks, they looked like animals walking upright; their breath filled the space in front of them, like plumes of volcanic smoke.

Tyrian watched them in silence. Every one of them stood still. Their blades were simple, straight talons of steel, but with chunks taken out here and there, as if they had never been cared for. Simple leather bindings covered the hilts, which the clumsy creatures gripped tightly.

Gabriel looked over at Tyrian and saw a madness in his eyes, then glanced down at the well-worn axe. "That thing will do you little good, Tyrian."

"You just watch!" he shouted, and with a burst of rage Tyrian charged the closest pirate, bringing his axe down and nearly cutting the creature's hand off. The pirate lurched back, screaming in pain as his hand dangled from the stump of his forearm.

The other two pirates charged forward, one at Tyrian and one at Gabriel. Gabriel easily parried a clumsy attack and cut his aggressor to the ground, bleeding and screaming. Tyrian took a step back as his attacker swung his sword in a wild arc. The breeze of the blade jolted him. But just as quickly he brought his axe sideways against the creature's thigh, carving a thick gash. The creature fell to its knees as Tyrian brought his axe down again into the center of his back. As if it were a stump of wood, he stepped down hard on the torso and yanked the tool out.

Tyrian froze briefly, staring down at the still creature. In all of his childhood squabbles he had never killed. He was amazed at how easily the Desert Pirate had fallen. Suddenly his heart both saddened and hardened. He thought of his mother's death and his father's sorrow; would some filthy wife and son mourn this sad creature's death?

"Get rid of that clumsy thing, boy!" Gabriel yelled. The boy turned and faced his next opponent, who lurched forward, blade piercing nothing but air. Tyrian brought his axe down and watched in dismay as the heavy wedged blade broke off and fell to the ground. Left with only a splintered piece of wood he swung it wild at the attacker's face, knocking him off-balance.

"Tyrian!" Gabriel yelled. "Put that stump down and grab a blade! You're going to get yourself killed!"

Tyrian threw what was left of his axe to the ground and retrieved a fallen sword. He gripped the hilt and swung it around several times. It felt lighter than his father's. It was rusted in spots and looked as if it had not been cleaned in ages. Still, it was a weapon.

Tyrian squatted slightly, mimicking Gabriel. He held the blade out before him in a defensive position. As the next pirate charged in Tyrian swung his blade clockwise, blocking an upward lunge and knocking the aggressor's sword into the air. Gabriel was stunned at the boy's strength. Left without sword, and mouth agape with fear, the creature stumbled backwards a few steps, only to be cut down by Gabriel. Tyrian breathed in and calmed himself. His movements became more controlled; he almost felt serene, as if drawing from his mentor's energy. Gabriel, for his part, stayed a few steps behind the boy, keeping him in his sights. Pirate after pirate charged in and Tyrian and Gabriel cut them down just as quickly as they attacked.

When Tyrian pushed one of the pirates back a few steps he saw Wolf emerge from hiding and move behind the creature, as he would do when they played games with the younger cousins. Tyrian moved forward, forcing the pirate to step backwards and tumble over the dog. Wolf locked his fangs on the fallen creature's throat, literally biting the life out of him.

Gabriel saw movement in the shadows of the trees and realized more Desert Pirates were approaching. He quickly grabbed the pouch from his breast and shoved it into Tyrian's hand.

"Tyrian, take this and run directly south along the river's edge. I will hold them off."

"You must come also, your Honor!"

"Stay close along the river bank. I will find you there. Now go!"

Tyrian hesitated for only a second, then turned and ran. Wolf followed close behind. Three Pirates followed them, but Gabriel blocked the first one by clipping his ankle; he then cut down the next two with lightning-fast lunges.

Tyrian had gone only a short distance when he found himself facing five more Desert Pirates, the lead one a short, stout creature about four feet high. He appeared to be in charge, as he stepped back and signaled to another. The taller creature inched his way towards Tyrian. The boy stood frozen, anticipating the attack. But suddenly, from behind, two thick arms wrapped him in a tight grip and he was forced to the ground. As he lay in the moist grass, he saw the pouch spill out from his cloak, dangling before him. The dwarfish pirate leader also spotted this and slithered towards the boy, snapped the pouch from around his neck and then disappeared through the semi-circle of fighters. Tyrian screamed in horror. Wolf appeared through the brush, barking and yelping as if in pain.

Tyrian felt the grip loosen around him momentarily and he burst forward, arms swinging back. His captor fell from the impact.

Tyrian saw Wolf lunge towards one of the pirates, clenching his jaws around the creature's calf like a steel gulley trap. The pirate's body became limp with pain as he collapsed into a heap on the ground.

Tyrian charged through the battle towards the run-away pirates, the pouch, and the end of the Great River Forest.

As Tyrian ran, the forest on either side became a dizzying mirage. He did not notice the trees becoming thinner, the air becoming cooler, and the descent of the ground growing steeper. He was lost in his own anger.

The sky above had opened up. Rocky cliffs rose above him on either side. Tyrian stopped for a quick breath and finally took in his surroundings: this was nothing like the forest he had known all of his life. But the fear Tyrian felt in his heart was unrecognized by the muscles of his legs, muscles that propelled him farther down the widening path into an open grassy field.

Tyrian pushed his thoughts aside. He did not look back to the forest, only forward. He saw more pirates up ahead, awaiting their brothers with the booty. They were gathered in a circle of wagons and horses in the center of the open field.

The chase had brought him to a wide, grassy clearing with rocky cliffs on both sides. He seemed to be descending a mountain. The boy stopped short, frozen by the sight before him—a hill of grass and a few trees. A few trees. The sky was completely exposed.

Tyrian closed in on the pirates, who were racing towards the others. The crowd of desert creatures was quickly gathering up their forest treasures, to make their escape. They looked back at the boy and hurried, seeing the fury in his eyes.

The air had become lighter, his breathing was freer. The naked air felt hotter than he was used to. He realized he could hear many sounds at once. The suddenly open space provided no insulation. Simultaneously he heard the horses up ahead, hitched to the pirate wagon, the calls of the pirates themselves, the wind up above, and finally Wolf behind him.

The dog called out to him. He was far behind and trying to close the gap, but Tyrian was being pushed by the fear of Gabriel's pouch being lost for good. His promise to Heir Theobald was in danger of being broken.

As Tyrian charged the wagon, he could see the three pirates surround the rear gate to the wagon, protecting whatever or whoever was inside. One of them was pushed to the back of the group, and this is the one that the boy guessed held the pouch.

The boy did not even slow his sprint. He lunged at one, then a second, and then a third pirate. Before they knew what had happened, three pirates had been killed and lay at the boy's feet.

The pirate who held the pouch jumped into the back of the wagon. Tyrian jumped in after him, then found himself surrounded by a small group of dazed, bound boys about his age. He looked up and was eye-to-eye with the disgusting desert demon. He reached down for the creature's throat, his eyes locked onto the pouch clasped tight within its claw-like hands. But suddenly he felt a cold rush of pain flood through his head and fell to the floor of the wagon. As he was losing consciousness, he thought he could see Wolf in the distance—running, barking, then disappearing.

# # #

As Gabriel moved to parry a frantic pirate lunging at him, his foot caught on one of his fallen victims and he tumbled to the mossy floor. He quickly rolled out of range of another attack. He sprang to his feet. He noticed that the pirates were fading back towards the edge of the forest. All except one— this pirate obviously had a lust for blood. The creature swung his sword down choppily, like disparate lightning strikes, no form or rhythm, no logic. Gabriel was moving backwards, a defensive tactic he rarely used.

Then, suddenly, the pirate dropped his blade altogether and his hands flew up in the air as he screamed a high-pitched song of death. Wolf, suddenly returning to Gabriel in the forest, had flung himself onto the creature's back and sunk his teeth into the nape of his neck. With the full weight of the dog on his back the pirate crashed to the ground, his dark, syrupy blood pouring out onto the damp forest floor.

Gabriel ended his assailant's struggle with one clean lunge through his spine. The forest was now empty, except for himself and the dog. Tyrian was out of sight. He saw the look of fear in the dog's eyes, unmistakable in such a beast as him, for it was a rare emotion.

"Where is Tyrian?" Gabriel asked. Wolf let out a series of helpless barks... then a growl. He looked towards the desert and howled.

"Then he was captured. And the dragon's teeth must be with him. We will go find your friend."

Wolf's snarl faded as he breathed in heavily, tongue lapping at the air. He turned towards the scent of his friend and steered Heir Gabriel across the threshold onto the green pasture that led to the open desert.

Chapter Five

Tyrian's head fell back against a wooden plank, jolting him into consciousness. His eyes shot open. The wagon was crammed with other boys, all shackled together. Tyrian pulled at the chains that bound him to the scrawny sullen boy next to him. The inside of the wagon stunk like urine and sweat. His head pulsated with currents of pain. Above him he could see clear blue sky and feel the burning heat of the naked sun.

It all came back to him. The chase down the mountainside; jumping into the wagon to retrieve the pouch. He realized now that he was a prisoner of the Desert Pirates.

He took in the faces that surrounded him. All of the boys were all his age or younger, with empty gazes of fear and disorientation. One of them, a freckle-faced boy of maybe thirteen years, with sun-bleached hair, wore a taut, angry stare.

"Where are we?" Tyrian asked. There was no answer. "Where are we going?" he tried again. All eyes were fixed blankly in different directions, except for the freckle-faced boy, who turned his attention to Tyrian.

"We on a' way t'be slaughtered... like pigs," the boy said.

"If they were going to slaughter us," Tyrian said, "why would they have not done it before? Why waste these poor horses' legs on taking us to be slaughtered? No, they have something else planned for us."

"You smart, forest dog! You see. They kill us like pigs and eat us in meat pies."

Tyrian closed his eyes again and looked down at his feet. He tried to clear his mind of thoughts, clear his vision of images and his ears of sound. He tried to bring vacancy to his consciousness, as Gabriel had taught him. But as his mind inched towards blackness, he suddenly imagined Wolf wandering the desert alone, thirsty and hungry. He tried to shake the thought from his mind. He concentrated again and worry faded into blackness, then a single, brief moment of stillness. But once again it was interrupted, this time by thoughts of his father, who he pictured sitting alone at the fire, praying for the safety of his son. Tyrian shook his head in frustration. Suddenly he felt the wagon come to a stop.

As the horses' clumsy march halted, a man opened the gate. He was wide and blocked the view of the outside by his sheer girth. With a long metal key he released a lock on a long sinewy chain that tied all the boys' individual chains together. In one long dramatic move, the foreigner pulled the chain back, snapping it in the air behind him like a rusted metal whip. Now the boys were free from each other, albeit still bound ankle to their own wrist.

The stout slave captain let the chain fall to the desert floor and began herding the captive boys forward towards the open wagon gate. One of the Desert Pirates began to motion frantically and barked unintelligible orders. He pulled the boys out, one by one, then stepped aside for a merchant—a bearded, burly man who wore a bright red hat that hung to one side—who spat directions in a garbled language that seemed to be made up of grunts and growls. His gravelly voice spilled out between his three remaining teeth.

The merchant began yanking the boys out one by one, pulling at the chains that linked their wrists and ankles. Tyrian shuffled through the narrow wagon as best he could when the foreman at the wagon gate lost patience; he reached his thick, tattooed arm into the wagon and grabbed the long chain that bound Tyrian and yanked it forward, sending the boy out of the wagon and onto the hot, cracked desert ground. Unable to catch himself, his forehead hit the ground and he winced at the pain. Blood trickled into his eye. The foreman leaned back, laughing heartily.

Tyrian lay for a moment in the sand, pulling at his bindings. His muscles ached at being restrained. His heart pumped faster. His breathing became heavy. He could not run, and all around him were men who seemed to be foreign agents. He looked up at the foreman outlined against the naked sky; he glared at the man, who smiled wryly in return.

Tyrian regained his feet in a rush of anger and charged the foreman, butting him square in the nose. The foreman fell backward onto his rear, dropping his staff and hiding his face in his round, puffy hands. His garbled barks became moans of pain. The captive boys gave a collective shriek as the foreman struggled to his feet. Suddenly other merchants, similarly dressed, surrounded the boys. They all held long, thick staffs and poked and prodded at the boys, pushing them all to the side of the wagon.

Tyrian was brought to his feet by two of the merchants, both wearing the same floppy red hat. As the other boys were ushered away he was pulled to one side, behind the wagon. The merchants tied his wrists and stripped him naked. One merchant jabbed him with a sharp wooden staff to keep him off balance while the other buckled his wrists onto two large, iron rings on the side of the wagon. The rings were spaced so that his arms were painfully spread apart. His legs were forced apart with the staff so he held a wide, tense position. A third merchant came around with a smaller stick, a worn-down baton with a narrow, almost flat end.

Tyrian rested his forehead against the wagon's side and saw in the distance a quick discussion between the Desert Pirates and one of the red-hatted merchants. There was an exchange of coins and handshakes and then his captors disappeared. With them went the pouch.

Tyrian's eyes welled up. He was watching Gabriel's prize disappear before him. He had failed. He was overcome with shame and he wanted nothing more than to tear that pouch from the dirty hands of the Desert Pirates. He wanted to make every one of them pay for his shame. Was he not strong enough? Or was he not smart enough? Neither answer gave him comfort. He wished Wolf were with him.

Tyrian's face was pressed tight against the rough, sun-burnt wood of the wagon. He squeezed his eyes shut, and stood in blind apprehension until he felt the baton strike the back of his right thigh. Then his left thigh. Then his right again. Alternating back and forth, each blow getting harder. Sweat poured down his face and his eyes watered as the stinging on his raw flesh became burning. His knees buckled and he slumped down, but the merchants lifted him back up. He let out a scream of pain and anger, but that was only met with laughter from his tormenters. Finally, the burning in his wounds became cold numbness; he felt a last brutal impact to his lower back. The merchants left him to collapse in his pain, still shackled to the iron rings.

A moment later he was hit with a rush of cold water. One of the merchants began wrapping his upper thighs with bandages made of rough, heavy material. Tyrian guessed that this was more to hide the wounds than to protect them. He was dressed in a long leather skirt. Finally, they clumsily replaced his iron shackles with leather bindings, pinning his wrists together. Then he was led away from the wagon and towards the open square.

His stride was slow and deliberate, revealing his pain. As they rounded the wagon and approached the open field, he saw a stage where all of the other boys, bound together by rope, wore the same leather skirts as his. They stared vacantly out at a gathering crowd of men.

Tyrian was nudged up on the stage platform and surveyed the entire trading encampment. It seemed to spread out like a slowly expanding pool of water, in no apparent logical direction. The tents and cabins were pushed up against each other, creating an absurd maze of alleyways.

He saw several different kinds of beasts, some carrying loads of goods, some wandering aimlessly, master-less. There were horses. There were two-humped creatures, which he later learned are called camels. He saw stray desert cats, wild dogs. And all of the animals looked viciously hungry.

Tyrian noticed a small caravan of wagons crawling back out to the desert. Off in another direction went another one. In the distance, still another. He did not know which one held his pouch. They all looked the same to him. But they were scattering out into the great, dry void.

The foreman stepped up to the front of the stage. Tyrian betrayed his thoughts with a smile, as he noticed the foreman's blood-shot eyes, and his skin turning a dark purple along the bridge of his nose. The foreman was barking out at the gathering of buyers just below the stage as he moved from boy to boy, pulling and poking at each of them. He had now taken on the role of auctioneer and was bellowing out the virtues of each young boy.

Tyrian could not understand the foreign words, but it was obvious by the auctioneer's gestures: this boy had sturdy legs for pulling carts and for pushing heavy harvest tools; that one had strong arms for lifting and stacking produce; another one had close eyes and was short, which meant he was good at herding animals.

As he finally approached Tyrian the auctioneer/foreman smiled widely, cunningly. He gave the boy a few firm slaps on the cheek and then looked out at the audience. His voice rose to a sing-song bellow as he gripped Tyrian's biceps tightly, then flexed his own and followed that by punching his fist into an open palm, showing that the boy was a hard worker and was strong.

The auctioneer spent a considerable amount of time showing off the strength and size of Tyrian; finally a man approached. The potential buyer was a tall man, dressed immaculately in a crimson velvet gown with a single gold medallion hanging over his chest. He stepped onto the stage and did not touch the boy, but examined him closely. Tyrian noticed that this man smelled of an exotic perfume and his face was clean and smooth of hair. Whereas the others smelled and looked as if they had not bathed in months, this man could have just dried himself and dressed.

Nodding at the boy's skirt, the stranger ordered, "Let's see his legs." The foreman bent down and lifted the leather skirt.

"Why are his legs bound up?" the stranger asked. The foreman answered with a confused look and some gibberish, which did not satisfy the stranger, who shook his head and walked away. Tyrian noticed, though, that he did not disappear—instead he retired to a bench a few strides from the auction stage and watched the proceedings. The stranger kept his eyes fixed on Tyrian.

Another potential buyer stepped up. He was a short, stocky man with a barrel chest and a long mane of snow-white hair. He limped along with a cane and did not attempt to ascend onto the stage. He jabbed his stick towards Tyrian and grunted some garbled words that matched the foreman's language. He was dressed equally as extravagantly as the first buyer, but this man looked soiled, and Tyrian could smell the sour odor of alcohol from where he stood. His movements were slow and clumsy; the man was as drunk as an Elder at New Moon Celebration.

The foreman and the stocky buyer negotiated in their crude language until the older man pulled out a handful of gold and silver pieces and slapped them onto the stage.

The foreman whispered his crude dialect into Tyrian's ear, and then stepped away with a laugh. Tyrian was unshackled and ushered off the stage by one of the other red-hatted merchants. As he descended the few steps, he noticed a group of young girls standing off to one side, waiting for their moment of sale. One girl stood off to the side by herself. She could not have been more than a few years younger than he.

When the girl saw Tyrian's kind gaze, her face widened as if smiling in all but her mouth. Her lips retained the slack maw of fear, but her eyes betrayed excitement. Tyrian gave her a subtle nod and she replied with an awkward curtsy-step, her tangled blonde mane falling into her face.

When Tyrian reached the bottom of the steps the old buyer took the chain from the merchant and jerked Tyrian towards him. He barked an order at the boy, then, in a very broken accent he yelled, "Come! Come! Walk, boy!" He pulled a small flask from his breast pocket and drank from it as he turned and began walking in the direction of the main square of tents and shacks.

Tyrian now saw that a whole settlement lay beyond. It sat in the middle of this great desert like a tiny island in the ocean. It was like a smaller, cruder version of Battgadl Square back home.

Now bound in rope, Tyrian inched his way along, and found himself being led into an alleyway of sorts. On either side stood tall shacks and tents, creating a narrow passageway that was shadowed and secluded. Tyrian abruptly stopped once he was out of view of the crowd behind him. When the slack of the rope ran out, the merchant was jerked back. He turned to the boy and was at first frightened by his obstinance and then angered. The new slave-owner wrapped the line a few times around his fist and then approached Tyrian. The older man hadn't realized how tall the boy was until now. He was forced to arch his fat neck upwards. Again, he spoke the only words he knew in Tyrian's language, "Walk, boy! Come! Come!" But Tyrian did not move. The merchant pulled at the rope but there was no give.

He pulled a leather crop from his knapsack, which he held out as a threat, then he pulled at the line again and repeated, "Come! Come, boy!" Still nothing. Finally, tired of this routine, he whipped Tyrian across the chest, leaving a long gash. Tyrian looked straight ahead. Again, the merchant lashed him across the chest, opening the wound wider.

Tyrian's eyes watered, but he made no sound. "Come! Walk!" And then another lashing. Blood began trickling down onto his stomach like a hot lava stream. The merchant took a sip from his flask as he studied the boy's face, then hurled a quick series of lashes across his chest and stomach—the old man's face was turning red.

Tyrian suddenly bolted towards the merchant, in an eruption of rage. Still bound, he clumsily attacked the old man, first butting his head with his own and then sinking his teeth into the man's cheek. The old man tried to jerk his head away, with his arms flailing about, but Tyrian's jaws were locked.

After a moment, Tyrian released his grip and stepped back. At the opposite end of the alley he saw a figure. It moved with a slow and confident gait, and as it grew closer, he recognized it as the figure of the stranger who had examined him on the stage. He could see the tall form becoming the handsome, broad-shouldered merchant, velvet gown flowing and sword drawn. Within moments the handsome stranger was upon them and stood directly behind the angry merchant.

The stranger said something in a low, calm voice, using the old man's language, although he made it sound less clumsy. The old man turned and looked up at the stranger and then laughed as he reached for his flask and drank again. He turned, spit, then grumbled a few words to the stranger. There was a short exchange; it began somewhat politely but quickly changed. In an instant, the stranger had the merchant by the throat and was pulling him away from Tyrian. Tyrian watched this as the rope fell to the ground; he was free to escape.

Tyrian took a few steps back. He turned as if to run, but then stopped. A surge of anger washed away his need to flee. He wanted to make the fat drunkard pay for treating him like an animal. But he stopped and watched in awe as he saw the stranger's elegance become violent.

The old man began flailing his arms, trying to fight the stranger, but to no avail.

Finally, the stranger released his grip, shoving the stout foreigner back against the wall of a shack and, suddenly, lunging his blade into the large round chest. The old man immediately went limp and fell to the ground, fighting for air as his torso spilled blood in heavy gushes. Gradually he slumped over, dead. The stranger then turned to Tyrian, and greeted him fluently in his own language.

"My name is Gorka Osa. I am a farmer and horse-breeder. I apologize for disposing of your purchaser here, but he insulted me."

"My name is Tyrian Fellhawk, and I am no slave."

"Well, you have successfully fooled the Desert Pirates and their merchant associates."

"It is not difficult to fool those desert idiots. I would punish each and every one of them if I had the time. And as for this drunken slob, if it were not you that killed him, I would have done so soon enough."

"I do not doubt that. Hold your hands out, and keep your arms still." Tyrian did this and Gorka Osa brought his blade down hard, splitting the leather bindings clean.

"You must be hungry," Gorka Osa said. "Let me buy you a meal and some ale."

Tyrian nodded, then followed him back in the direction of the market. He was silent and kept his head down as he shadowed Gorka Osa round the corner towards the inn. As he climbed the steps to the inn, Tyrian turned back to see the young girl being led by a merchant, just as he had been moments before. He stopped and caught her gaze as she was led to a horse-driven cart full of pigs. As her purchaser lifted her into the cart with the pigs, she turned her head away from Tyrian, unwilling to make eye contact. The old man handed a few coins to a nearby boy to watch her, then turned towards the direction of the inn.

"My friend, food and drink await you," Gorka Osa said to Tyrian.

The inn's café was dark, hinting at neither the chaos nor the bright sunlight outside. Several lamps placed sparsely around the room gave off little light. A bar and kitchen could be seen in the back of the inn—the rest of the area was filled with tables and chairs. A wandering musician moved from table to table, playing a strange stringed instrument with tiny bells attached to it.

Gorka Osa and Tyrian found an empty corner table and were sitting down when the barkeep yelled from across the room, first in the crude desert language and then in Tyrian's own language, "No slaves allowed in here!"

"My friend is no slave," Gorka Osa yelled back.

"He wears the skirt of a slave!"

"He has just been freed. I would appreciate a pitcher of apology for him!"

The hushed crowd went back to their business. Gorka Osa and Tyrian settled into drink and plates full of overcooked camel steaks and a stew of potatoes and bitter desert plants. Tyrian had never tasted such flavors before. His palate had been formed by sixteen years in the forest and the spices he ate there normally varied from bitter to less bitter. Here was a stew full of exotic ingrediaents that made him sweat. He drank his ale down quickly, soothing the burning on his tongue and in his throat. Gorka Osa smiled and watched him devour his food as if he hadn't eaten in weeks.

"You eat like a slave; you must have been travelling for days. Your accent is curious. It sounds like that of the Great River Forest, but you are far from there."

"My accent, as well as I, come from the forest."

"And how did you end up on the slave block? Even the Desert Pirates fear your barbarian brethren."

"I was riding with—" Tyrian stopped himself, suddenly thinking better of revealing anything further.

"I got lost," he continued. "I was on a hunting trip with my dog and we got lost. The Desert Pirates attacked us at the southern edge of the forest."

Gorka Osa watched the boy's eyes wander across the inn and then drop down to his meal. He smiled and left the boy to his thoughts. Tyrian finished his stew and picked at the last remaining piece of camel steak, then looked up at Gorka Osa.

"Why did you free me?" Tyrian asked.

"He was a foolish drunk. He would have wasted your gifts on lifting bales of wheat or stacking his wine."

"You chose not to purchase me."

"I saw how the merchant looked at you; there was fear in his eyes. He was wary of you because you fought him. Any man who fights against captivity will not stay captive for long. If I were to purchase you and enslave you, you would undoubtedly slay me in my sleep one night, the same punishment as you would have given that fool."

"It is true!" Tyrian laughed.

Gorka Osa rose and dropped three gold coins on the table as he gathered his cloak and his pack. Tyrian took one of the gold coins and held it close to his face, studying it. The forest clans had no need for gold coins. The commerce of the Great River Forest was trade and bartering; meat, wood, fur— these were the things of value to them.

"I can provide you with a bed and a roof tonight."

Tyrian hesitated; he had no horse and no supplies. He had no idea how far into the desert he was.

"Are you far from here?"

"We will be there before the sun sets."

"The Desert Pirates took something from me. Something I cannot lose."

"You will not reach them before sundown. You will have to resume your chase tomorrow."

"I do not even know where to look tomorrow."

"I can help you with that. For tonight, you need rest."

"I would greatly appreciate a soft bed tonight," Tyrian finally replied, as he followed Gorka Osa back into the overbearing sunlight.

As they rounded a corner and entered an alleyway, Tyrian looked back and saw the same ratty-haired slave girl, sitting as before in the wagon with the pigs. Her face had not yet resigned itself to the fate of a slave, and she pulled at the chain that kept her tethered to the wagon. She hissed at the pigs to leave her be, as they sniffed and nudged her with their snouts.

"Give me your sword," Tyrian said. Gorka Osa looked at him, confused, and then gave him his blade.

Tyrian ran towards the girl. Gorka Osa watched the boy as he pulled open the short gate to the wagon and clapped his hands, sending the pigs out, one by one, scattering across the dusty square in confusion.

Tyrian pulled at the tattered leather binding that held the girl.

"Hold your hands apart, girl! Look away!" He moved the girl's hands apart, realizing she did not understand. He swung Gorka Osa's blade up in a wide arc and brought it down, splitting the binding. The girl was free. She looked at him, eyes wide and unsure.

She took a step forward towards him, grasping his wrists in a tight grip.

"Go!" he yelled, forcing her out of the wagon. He grabbed her by her narrow waist and pulled her up to her feet. She reached out and cluthed his arms tightly. He tried to pull away, but she held tight. Her eyes spoke the words which her language could not: 'Where will I go?'

He pushed her towards the open desert. "Go to your home, girl!" Even as he shouted the order, he realized how ridiculous it sounded. And then his rescue of the girl seemed suddenly futile. He turned back to Gorka Osa, who lowered his eyes from the boy's stare and shook his head slowly, no.

The girl wrapped her arms around his wide torso, as if pleading. He broke free of her grip and then shoved her in no specific direction.

"Go! Run! You are free!"

She stepped decidedly away from him and spit at the ground, then turned and walked, slowly, firmly, away from him.

"But she is free now," Tyrian said helplessly.

"Free?" Gorka Osa asked.

"She does not sit with filthy swine, like another animal. She walks free."

"I cannot take her, Tyrian."

"Why can you not offer her the same refuge that you offer me?"

"My offer is admittedly selfish. You have something to offer me. You have strength and cunning. She is young and there is no man near me that I could marry her off to. She would be a burden. You freed her. Let it be enough. Believe that she will gain safety and comfort and clear it from your mind. You can do nothing further."

Tyrian and Gorka Osa turned into the alleyway.

# # #

Gorka Osa and Tyrian arrived several hours later at the estate. Gorka Osa slowed the horse to a trot as Tyrian took in his surroundings. Tyrian jumped from the back of the horse onto the soft estate grounds.

Tyrian had never seen anything like this arranged and manicured landscape, the sheer beauty. The Fellhawk Compound was large, but it was dark and the grounds were muddied from work and horses and wagon traffic. That yard was filled with abandoned tools and woodsheds and spare wagon parts. It was, at best, functional.

Gorka Osa, living alone on such a vast estate, took care to tend his land for beauty over functionality. The pathway to the house was lined on either side with deep green fields, broken up here and there by patches of flowers or small, well-trimmed shrubs. The house itself stood in the shadows of several large shade trees. It was made of white stone and decorative Avajian tiles. The house had three levels and the second level opened onto a wide patio that stretched out over the front entrance.

As Gorka Osa brought the horse to a full stop, Tyrian dropped to the ground and wandered into the yard, smelling flowers he had never encountered before. He marveled at how the trees were cared for, compared to the trees in the Great River Forest were never looked at for their beauty but only for their purpose. Indeed, everything about his homeland was about purpose. Gorka Osa lived with a luxury that the boy had never known.

Gorka Osa walked his horse to the back of the house and soon returned to find Tyrian sitting in the grassy yard, eating an orange from a tree. Watching the boy's delight at the beautiful estate, Gorka Osa found a renewed appreciation that he had lost. Waking up day after day in this place, he had gradually forgotten its splendor. He took a moment to breathe in the fragrant air, as the slight breeze carried with it the aromas of the many flowers and fruits.

The sun was beginning to set over the long narrow horse stable that fenced in the western side of his yard. He motioned Tyrian to follow him into the house.

As they entered, Gorka Osa removed his shoes and motioned Tyrian to do the same. The stone floor felt cool upon Tyrian's feet and he found himself suddenly calmed and comforted being away from the chaos of the desert.

The house's interior was another wonder. The floors were tiled with sun-baked red stone. The lower level was marked by tall shutter-less windows, which guided in soft breezes that moved the gauzy curtains like dancing specters.

"You can draw a bath upstairs," Gorka Osa said. "You will find me in the library downstairs when you are done. There are robes in the bedchamber just down the hall."

Tyrian found a long, deep tub set in the center of the bathing chamber. In the corner of the room was a short cast-iron stove with a pot of water atop it. Tyrian built a fire in the stove and sat patiently waiting for the water to come to a boil. Next to the stove was a long vat of fresh, cold water. On the surface of the water lay petals of roses and other flowers. He wondered who maintained this place. He saw no sign of servants, but the upkeep at Gorka Osa's estate surely required more than just one person. Finally, after the water had come to a boil, he poured it in, heating the bath and lowered himself in.

As he lay back in the warm water, he watched the steam rise from the surface into the air before him and he closed his eyes. He tried to clear his mind. Once again, he searched for that elusive vacancy of thought and image. He slowed his breathing, as Heir Theobald had told him. He kept his body still and let the warm water roll over him. Try as he might, each time his mind drifted into blackness Wolf appeared, or Heir Theobald, or his father. Then he thought about the pouch with the dragon's teeth. A wave of shame overcame him. He had let Gabriel down. He dunked his head into the water and tried to forget everything. Maybe he would wake up the next morning and take Gorka Osa's horse and return to the Great River Forest. Maybe Theobald had already retrieved the pouch. No matter, he was a woodcutter, not an adventurer.

As the water cooled, Tyrian climbed out of the tub and found a towel and robe. He wandered through the hallways, peeking in chamber after chamber, marveling at the spaciousness and the furnishings. This estate was certainly meant to house many people.

Tyrian found a room to his liking, of modest size and at the corner of the floor, overlooking the courtyard and horse barn. A giant bed covered in velvet and silk was the main piece of furniture.

Against the wall at the foot of the bed was a long cabinet with neatly folded piles of blankets and towels. He lay back on the bed, hair still wet, and closed his eyes; gradually the blackness became his passage into slumber.

The only known dream-world for Tyrian was that of fighting the dark demons in the Great River Forest, with his trusted companion at his side. But, strangely, now in his subconscious, he stood alone. Sword drawn and ready, but alone. There was no Wolf at his side and there were no enemies in sight. The once-mysterious sounds that bounced back and forth in the dark were now heard as playful and benign. Critters perched on fallen logs, where once panthers prowled and serpents slithered. He was motionless, not with fear but in peace. No aggressors and no dangers in sight, he found himself still, at peace.

Hours later Tyrian woke to the stinging chill of the breeze from an open window. He jumped to his feet, shivering, and pulled his robe tight around himself.

Tyrian found a simple tunic and trousers in a dresser drawer and dressed quickly. In a nearby walk-in closet, he found several intricate robes hanging. He pulled one off of its hanger and covered himself before making his way downstairs.

The sun had set some hours before and the house was mostly dark. There were occasional pockets of orange glow where lanterns hung or candles sat inlaid in the walls.

Tyrian found Gorka Osa in the library, sitting beside a healthy fire in a deep leather chair. He read from a large hardbound book that sat in his lap. On a table in the center of the room was a carafe of red wine.

"You fell asleep," Gorka Osa's deep voice filled the cluttered room. Tyrian noticed that this was the only room he had seen in any sort of disarray.

"Yes. I've not bathed in such a room ever, my lord. For all my grandfather's battles and life troubles, this could be his heaven."

Gorka Osa rose and crossed to the table, where he poured two glasses of wine and handed one to Tyrian. He then took his seat again and set the book upon a nearby shelf.

"Do you ride with a militia, sir?" Tyrian asked.

After a brief pause, studying the boy, Gorka Osa answered, "I fight for no militia. My time is better spent gardening or brushing my horses than fighting for the false honor of a dishonorable king."

Tyrian had never heard such words before. "Every few months the King's agents come for his taxes and I run them off," Gorka Osa continued. "They have come to arrest me a few times, to no avail. I suppose some day they will tire of this game and send a local militia to burn my estate down, but until that day, I am happy in my position. There is a higher order than the one the King pronounces. And his days are numbered."

"But how long can you defy the order of his word?"

"I will gamble that I can defy his throne longer than he can hold it. I believe in anarchy, Tyrian—the free will of man. According to my philosophy, the concept of a law of property is absurd; there can be no theft because man has not natural claim on land. I did not purchase this land, so no law can take it from me. When a man can defeat me in battle, he can have it. But until that day, it is mine, and I pay no taxes for its stewardship."

"But there must be order," Tyrian said. "Should there not? Even in our dark part of the world, the savages come to my family to settle disputes. Even in our land of vandals, we know that to have no order is to have chaos and destruction."

"Anarchy does not have to be chaos. It is true the hearts of most men contain rage and anger, but not always. My anarchy is only aggressive when it needs to be. When no man threatens me, I am at peace."

Tyrian was silent. He wondered how his barbarian townspeople would be without the anchor of his family. "Where did you get such wealth, if I may ask?" Tyrian finally spoke.

"During the Kazhan Years, the Time of Upheaval when the King's armies were devouring villages and states, my home was attacked. My father sent me off with all of his treasures and begged that I never return. I defied him just one year later and found my family dead and my home destroyed. I took what my father had given me to start a small horse-trading business, and … found this estate. I pledge allegiance to no man, Tyrian. This world is not worthy of a leader."

Tyrian sipped his wine and stared into the fire. His thoughts again wandered to his friend Wolf and to Heir Gabriel Theobald. He must leave at daylight to find the treasure he had lost to the Desert Pirates.

"I could use some help around here. I could pay you well, and you can learn the trade," Gorka Osa offered.

"Thank you, sir. But I will bother you for one night only and then I must move on."

"Where did you learn to speak so well? And such manners! You do not speak like the barbarians I know of in the Great River Forest."

"You are familiar with my homeland?"

"My adventures have taken me through there, yes. That is one of the most rugged and dangerous places I've been through, I must say."

"Our family is well-regarded in the forest, Gorka Osa. My grandfather rode with the militia when it existed. And my uncle reaches out to our people often. My father has taught me words and how to use them, as well as a sword and how to use that."

"He has done well. You are both well-mannered and have a reasonable mind."

Gorka Osa fell silent again. Tyrian looked away, pondering the shelves of books and papers, as if searching for a specific title. Gorka Osa cleared his throat and then continued, "I offer you not only coin for self-reliance, but the faith to truly rely only on yourself. My secrets cannot be given to you by a church or a state, because they are the opposite of church and state. Anarchy is truly being independent of any ruler, my boy. My offer will be open-ended, should you change your mind. I could use a strong boy like you who learns quickly."

"Thank you, sir." Tyrian finished his glass of wine and then stood in the doorway, pausing for a moment.

"What is it?" Gorka Osa asked.

"I must find the Desert Pirates who captured me. They took something of great value from me and I must retrieve it."

Gorka Osa laughed to himself and then replied, "You are certainly to be the first to escape capture and slavery only to return and face his captors. You have the heart of a giant, to be sure."

"I must," he said, and then suddenly considered the danger of his journey. "What will happen if they catch me again? Will they try to sell me once more, or will they kill me?"

"They cannot hold you, Tyrian, that is for sure. But it is a dangerous quest you go on."

"I must," the boy repeated. "Where will I find them?"

"A place called the Vilzcyys Tents. It is as close to a home as those sand beasts will ever have. Every third day the Desert Pirate expeditions return, to unload their booty."

"And I will find my treasure there?"

"It should be there still. They do not sell or barter their stolen goods until they've fully appraised them. This sometimes takes weeks. You have time. You will find the Vilzcyys Tents on the southwestern edge of the desert. You must find the jagged ridges of the Khozjik Mountains, then let them lead you to where the sand ends. This is where you will find the tent village. It is about a day's ride from here. You will do fine. What is this treasure you are retrieving, may I ask?"

Tyrian looked down at his feet, suddenly uneasy. He was fearful of his secret being revealed. Looking up again he quickly said, "Thank you again for your hospitality, sir. Goodnight."

Tyrian had been asleep for several hours when he woke to the sound of horse hooves clapping on the tiles of the house yard. He rose and looked outside. Out the window he saw three men standing in the courtyard below, fully lit by the naked moonlight.

# # #

The sun had vanished hours before and the moon was now ascending to its nighttime perch. Gorka Osa was saddling his horse when two other steeds approached him on the cobblestone path of his estate. He led his horse out into the open where, beneath the yellowish light of the desert eye, he met the two armed and helmeted riders. They looked like knights in some foreign army. One had a helmet with a single horn protruding from the forehead. This was Babbel, a stocky, robust warrior with few decorations or adornments to his attire—a drab riding gown covered by chain mail and broadsword on his back. Babbel hailed from the foothills of the Jotun Peaks—icy fields and snowswept, unforgiving land. He was quick to anger and answered to no man, save Gorka Osa.

The second rider was Dò bbeldam, a tall man although his height was disguised by his bowed posture. His recent bout of stomach pains bent him into a perpetual tormented position and he was given to fits of violent coughing. It was obvious to all three men that his days among the living were few. Gorka Osa and Babbel could see it in his eyes. Dò bbeldam heard it in his own voice when he spoke. His illness had reached into all parts of his body, and although he still fought like a man several years his junior, his combat was driven by his spirit. Even the hours of simple riding took their toll.

Dò bbeldam's father had been a tribal leader in his village and as a youth Dò bbeldam had trained in the much-respected discipline of archery. On his back hung a quiver of arrows and a long bow. Sheathed in his horse's saddle he kept a short, thin blade used for close combat, in which he almost never engaged.

Gorka Osa had met the two riders decades before, when he was leading a group of rebels fighting King Azjik's armies in the Grytician Valley. Gorka Osa's army was attacking small bands of soldiers as they journeyed back to their camp to be replaced by reinforcements. Hiding in the mountains and staying well-rested and well-fed, his strategy was to overpower soldiers tired and weary from battle, rather than engage new forces. This way, Azjik's forces were slowly depleted over many months. Gorka Osa had the gift of patience.

One night a scout approached his camp with a request for help from Babbel, who was leading a frail army of resistant villagers. Gorka Osa led his men into the valley where to his dismay, he found Babbel's army all but destroyed; only Babbel and a few others were left standing. Babbel's men had fought bravely, but were no match for the King's many platoons. Angry and vengeful, Babbel joined Gorka Osa and over the years became a trusted general.

Several years later Dò bbeldam, having heard about Gorka Osa's mercenary campaigns, commissioned him to help drive out Azjik's army from his home village, which had been overtaken not a year before. His father was beheaded for his refusal to surrender to Azjik, but not before he had implored all of his men to kill themselves rather than surrender. As the first born, Dò bbeldam was required to go into hiding to avenge his father's loss.

Gorka Osa accepted Dò bbeldam's commission with passion. With Babbel and Dò bbeldam at his side, he stormed into the village, leading the largest group of men he had ever commanded. They were all battle-hardened and angry. They answered his call with fury. Gorka Osa was successful once again in driving out Azjik's forces. But what they had won was a mere shell of what it was before. Half of the villagers had either been killed or had fled. The shallow river that ran through the village, their only water source, was contaminated with dead soldiers. The women and children were sent way to a neighboring village while most of the remaining healthy men chose to ride with Gorka Osa in campaigns against Azjik.

For years Gorka Osa led his new army through the mountains and plains, attacking the King's Regular Stand Army with Babbel and Dò bbeldam, his two generals. But, over the years, men died and men left. And now, even the mighty Dò bbeldam was nearing his end.

It was a meeting between Gorka Osa and the priest Roserie Argaune, arranged by Farafah Fruz at Argaune's request, held on the beaches of the Blood Sea, that had changed the course of rebellion for the rogue assassin and his generals. Argaune convinced Gorka Osa that his campaigns were "pin-pricks to the shell of a giant, whereas an infection from the belly is what will truly kill this monster."

Together the Three Riders fought with allegiance only to themselves. Their common bond was a hatred for the King and a love of gold. Babbel and Dò bbeldam followed Gorka Osa where he directed and he occasionally let them solicit their own missions of assassination or thievery. Their leader's close ties to the wizard Roserie Argaune always kept them employed with a job that contained equal parts darkness, danger and riches.

What Babbel and Dò bbeldam did not know was that Gorka Osa's ties to Argaune went beyond just those of an assassin and his benefactor. Their relationship was more than business associates. In the shadows of a violent kingdom, Gorka Osa was a protector of sorts for the aging priest. Babbel and Dò bbeldam never questioned the long periods when their leader disappeared without a word, sometimes for a year at a time. These were secret assignments, when Gorka Osa would track down enemies of Argaune for assassination or to retrieve information. In exchange, Gorka Osa waited patiently for the day that Argaune's plans for the King's demise would come to fruition. On that day, Argaune assured him, the princes would fall, and with them, the Order of the Heirs. The line of ascension would mean nothing, as militias battled each other, heirs slayed heirs... chaos!

The older man guaranteed Gorka Osa that he had secret agents within the King's Council of Elders. His plans had been developed in concert with others.

In moments of rest, as Argaune and Gorka Osa would share a meal, Roserie spoke eloquently of the frailty of the command King Azjik held over his vast kingdom.

"The routines of our fellow men are like parchment that can easily be pricked through," Argaune once told him. "And underneath live the chaos and violence that are all too ready to usurp the false order."

Gorka Osa would listen intently to the reasons for the unrest: the decree of Azjik's One Disciple; the collection of taxes; the Order of Heirs, constantly kept the generals at odds with each other.

Slowly, over the years, Argaune had hinted at his plans of chaos and unrest. Upon the King's death the sons would also be assassinated and then, after Argaune had planted the seeds of mistrust between heirs, years of war between the militias would ensue. Heir Volkummen would quickly (and, unbeknownst to him, temporarily) rise to the monarchy; he was the only heir ruthless enough to bring order. "He is the one with the stained heart and dark soul," Argaune liked to say. Volkummen's monarchy eventually was to give way to a new structure. This is where Argaune's details became vague. Gorka Osa was satisfied at the thought of Azjik's demise. Argaune had promised him his own independence outside the borders of the new kingdom. It was a strange marriage—Argaune's dreams of power and dominance fed Gorka Osa's dreams of isolation.

Gorka Osa's attention was brought back to the present by the glare in the sky: the yellow moon, his only god. He fastened his saddle and sheathed his broadsword atop his horse; the three men exchanged formal greetings. Gorka Osa looked up into the starry night sky and spotted the mysterious hawk, his surrogate guide, sent from Roserie Argaune. He watched as it circled overhead, as if waiting for him. He put on his battle helmet and suddenly became the mysterious and sinister rider. The moon shone against his helmet, glimmering on the two well-polished horns on either side of the top. Without a word he mounted his horse and pushed her into the night, Babbel and Dò bbeldam close behind.

# # #

From the second story window of his guest room, Tyrian, still groggy, could not make out who the men were, just three figures riding into the dark desert night. He had the fog of sleep still in his head and was not sure if it was a dream or if it was real.

As the three figures disappeared into the darkness beyond the estate, Tyrian fell back into the plush cradle of Gorka Osa's guest bed, the soft breeze of the cold desert air sweeping over him now and then. He wondered if he would not be happier living here and working for Gorka Osa.

Chapter Six

Heir Gabriel Theobald and Wolf arrived at the Desert Trading Post just as the sun was melting into the western horizon. As they waded into the camp from the vast emptiness of the desert, through the invisible borders of the trading encampment, the bright glow of the desert floor was giving way to the dark mirror of the night sky. Blackness was pricked here and there with torches that lit the entrances to small inns and brothels. The encampment denizens were now hiding in tents or, more likely, huddling in the main inn and saloon.

Gabriel noticed a well near the slave auction stage and led the dog to it. He lowered the bucket down, feeling its weight increase as it filled. When he pulled it up and onto the ground Wolf dunked his head into it, lapping up the water, filling the air with the sounds of his thirsty tongue.

Gabriel strode to the inn at the center of the square, Wolf in tow. He squatted down in front of Wolf at the entrance and stroked the back of his neck.

"My friend, you stay here. I won't be long."

Wolf sat, as if to guard the foot of the stairs, but was soon on his belly, fighting sleep.

Gabriel entered the chaos of the inn and found his way directly to the bar. He took a seat and motioned for the barkeep, a bearish, toothless man who leaned in close over the bar, sharing with Gabriel his sour breath—a concoction of odors mingled too long ago to recognize.

"What'llya have?" The barkeep leaned back as he pointed at the wall menu.

"I'll have two of your roasts and a mug of ale," Gabriel replied, suddenly realizing that his royal medallion was hanging through his robes. He tucked it back in and smiled at the barkeep.

"By 'is majesty's order, Yer Honor, I must feed you free of coinage."

"There will be no need for that, barkeep. In fact, if you keep my status a secret, and you pack up that second roast, my pay will be more generous."

The barkeep winked his bloodshot eye and smiled widely. "O' course, Yer Honor."

When the man returned with the food and ale, Gabriel dropped four gold coins on the bar top in front of him, and let dangle a fifth in his fingertips. The barkeep's eyes closed in on it, and sparkled with greed. "Can I get you anything else, Yer Honor?"

"Yes. You can tell me about the slave sale today. Were there any especially high sales? Anything of exceptional interest?"

"There were a murder 'round the corner this ev'nin!"

Gabriel leaned in closer, "Tell me more."

The barkeep cleared his throat and looked up at the ceiling dramatically, as if to recall the details. "Well, to be honest, not sure I remember much o' what me 'eard!"

Gabriel slid another gold coin across the wooden bar, letting it rest against the barkeep's fat and cracked sausage-fingers. The Barkeep suddenly gave a look of clarity and he leaned in towards the knight.

"Right, right, now it comes to me! There were a tall boy, with white skin. Very white skin, mi'lord. He were very tall and he were bought by a fancy man with lots of coinage! But the boy killed him in the alley 'round the corner there! That was all!"

"Was there anyone with him?"

"He was seen dining with another man, later, but they both disappeared into the night, Yer Honor!"

"Thank you, my friend."

Gabriel found Wolf fast asleep in the shadows of the inn. He knelt down and set the roast in front of him. The dog devoured it hungrily.

When Wolf was finished, Gabriel pulled a torch from its holder by the stairs and led Wolf towards the alleyway that the barkeep had spoken of.

Wolf sniffed at the dirt, examining every scent. The dirt retained the ghosts of thousands of creatures, as the encampment was a meeting place for just about every culture in Azjik's kingdom. Wolf's nose was working furiously at the criss-crossing aromas of human, animal, and other unknown beings. All the while Gabriel searched for footprints, hoofprints, metal chips, or anything else left in evidence. He held his torch down low towards the ground, squinting through the darkness.

Wolf began growling quietly as he stopped at a certain spot where the ground met the wall of a building. Gabriel rushed over and lowered the torch close to the ground, and there he saw dried blood. Only hours old, he guessed, but already baked dry by the unforgiving desert heat.

Wolf had moved on to another spot nearby, where he began barking wildly. His head bobbed up and down and his shoulders jerked in spasms, as if he was tethered to this spot. There were new bloodstains on the dirt here, but Wolf knew it was not the same blood. This was Tyrian's. He knew the scent well; he had licked clean the boy's wounds long enough to recognize the odor of his blood and his sweat. His friend had been here.

In the quiet of the desert night, beyond the muffled howls inside the inn, Gabriel realized he could hear the distant snort of horses. It caught his attention because in this dangerous place men stayed indoors once the sun went down.

Gabriel found two pair of footprints leading away from the spot. Where they stopped there was confusion, a circle of activity. But beyond that point the two sets of prints walked away in a seemingly casual manner, as if the struggle had been resolved. One pair was bare feet, which he guessed were

Tyrian's. The second pair was a pair of wide and heavy boots. They had made deep imprints, with no marking on the sole: well-made and expensive.

Gabriel tossed the torch to the ground and extinguished it with the dirt, then called to Wolf. The poor dog was tied to Tyrian's scent, as if his friend might return, but he obeyed.

The man and dog reached the end of the alley and Gabriel felt at the ground with his sword, finding the edge of the building next to him. Gabriel looked back and saw three dark figures, against the moonlight at the opposite end of the passage. In silhouette, they had almost no form, yet it was apparent to the heir who they were. Unmistakably, the Three Riders: Gorka Osa, Babbel and Dò bbeldam.

Gabriel saw Gorka Osa signal to the other two to split up; each moved around the buildings on either side. Gorka Osa himself kept a slow march down the center of the alley, hidden by the darkness.

Wolf growled and nudged Gabriel's leg with his nose to alert him, but Gabriel had already drawn his sword. He stepped back slowly, his back hugging the wall behind him. He motioned Wolf to hide.

Wolf moved deeper into the darkness of the street. He was no farther away than the length of a horse and carriage, but the denseness of the night cloaked him. He crouched low against the cold sand and locked his gaze on Gabriel, who stood just outside the lamplight. Wolf could see Gorka Osa moving down the alley. And on the other side he could see Babbel creeping slowly from the rear of the square, while on the north side Dò bbeldam approached.

The wolf-dog growled. He scuttled a bit towards Babbel but then stopped. As the assassin drew closer Wolf rounded the arc of dim light, staying in the darkness and sounding like nothing more than a stray dog. He stopped and crouched, ready to pounce, still unseen. Then, in an instant, he lunged forward, sinking his teeth into the back of Babbel's leg, ripping muscle and tendons in a vicious grip. The assassin screamed as he dropped his sword and flailed about.

Gabriel took advantage of Wolf's surprise attack to launch his own attack. He charged Dò bbeldam in a full-out sprint, tossing his blade to the side at the last second and falling to the ground in a ball, hitting the confused mercenary in the knees with his shoulder. Dò bbeldam tumbled to the ground. Gabriel quickly regained his feet and retrieved his sword. He leapt towards Gorka Osa, who was now lunging forward. Their blades clashed with a spark and Gabriel's hands stung from the vibration. Gabriel spun back to block a forward lunge, then in a quick flash forced his own attack, denting the metal plate that covered Gorka Osa's bicep.

A short distance away Babbel continued to struggle with Wolf, who pulled at his leg, keeping the burly fighter continually off balance.

Gorka Osa took a few steps back, finding himself defending against a flurry of attacks from the aggressive knight. Gabriel swung his sword in small arcs left to right, then right to left, never letting

Gorka Osa find a rhythm. Gorka Osa was momentarily overwhelmed by the onslaught but eventually regained his position, forcing Gabriel to step back.

Suddenly, Gabriel found himself unable to move, his arms bound to his sides in a bear hug by Dò bbeldam, who held him from behind. Gabriel forced his body sideways to avoid the blade of Gorka Osa and then tried to break free, but to no avail. Abruptly he leaned back onto the assassin, throwing both feet up and shoving Gorka Osa directly in the center of his chest. Gabriel and Dò bbeldam both tumbled backwards onto the ground, the impact setting Gabriel free.

Dò bbeldam rolled to the side, retrieving his sword. Gabriel sprang to his feet and dropped his heavy boot onto Dò bbeldam's wrist, forcing him to release the grip on his weapon. As Gabriel reached down and tossed it to the side, Gorka Osa tackled him and forced him onto the desert floor. As they struggled for control, Gorka Osa reached into his boot and pulled out a dagger; he arched back, ready to bring it down into Gabriel's chest. But Gabriel had managed to work his knee up in between them and, straightening his leg, pushed the mercenary off. Gabriel pounced on him and again they struggled for control, this time with Gabriel in the stronger position.

Gabriel threw a quick fist just below Gorka Osa's battle helmet, sinking it into his throat. He jumped to his feet and turned to see a stumbling and bloodied Babbel holding Wolf by the throat. The poor beast was squealing, his eyes bulging and his mouth frothing with a mixture of saliva and blood.

Gabriel rushed to the dog's aid, driving the tip of his sword into the back of Babbel's leg with such strength that it came out the other side. In the rush of pain, Babbel released his grip on the dog and fell to the ground. Gabriel pulled the blade back out. Wolf fell to the ground on all fours and shook his head, trying to rid himself of the pain. His mouth curled immediately into a snarl and Gabriel knew he was about to attack again. He called out to stop him.

"Wolf! No!"

The dog glared at him. Gabriel whistled to the dog as he turned and ran. Wolf sprinted right behind him. As they rushed into the trading square he looked back to see only one of the mercenaries chasing after them—Gorka Osa. In all of his travels, Gabriel had heard of the Three Riders but had never faced them in battle. They were a nuisance to The Order of Heirs, if anything. They were seasoned fighters, to be sure, and although he could have bested them eventually, now was not the time.

Gabriel and Wolf moved swiftly towards the center of the encampment. Soon the darkness swallowed them and Gorka Osa gave up his chase. He stopped, caught his breath, then turned and walked back to his partners.

Babbel was on his knees, tying torn pieces of his tunic around the bleeding wounds on his legs. Dò bbeldam hunched over him. Babbel looked up at the tall figure of Gorka Osa.

"I am sorry, General Osa," Babbel pleaded. "Please forgive me."

"No matter," Gorka Osa struggled to get the words out. "We are not trained... in fighting rabid dogs. Let us retreat for the night."

Gorka Osa looked up just in time to see the hawk circling against the light of the moon; it made a wide arc southward and disappeared into the black sky. He turned and entered the dark alley leading back to his horse. Babbel and Dò bbeldam followed right behind. Dò bbeldam could be heard coughing as he walked—a deep wet cough—and then spitting onto the ground.

# # #

As the birds began their melodious morning dialogues, the sun could not yet be seen, still hidden by the height of the trees and shrubbery that surrounded Gorka Osa's estate. Tyrian rose out of the comfort of his bed and crossed the marbled floor to the window. There were flurries of action in the trees as birds rushed to and fro, beginning their own morning rituals.

He remembered the three figures from the night before, still unsure if they were real or imagined.

Tyrian found a tunic and trousers laid out for him by the bed. He dressed quickly and descended the wide staircase to the main floor of Gorka Osa's mansion. Once again, all of the windows and doors stood open to allow a cross-current of breezes to move through the house. Tyrian stepped out onto the wet, dewy tiles of the entrance patio. He was surprised to find Gorka Osa kneeling in a patch of flowers, pruning the stems and pulling weeds from the surrounding dirt. The older man looked peaceful and focused and did not notice the boy at first.

"Good morning, sir," Tyrian said softly.

"Well, look at you," Gorka Osa replied. "I thought you'd sleep for days, you looked so tired."

"I must go. I cannot afford the amount of days that would be needed to refresh me. I must move on."

"Very well. You must eat first. I have some breakfast stew cooking, and juice. Won't you join me?"

"Thank you, sir. Your hospitality has been gracious, but I must go."

"As you wish. I will at least pack you some fruit and bread. You must nourish yourself early, it sets your body for the day's journey. And I also have some gifts." He entered a shed just off the main yard. Tyrian followed him in.

Gorka Osa reached into a cabinet and then turned back to the boy, presenting him with a long sword and belt with a sheath.

"This is for me?" Tyrian's eyes widened.

"You will need it. It is a dangerous land out there. Please take this. And I have a young horse for you to take with you."

"I cannot possibly accept these gifts, sir."

"You must accept them. It is a long journey that you are starting. You'll need stronger legs and a blade to get you there. But remember my offer, boy, it is always open. I could use an apprentice."

"In horse-breeding?"

"And tillage, the cultivation of the land. I can teach you a great many things. And I can help you gain riches as well. Come back when you decide my offer is worthy of your blood and sweat."

Tyrian took the blade from its sheath and held it out before him. The handle had a soft grip of leather over a layer of horse mane. The long, sharp blade shone as if it had never been used. He wrapped the belt round his waist and slid the sword carefully into the sheath.

"Thank you, sir. Thank you," the boy repeated.

Gorka Osa walked Tyrian to another shed, where a single brown horse stood. Its muscles rippled through the velvet of its short hair. As Gorka Osa patted the back of the horse he told Tyrian, "She is young and strong. Treat her well and she'll treat you well."

Tyrian saw leather packs slung over each side.

"I've packed you food and drink for four days," Gorka Osa said. "Use it sparingly and you can stretch it to five or six."

Tyrian looked down the path leading away from the estate. Gorka Osa took note of his wandering gaze.

"You will be fine, boy. Just follow this pathway out to the desert, then ride towards the sun; by midday you will see the mountain range. Once you are within reach of the foothills, turn southward until the sand ends and you will find the Desert Pirates' home. You are brave, Tyrian. You ride into certain danger, but something tells me you'll survive. My advice to you, my potential apprentice, is to only fight if need be, never announce yourself, be stealthy, be quiet, and be strong."

The boy walked the steed out into the open. He bowed low on one knee to Gorka Osa. "Your kindness will not be forgotten, Mr. Osa. I will repay you someday."

"We will meet again, Tyrian."

Tyrian mounted the horse and took the reins, driving the steed forward along the dirt path leading away from Gorka Osa's estate. Soon the boy was gone, vanished into the arid air of the thirsty desert.

Chapter Seven

Tyrian reached the end of Gorka Osa's estate. As if waking from a dream, he saw the soft, dark-brown soil and the lush green grass fade away into white sand. He then led his horse on foot, to feel the dirt beneath his feet. It reminded him of the Fellhawk Road, soft and forgiving.

Now he found himself at the edge of the desert once again, although this time, not under chase. He had a young horse, fresh supplies, and a brand new blade. He stared out at the great dry ocean before him. It seemed to never end. It looked different from this vantage point, and from this moment of calm. It seemed to be the end of the world. He could see nothing but sand in any direction east, south or north.

For a moment he considered riding back to the Fellhawk Compound. Had Wolf returned home? Perhaps Heir Theobald had already retrieved the pouch and was returning to the kingdom.

Tyrian mounted his horse and looked back to the road that led to Gorka Osa's mansion, then out towards the open desert again. He took in a few last breaths of the sweet floral scents of Gorka Osa's estate before pushing his horse into a healthy gallop.

The heat of the naked sun hit him immediately. After a short distance he pulled his horse to a stop and dropped down to the sand. He dug into the pouches to see what Gorka Osa had packed for him. He found a loose, light hat to protect him against the sun. He took a quick drink of water and then remounted.

Tyrian pushed the young horse into a sprint eastward, chasing the rising sun. The scorching yellow orb crawled slowly into the sky, following Tyrian like an oppressive captor.

He rode for the better part of the morning. The sun had almost made its final ascent when something caught Tyrian's eye. He pulled the horse to a halt and dismounted.

The sand was littered with long splinters of wood and hoof-prints, wheel tracks and scraps of dirty cloth.

"This mess must have come from a Desert Pirate party," he said to himself.

The wheel tracks were shallow, he noticed. They had sold their slaves and whores, he thought. They were returning with coins and jewelry only. And perhaps the pouch of dragon's teeth.

In the distance he saw an old cracked wheel. There had been no struggle, no attack. Just a maintenance stop. The prints were still very defined, so they must not be far, he thought.

Tyrian felt a surge of excitement. After giving himself and his horse a quick drink of water, he started off in the direction of the tracks. He pushed the animal faster.

They rode against a breeze that had arisen. The horse struggled a bit, but she was young and strong. Tyrian feared that with the wind picking up, the sand would cover the tracks. He pushed his mount even harder. He wanted to catch The Desert Pirates in the open desert, before they reached their "home."

Tyrian was losing his sense of direction, as the sun was directly overhead now. But he kept on, following the increasingly disappearing tracks. He looked out into the distance ahead and still could see only barren sand.

The trail he was following was becoming fainter. He pulled the reins, stopping the horse. He jumped down and knelt. The tracks were quickly being covered by the windswept sand. He took a chug of water from his pack, gave some to his horse, then remounted and rode even faster eastward.

After Tyrian had been riding for a while he suddenly saw what he thought were the tracks, but as he squinted and slowed the horse he realized they had now completely vanished. He knelt down and brushed the sand aside, as if the wheel tracks were still hidden beneath, but he saw nothing.

He ran ahead a short distance and looked in all directions. He ran back towards his horse, making wide circles, trying frantically to uncover the trail. There was only sand and a gust of wind that picked up now and again. Against the horizon, only a thin line showed where the sky met the desert. From up above he could feel the piercing, yellow midday sun.

Tyrian dropped to his knees. Tears came to his eyes and his heart became numb with despair. He watched his horse, so beautiful and healthy, dancing in its place not far from him. It taunted him. Perhaps this was a trap and Gorka Osa had sent him on a path of folly.

After a moment Tyrian calmed himself, then rose to his feet and walked back to the horse. He pulled out some more water and gave some to the animal, then drank from the leather water- vessel himself. He found some cured meat and took out a few bites to chew on.

Perhaps the whole adventure was absurd. He wondered if the dragon's teeth were even real. He remembered the dead boy in the forest, from whose body he had extracted those teeth. Heir Theobald had told him the boy had sacrificed himself as a vessel.

Tyrian sat down cross-legged on the grainy ground. He became completely still. He listened to his breathing and slowed it as best he could. He let go of his thoughts, his feelings of shame and fear. At first he tried to shut out the sounds coming to him: his horse's snorting, the wind, his own breathing. But then he tried the opposite: he tried to hear them more clearly. He welcomed them. And soon they wound into one single melody in his head. And just as soon as they were heard, they dissolved into his consciousness, like the words sung at the campfire by his Uncle Petter, in his deep sorrowful voice. The sounds around him were present, but no longer a distraction; they were a guide.

Now Tyrian focused his mind on emptiness. He could feel the heat of the dry wind against his cheeks. He heard no voices, as Heir Theobald had said would happen. But then he saw a faint picture of a mountain range. It was distant and hazy and he thought it could have come from his imagination. He sensed that the mountain range he was to follow lay straight ahead, just beyond the horizon. And he realized his only option was to trust in Gorka Osa's directions—to ride towards the sun and look for the mountain range.

A moment later Tyrian sat perched atop his horse again, riding towards the mountain range he had seen in his vision. The horse seemed to sense his urgency as they pushed deeper into the desert. Tyrian wiped away the tears matted with dust on his face. He adjusted his hat against the sun and felt suddenly confident about his direction.

He rode for some time, long enough to feel the sun's heat on his back. He finally saw a thin line of dark, jagged edges protruding from the horizon. He lifted himself on his haunches, trying to see further into the distance, then snapped the reins, pushing his horse on harder.

As he rode, the dark, uneven line began to take shape and he could see that it was, indeed, a mountain range. Just as Gorka Osa had told him. He was close; behind him, the sun had moved halfway to its destination on the western skyline. He still had several hours of daylight ahead.

The wind had stopped. As he approached the very edges of foothills he saw in the sand directly ahead of him what he thought could be a carriage and horse tracks again.

Tyrian leaned forward in excitement as he took up the chase, moving along the deepening trail of hooves and wagon wheels.

Several minutes later, he saw a dust cloud ahead, a good distance away. He guessed that it was a Desert Pirate expedition.

Tyrian was closing the distance quickly, but still remained unseen by the creatures. He pulled back on the reins, trying to hold a safe distance so as not to be discovered. He wondered how close they were to the Vilczcyyz Tents, the Desert Pirates' home.

As he drew nearer, he could make out the figures: two on foot, one on horseback leading the carriage. Three Desert Pirates. He could take them. His first instinct was to charge in, but then he remembered Gorka Osa's words of advice—be quiet, stealthy, only fight if necessary.

Tyrian decided to follow them back to their camp. The sun would be setting soon and he would have the cover of night to hide under.

The trio of pirates led him, unknowingly, for a while longer. Because of generations of in-breeding and poor living conditions, the Desert Pirates were genetically crippled in many ways. Simple things that humans took for granted—breathing, seeing, smelling, speaking—were all challenges to these desert creatures. This allowed Tyrian to follow at a safe distance, undetected, through the daylight.

Tyrian could see the outline of a series of tents and slumped structures in the distance, just as the sun was approaching the western horizon.

He slowed his horse even more, letting the trio of pirates leave his sight. He decided to wait out the remainder of sunlight to go into "The Tents" undetected. He used the time to have a bit of food and feed his horse. Tyrian sat on the desert ground, the sand starting to cool as the sun began its departure.

The Tents were a short distance away. He knew he would have to ride in before nightfall, but he wanted to move under as little light as possible.

Tyrian stood up. He kicked the sand. There was so much of it. He wanted to be rid of the dry, grainy stuff. He wanted to go back to his deep rich soil in the forest. Sighing, he returned to his horse.

Soon it would be dark. His horse took a few steps forward, towards the tent village, almost unconsciously. Tyrian looked westward, at the dimming horizon. He looked back northward where, somewhere beyond the vast skyscape, lay the Great River Forest.

If what Heir Gabriel Theobald had told him was true, if that pouch held the secret to a near immortal army, then he did have a duty. He remembered his question to Uncle Petter, "what if one chooses to live a life of war so that others can live in peace?" Did he truly believe that? He gently kicked the horse in the side, moving it forward lazily. Yes, he did believe in that.

Tyrian rode slowly towards the Vilzcyyz Tents. The complex was beginning to take shape before him. He realized it spanned a great distance. There were tents that looked abandoned, and some that had apparently just been put up haphazardly. It was quiet. The tents and shacks on the outskirts were dark, either empty or the inhabitants sleeping.

Near a grouping of the dark tents, Tyrian found a small fence to tie his horse to. He guessed this had once been an active corner of the village, but now it was deserted. The tents were empty and there were no horses tied up. Is this how these creatures lived? They just departed (or died?) and their homes were left vacant?

He felt through the packs on the horse and found a small dagger. He marveled at Gorka Osa. In these two small bags he had crammed everything the boy would need. It was as if the horse-breeder had made this trip himself before. He also found a long, hooded cloak tied to the horse's hind end. He unwrapped it and covered himself.

Tyrian plunged into the maze of tents, cloaked by darkness and his hooded cape, dagger in hand.

He felt uneasy over how quiet it was. There was still just enough daylight for him to see the little pathways. He could see no logic to the complex's design, but he figured the dirt streets had to lead him somewhere.

After a few minutes of walking, he found a long tent standing on its own, across from another series of smaller tents. He discovered a small opening at one end, as if this was the official entrance. He pulled at the tattered cloth of the tent; it was tied shut from the inside. He used his dagger to tear a peephole in the material with the dagger and looked inside. It was a mess tent, dining quarters. He could see tables littered with the remains of the most recent meals and pitchers and mugs of ale. Slung over the tables he saw an array of Desert Pirates sleeping soundly, or in some cases, not so soundly.

Tyrian continued on down the alleyway, suddenly realizing this whole place smelled horrible. He wondered if it was the odor of sewage, or death, or a combination. He pulled his cloak higher, over his nose, and continued on.

At the far end of the dining tent he came to a dead-end, and found himself staring at a stone wall. One end of the wall appeared to have been torn down; the other end stood firm, as if holding up an unseen structure. Strange. Perhaps at one time there was an actual castle here, and the pirates had overtaken it and neglected to do any renovation. He followed along the wall, feeling his way, as the darkness was starting to deepen quickly.

Across the pathway he saw another long tent. He peaked in through the tent opening and saw another mess full of sleeping or drunken creatures laid out all across the tent. This village seemed to shut down abruptly when the sun went down.

Suddenly, though, there was movement. He quickly turned away from the opening and slipped back around the corner of the tent. He heard someone exit the tent.

Tyrian pushed himself up against the outer wall of the tent and held his breath. The creature stumbled around the corner and looked down the alleyway in his direction. The boy was not far from the pirate and could see his outline clearly. But Tyrian was cloaked by the dim light and the pirate was handicapped by his genetic defects, unable to detect Tyrian's presence by sight, sound or scent. Soon, the boy saw the figure disappear around the corner and he heard him pass back into the tent.

Tyrian could see a figure who seemed to be standing guard outside of a round tent nearby. It stood out from the other tents, because of its shape as well as the presence of a sentry. This must be where they keep their treasure, he thought. The boy froze. The pirate-guard was still not aware of him. If this was indeed the only guard, entrance would be simple. Tyrian stayed where he was and watched. There was no movement. The guard made no signs to anyone else. He must be the only guard.

He approached the guard slowly, quietly. Each placement of his foot was separate and deliberate. He took a step, then waited for a reaction. Nothing. Each step brought him closer.

Tyrian silently crossed the dirt street and moved along the curved side of the tent. He crouched, pulling at the bottom of the tent, but it was fastened snugly from the inside. He moved stealthily along the dirt street, back towards the front. There was still no movement from the guard. The boy inched closer, within striking distance, and there was still no movement. These poor beasts counted on the fact that no one ever invaded their tent village because of the filth. They certainly did not expect to have to actually protect their treasure from anyone.

As Tyrian came upon the entrance, the creature finally sensed something and swung his short blade in a wide arc, just above Tyrian's head. Tyrian was still crouched, at the pirate's feet. The pirate sniffed at the air, grasping at the nothingness around him with his left hand.

Tyrian reached up quickly, grabbing the pirate's wrist, squeezing until it dropped its sword. The boy pulled the creature down to the desert floor, covering his mouth with his hand. Tyrian immediately pounced on the guard, pinning the sword hand to the ground with a knee as he pulled out his dagger and slit the beast's throat. There was no time for struggle or noise. The horrible, strained breathing noises quickly came to an end.

Tyrian wiped his sword on the pirate's pants and resheathed it, then entered the tent. It was barely lit with two torches. He saw one pirate at the far end, at a table. He looked old, as much as the boy could distinguish this creature from any of the other pirates. The pirate was just as surprised at Tyrian's presence as the boy was of his. The creature sat frozen in his seat. No doubt the creature feared for his life.

Tyrian sprang across the tent, grabbing the creature by his cloak, covering his mouth. He knew that speaking was useless; he could make nothing of their crude language. He looked around at tables and tables piled high with jewelry, gold, blades, all kinds of riches. The frail, old desert pirate struggled as best he could, but he was no match for the young, strong woodcutter. The pirate moaned and pleaded. Tyrian took a rag from the table and shoved it in the pirate's mouth, tying it with the belt from his cloak, tight around the old creature's head. Then he pulled the belt from the pirate's own trousers and tied his wrists behind his back. Once the boy let go of him, the creature stopped struggling. He lay still and silent, closing his eyes.

There were so many tables, and there was no logic to the riches. They were piled high in no apparent order. He did not know how long he would be alone so he turned to the nearest table and started throwing things to the floor: vases, necklaces, medallions, daggers, chalices, mirrors. He stopped, looked back at the silent desert pirate, looked again at the room filled with stolen treasure. He could not get through this whole tent by the time the sun came up. He went back to his prisoner and lifted him up. At the boy's touch, the captive resumed his whimpers and moans. Tyrian propped him back up in his chair.

"There was a pouch. From the Great River Forest! The Great River Forest!"

The creature whimpered. He shook his head as if not understanding.

"There was a group who came from The Great River Forest, do you remember?"

"Fo'est. 'e tree wuld. Tree wuld. Yes, 'e fo'est," the captive slurred in his garbled accent. He nodded his forehead at a far table. Tyrian let the pirate go and rushed over to the table. He went through the riches, throwing to the floor the coins, belts, and helmets. They were nothing of value to the boy. There was no pouch. He dug through every pocket of every cloak, inside every helmet. There was no sign of it. He was losing hope. He rushed back to the tied-up pirate and shook him.

"There was a pouch! A small bag! I need the pouch from the Great River Forest!"

The pirate stared at him with a blank look. He shrugged his shoulders and nodded back at the table, "Fo'est. Fo'est!"

Tyrian looked down at the pirate's jacket. It was tucked in and buttoned up tight against his neck. The boy pulled the jacket apart, letting fly buttons across the room. The creature wriggled back, trying to get away. Tyrian reached around inside the jacket and finally felt a packet, bunched up in his armpit.

Tyrian stepped aside and held the pouch tightly in his fist; he knew what it was at first touch. He opened it and there were the dragon's teeth. He pulled them out and held them in his hand for a moment. They glowed as they absorbed the warmth of his palm. He could feel the Pirate move in closer, holding his breath and gasping. The greedy creature had no doubt been spellbound by their brilliance and hoped to keep them for himself.

The decrepit desert pirate struggled now, trying to wriggle free. Tyrian shoved him back, sending him falling backwards in his chair. Tyrian swept across one of the tables, snatching up a handful of coins, but mostly knocking them to the floor.

As Tyrian bolted from the tent he could hear the creature whimpering and crying. He stepped back out into the cold darkness. The one guard still lay at the foot of the tent entrance. Tyrian could detect no movement or sounds along the tiny alleyways that made up the tent village. There was nothing.

He rushed back down the way he had come. He felt his way along the structureless wall, against the second and then the first dining tent he had passed earlier. He found himself back out in the open, where he heard his horse whinny.

Tyrian was ecstatic. He felt his father's absence the most at this moment. There was a void in the pride of an accomplishment as it was unknown to anyone but him. He was right to have gone after the pouch.

Tyrian mounted his horse and urged it out into the cold darkness. He rode in what he hoped was a northward direction, unseen in the desert darkness. At first they galloped at a frantic pace, but as the distance grew they slowed to a comfortable stride. He felt the pouch, tucked against his breast inside his cloak, and his heart pumped excitedly. He could not wait to tell his young cousin Djuri of the Desert Pirates' horrible village.

The night lay before him like a deep, black ocean.

Chapter Eight

The men of Heir Volkummen's militia had grown anxious. They were feeding off of their general's impatience; Volkummen's anger was betrayed by his restlessness. He took long walks but spoke not a word. At night he would walk circles around Roserie Argaune's tent, never entering.

The militia was on rations of one meal a day and they were nearly out of ale. Some of the men quietly threatened mutiny, while others knew they were empty threats and no one would desert Heir Volkummen's militia. Others passed the hours telling stories to the younger boys about long-ago battles.

As morning faded into noon, Greit Shultheis made his rounds. He drank his morning tea as he went from tent to tent. Never uttering a word, he looked his men in the eye, nodded to them and then moved on. As he was rounding the last tent he heard a horse ride up to the camp. He immediately drew his sword and then saw the figure of Gorka Osa dismounting.

As his heavy leather boots hit the loose dirt below, Gorka Osa pulled off his horned helmet, hitching it to his saddle. His long hair was pulled back into a tail and he wore riding pants and an open shirt beneath his cape. He tossed the cape over his saddle and approached Roserie Argaune's tent.

Greit watched Heir Volkummen. The general turned his gaze on Gorka Osa as the assassin disappeared into the darkness of the wizard's tent.

Volkummen despised the Three Riders. They represented disorder, which equaled narcissism and weakness as far as he was concerned. He had never come face-to-face with Babbel or Dò bbeldam, but had seen Gorka Osa several times over the years. Although their meetings were formal and never cordial, the men had never crossed swords. Secretly, though, Volkummen had always sized up the loner, looking for weaknesses.

He had watched the bond between Gorka Osa and Argaune grow stronger over the years. He felt a touch of jealousy and competition in his heart. He did not know where Gorka Osa fit into the wizard's plans, nor did he know the full extent of the assassin's commission. He brushed it off as the relationship between a mercenary and his benefactor. He was wise enough to keep Gorka Osa sufficiently close to monitor. He had promised on occasion to arrest Gorka Osa as a threat to the King's security, but Argaune had always pled a good case for the rider.

Likewise, Gorka Osa saw Volkummen as a violent tool of King Azjik's empire. He was careful not to underestimate Volkummen's strength or position; indeed, he kept his distance. But he harbored more disgust than fear for the northern-born thug. He detested how Volkummen forced his men into submission. Gorka Osa saw much more value in coaxing allegiance from his men.

Gorka Osa knelt a short distance from Argaune. As the wizard sensed the assassin's presence, or rather smelled the perfume of his hair, he gently pulled his God-twin from the bird and far away, across the desert, guided the hawk ever so slowly to a perch on a cliff on the Adrujian Coast.

Argaune roused himself from the trance and rose to his full height. He stretched and yawned, as if waking from a deep sleep.

"Welcome, my friend," Argaune held out his bony wrinkled hand. Gorka Osa took it in his own and shook it firmly.

"Thank you, Argaune. Your guide has led us well. But we were not so lucky when we found your countryman in the Desert Trade Encampment. Heir Theobald is a formidable knight and his pet beast nearly dismembered poor Babbel. It will take him some days to recover."

"And what of Dò bbeldam?" Argaune asked, sensing a delicate subject.

Gorka Osa looked away and sighed, "I fear his better days are behind him, Argaune."

Argaune studied him intently, letting the silence permeate the tent like a cloud. These were the moments when Gorka Osa felt the power of Argaune—he had the ability to sit in silence and use it to his advantage. Finally, as if out of mercy, Argaune spoke, "And what of your generals, Gorka Osa? Are they still an asset to our campaign?"

"I fear they are becoming a burden. I have seen the signs when they fight, Argaune, and they will most assuredly die in battle soon."

Gorka Osa quickly changed the subject, "I may have found an apprentice. A boy, who at a young age, has the combined strength and skills of both of my generals."

"Who is this boy?" Argaune moved closer to Gorka Osa and lowered his voice, his interest piqued.

"He was captured at the edge of the Great River Forest by Desert Pirates and was sold off to a drunk for slavery. I rescued him and gave him a night's lodging. He was very grateful but was determined to push on. He was seeking something stolen from him by the desert vermin. There was something about him, though. There was something hidden. He was careful with his words."

"My friend, I've learned in my years that the fewer words a man speaks, the more he has to say."

"Indeed, there was something in the way that he looked at me that said he could not speak freely."

"There may be a connection between this boy and Heir Theobald. It is no coincidence. We must keep our eyes on both of them. You have done well, Gorka Osa. If Heir Theobald does not hold the teeth of the Green Kaditz Dragon then he most assuredly will possess them soon enough. He will deliver them to Azjik's compound and he can only get there by the Road of Fathers."

Gorka Osa watched as the old man's gaze drifted up towards the roof of the tent. His mind plotted schemes as casually other mens' minds counted coins in their pocket.

"Now," Argaune continued, "I hope you will go home and rest. I will advise our friend, Heir Volkummen, to find them on the Road of Fathers."

"But how will Volkummen engage Theobald? By Azjik's decree, even an heir cannot fight an heir unless called upon by the king himself."

"Leave that to me, my friend. You will be needed soon. I will send you notice by courier when the time has come. You will have your second chance at besting Heir Theobald. For now, you must retire to your wonderful estate and tend to your wounds."

Gorka Osa stood slowly, then bowed to the sorcerer before leaving.

Argaune sat back and listened to the soft drumbeat of Gorka Osa's horse riding off. A few moments later the sunlight beamed in again, as Heir Volkummen entered.

"My patience has worn thin, Master Argaune," Volkummen bellowed in his low, thunderous voice. "Your damned hawk has been circling the skies night after night, while you sit here in your trance. I want to know where my treasure is!"

"Your fellow heir will lead us to our treasure," the wizard said calmly. "He will not release our prize willingly. And seeing as how you are an heir, you and he cannot legally engage in confrontation. But you could come to his aid. And, in doing so, you could fall into possession of our prize."

"Speak directly, sorcerer! I've had enough of your riddles!"

"Directly speaking, Heir Volkummen, the only way back to King Azjik is along the Road of Fathers. In two days' time, I can assure you that Heir Theobald will be under attack by a horde of Desert Pirates. He will need your help. You can come to his aid and strip him of his delivery."

"In two days' time…," Heir Volkummen considered this. He pulled at his long red beard, cleared his throat, and then nodded in agreement. Without another word he turned and exited the tent.

Volkummen approached the main fire at the head of the camp and took a leg of meat from the fire. Moments later, Greit approached him.

"Your Honor," Greit Schultheis bowed.

"Greit!" Volkummen said, his voice rising. "Get these dogs to pack up the camp. We're heading to meet our brothers at the green cliffs. From there we will ride home to Azjik!"

Loud cheers filled the open desert air. But Volkummen leaned in to Greit, "Be sure they are ready for battle. I have a feeling we will be running into a horde of Desert Pirates along the way."

# # #

Tyrian had ridden most of the night, but his pace was slow. He sat firmly atop the horse, self-confident. He had never been in command of such a beautiful beast as this. The animals at the Fellhawk Compound (except for Wolf) were dumb and trained only for simple jobs. It took nothing to get them to move. But this beast was to be coaxed and reasoned with.

The sun was just rising and Tyrian could now see his path westward. He held the pouch close to his breast, tracing the outline of it inside his cloak to give himself comfort. He would ride to the Desert Trading town and hopefully find Heir Theobald and Wolf there. It seemed as good a place as any to begin.

Tyrian yanked the reins and squeezed his knees tightly as he turned westward. Obeying Tyrian's unspoken command, the horse charged towards the Desert Market.

Tyrian did not know what he would do when he reached the encampment, but he was certain to find direction there. Perhaps Heir Theobald had come looking for him, or was even waiting there for him. Perhaps someone knew the Heir of Coteville and would direct Tyrian to him. Or perhaps he could get directions to Coteville and find Heir Theobald in his home village. Whichever was the correct answer, it was sure to come to him in some form at the desert trade encampment, as much as he despised that place.

At midday he began to tire, and pulled his horse to a stop. He guessed that he was still several hours from the encampment but could reach it by early afternoon. His buttocks were sore from the ride and it felt good to walk. He took off his boots and let his feet be massaged by the warm sand. He pulled from his pack a piece of jerky that Gorka Osa had given him.

Tyrian climbed a slight incline in the sand for a view of the expanse before him. He saw, down in a wide basin, a small band of Desert Pirates. The vermin were scattered across the oval- shaped depression like flies, and to get around them he realized he had to traverse a long trail that led into a bed of rocks and desert foliage. He scanned the area for the safest route.

Tyrian had learned that the Desert Pirates were poorly equipped and were negligent about the care of their animals. They seemed barely evolved from the mangy animals they kept.

Tyrian decided on an alternate route around the basin. He mounted his horse and took a northern arc around the wide dip, keeping the small caravan in sight. He rode at an easy pace, very methodically, to watch every movement of the group. Suddenly he saw some commotion. He heard distant calls back and forth that were muffled by the distance. He saw the lead figure frantically pointing up towards Tyrian and the others scurrying around, hoisting their captives into the carriage as they can. The others were pushed along at a quicker pace.

Tyrian started down the descent into the plateau bed, where he could see the pirates more clearly. There were only four of them, and they seemed agitated. As he got closer, Tyrian saw that all of the captives were women and girls. They were in ragged tunics that covered them from the sun.

As his horse descended further, he could make out faces. The Desert Pirates were wrapped in their filthy scarves and tattered hoods, appearing to be faceless beasts. The captives looked either terrified or frozen still in a lethargic state. But there was a face that he recognized—the young blonde girl from the trading post. His eyes narrowed, at first not trusting his vision; perhaps all girls looked the same where she came from.

As if his horse had sensed his anger before he did, it charged down towards the caravan. Tyrian held on to the reins tightly with one hand as he drew his sword with the other, his rage swelling. He held his blade up high before him, as if to warn the pirates of their impending demise.

The Desert Pirates scurried about, pulling their tired horses harder, trying to get them into a sprint, to no avail.

Like a boulder in an avalanche, Tyrian and his horse crashed into the caravan, knocking the lead pirate to the ground screaming. As his horse turned and charged in the opposite direction, Tyrian stretched out his body, holding tightly to the reins with one hand while using the other to swing his blade in a wide arc as he passed, cleanly slicing free the arm of a pirate. The pirate fell to the ground shrieking a horrific bellow that sounded half-animal.

As he brought his horse to a halt again, Tyrian dropped to the ground. The women and girls were all silent in fear. One of the Desert Pirates, a tall and wiry beast, stood close to them holding a bent and rusted metal lance, shaking and scared. Another pirate nearby approached cautiously, his long blade held out before him.

Tyrian lunged forward, knocking the tall pirate's lance from his hands. The creature stepped back, his hands stinging from the vibrations as he stumbled. Tyrian thrust his sword into the pirate's torso, releasing a torrent of blood accompanied by a howl.

Tyrian turned to the one holding the lance, who was jabbing it at him almost comically. The boy easily deflected the jabs with quick but firm parries. He sensed another pirate approaching behind him; the creature had regained his feet and was on the attack. In an instant Tyrian turned around and charged headlong at the pirate attacking from his rear. With a scream of fury, he brought his blade round in a wide arc, slicing the would-be attacker's head from his shoulders. The headless body collapsed in a heap to the ground, the head settling nearby.

Within seconds, Tyrian was charging towards the two remaining Desert Pirates. The lead pirate, who held the lance, was moving backwards even as Tyrian was on him. Tyrian brought crushing blows downward against the long weapon, making it impossible for the creature to lunge. Tyrian also kept an eye on the second pirate, who was still standing in front of the women and girls. Tyrian worked himself close enough to his prey to throw a kick hard into its groin. The creature bent over in pain and Tyrian saw the lance loosen in his grip. He stepped back and unleashed a shower of attacks on the lance, tiring the pirate's arms.

Tyrian moved in closer again, weilding another kick. The impact was enough for the Desert Pirate to drop the lance altogether and fall to the ground, holding onto his injured leg. Once the filthy beast was down, Tyrian unleashed a series of vicious kicks to its leg.

Convinced the creature was no longer a threat, Tyrian turned towards the last pirate. The adrenaline was pulsing through his body and he rushed forward; the second pirate had no defense but to crouch down holding his blade over his head with two hands, absorbing each blow. In the end, it was too much, and finally Tyrian overpowered him. The filthy beast could not keep his grip and let go of his blade, covering himself as best he could as Tyrian cut into him with savagery.

Painted with blood and heaving with exhaustion, Tyrian surveyed the scene. The injured pirate lay at the side of the carriage, holding his broken leg and whimpering. The captive females huddled together in the carriage bed and underneath it. Tyrian found the key to the shackle locks on the belt of the slain guard. He tossed it to the oldest woman, who immediately freed herself and the others. Meanwhile, Tyrian went through the carriage and all of its clutter, separating supplies from garbage. He found water and some food, but the rest was useless. The Desert Pirates were more than just slave hunters; they were hoarders of useless items that they tried to sell.

Tyrian quickly looked the youngest girls over for injuries, and once satisfied he covered them with a ratty blanket for safety from the dry air. He motioned them to squeeze in tight, which they had no trouble doing, as they were locked in each other's arms, a small comfort against their horrors. Left standing beside the carriage were two figures—the first, an older woman whose stark, drawn face showed her years of hard work, and the second, the same young blonde girl who Tyrian had rescued days before.

Tyrian grabbed the older woman in his arms and lifted her onto one of the carriage horses. He grabbed her hands forcefully and put them on the reins, signaling for her to hold on to them. Then he turned to the blonde girl, but she stepped back from him. Her eyes turned from fear to anger. He reached out his hands. "Here. Here," his hands jerking towards her in offering. His eyes turned to the horse and back to her.

The girl slapped his hands away and then went to the horse, fixing her foot into the stirrup and attempting to pull herself up. She was much too small, the horse much too large. Her thin arms grabbed the saddle and pulled to no avail. The horse snorted and shook its mane, as if in disgust. Tyrian let out a loud laugh.

The girl refused to look at Tyrian. Instead she looked to the older woman who, hiding her own smile, dismounted and helped the girl up into the saddle of Tyrian's horse. Only then, securely in place, did the girl look back to Tyrian, again with the razor-thin eyes of anger. The old woman then remounted and gave Tyrian a look of approval.

The boy bowed to her, then grabbed the bridle of the wagon horses and directed them westward. He smacked the lead horse on the hind legs, calling out to them to move. The tired, beaten horses begrudgingly started their slow lazy march back to where they had just come from.

As the small caravan took up its journey, Tyrian climbed into the saddle in front of the angry girl and pushed his horse onward. He quickly caught up with the carriage and noticed that the older woman was relaxed and confident. The younger girls were still wide-eyed with fear. The woman riding the lead horse had taken the reins firmly and, to his surprise, she was forcing the horses to pick up speed.

The girl behind him held onto his waist lightly, as if keeping a small distance between them. The gap gradually closed as they made their way through the desert and she tired. Soon her head bounced lazily against the center of his back. He turned and saw that her eyes were closed.

"What is your name?" Tyrian called back. There was no answer. He looked back again and saw her staring at him coldly. "I don't suppose we speak the same language. I am Tyrian." He let go of the reins with one hand and pointed to himself, "Tyrian. Tyrian Fellhawk." Then he pointed his thumb back at her with a questioning look.

Her head popped up, as she suddenly understood. "Serena! Serena!" Then she laughed self-consciously. "Serena," she pointed to herself. Then, as she pointed to Tyrian, "Tyrian." He threw his head back, laughing. "Yes! We are acquainted now!"

Tyrian turned his attention back to the western horizon. And as he sat forward, he felt Serena's grip tighten around his waist and her head rest against his back.

Chapter Nine

In her disjointed sleep, Serena held onto Tyrian's waist tightly, as if she were holding onto the sweetness of her dream.

Her dreams were weaving in and out with the motion of the horse and the warm air around her. She dreamt she was in a carriage, riding through her father's garden, a reality long since vanished.

She remembered the constant dips and rises in the roads, the surface never level, and the comforting smells of the floral shrubs that lined the pathways. She remembered, too, the soft comfort of her father's belly as she snuggled up to him for warmth.

Serena grew up the youngest child after four brothers. Her father owned a very successful spice-trading business and so the family was quite well-off; well enough off to pay the local heir for her brothers to avoid the local militia. For her part, Serena was expected to marry into a family of equal wealth.

Serena's family lived at the edge of a shallow but wide cold-water lake. Their main residence was a modest two-level abode which sat along the shore, with one smaller cabin for the servants beyond. The servants' quarters abutted a small wooded area and housed two families.

Serena spent her childhood wandering through the woods with Inchiru, the son of her nursemaid. In their games they played as hunters chasing down wild boars or dirt dragons.

Their friendship was looked upon innocently by the adults as nothing more than a bond of youth. But as they grew older, and as Serena's adult responsibilities began to take shape, her parents started to draw her away from Inchiru and towards more "appropriate activities": music lessons, letters, recitation; the qualities that would define Serena as a lady. But she rebelled.

Even as Serena and Inchiru neared adolescence, they thought very little would change in their day-to-day games. To them there seemed to be no other future possible, for in youth one has little heartbreak or sorrow to base one's future emotions on. So this was the existence that Serena and Inchiru imagined.

But on his fifteenth year, Inchiru was required to report to the town square for training in the militia.

As that day approached, the reality of their future apart had become all too clear to them. The separation of their classes meant that once Inchiru joined the militia, King Azjik's military whims would define his life. And custom required that Serena's life be spent within the walls of her future husband's house, that home becoming her own prison.

At first they ignored their coming separation. But, as the future grew closer they began to talk about it with despair. Neither of them comprehended loss such as this.

Finally, Serena planned their escape. With no thought to the consequences, the young girl packed up some food and blankets and they stole away into the night. Together they ran into the cover of the dark forest and hid. Her plan consisted of that and that alone.

The next morning, as day was breaking, Inchiru took charge and led them further into the forest—still not sure of where they were going. But the fear of losing each other kept them on the move.

They made little progress, but they kept moving until the night, nearly a week into their journey, that Serena's father and brothers found them. The young pair was found hidden inside their make-shift tent.

Her father approached, but then stopped, terrified of what he might see.

"Come out of there, Serena!" her father called. There was no answer.

He turned and ordered his oldest son to wake them. When the son passed through the crude tent opening, he saw what he thought was two naked bodies intertwined. In reality, he had looked away quickly for fear of seeing his sister unclothed.

The son stepped away as the father bellowed in a voice that woke the forest from its peacefulness, "Out of there! Clothe yourself immediately and address me!"

Two children quickly appeared, shaking and pale with fear. The father handed the oldest son a long, curved dagger and nodded to him. Following wordless orders, the son approached Inchiru directly, gripped his shoulder with tightly and jabbed the dagger into his stomach. The boy fell to his knees in a silent scream, collapsing at Serena's feet. Her scream was not silent and penetrated the silence of the forest. Serena's shriek continued as the second oldest brother swooped her up and put her on his horse.

The brooding family returned to their house, leaving the cold, lifeless body of young Inchiru to the burial ceremonies that only nature could provide.

Serena's father believed that she had dishonored him and sullied his name, and, immediately upon their return, he gave Serena away to their heir as a gift to the King. Her life now was to be that of a Night Widow, sent off with a Burial March into the remains of a battle in a nearby land. Her honor would now be given as a marriage seal to a dead soldier for his entry into heaven. The young girl was devastated.

The trip to the Night Widow convent was a long and torturous one. Serena sat in a plain wagon with five other girls about her age. They wore matching cloaks and scarves that covered their heads. The girls were not allowed to sleep; kept constantly awake by loud bells clanging every so often, they were given small books of prayer to recite from in a constant repetition. Early in the journey her fatigue and confusion caused Serena to break into tears. But gradually, she became used to the fatigue and grew numb to the confusion.

The convent itself consisted of a modest boarding house with wide (and cold) sleeping dormitories and one large kitchen and dining hall. Because meals were to be eaten in silence, the kitchen became the only refuge for the girls to draw comfort from each other's company. The hours of the day were spent in the practice of sewing, cooking, washing, and other equally mindless chores.

Serena only spent five weeks at the convent before she managed to escape in the dark of night. With the clothes she wore, and a few knives and whatever food she could carry in her arms, she slipped out of the window of the dormitory and into the cool, wilderness.

After wandering for several days she found herself on the edges of the desert, searching for foliage and water. She took refuge for a night in an abandoned horse barn and then moved on, in no particular direction, following the path of migrating birds.

One morning, early, just hours after the sun had risen, she was captured by a band of Desert Pirates and within days was sold into prostitution.

# # #

Tyrian shook the poor girl awake. She was saved from the darkest part of her memories by sudden consciousness. As Tyrian jumped to the ground and stretched his legs, Serena squinted into the midday sun, quickly remembering all that had occurred since Tyrian had first found her. She looked over to the other girls in the carriage, then at the older woman who rode the lead horse. The woman motioned to the girls to stay in the carriage. Tyrian was pacing back and forth in the hot sand. As the fog of sleep dissipated fully, she realized why Tyrian was pacing the desert floor—she saw corpses of Desert Pirates everywhere, some dismembered, some beheaded; none of them left in peace.

Serena watched as Tyrian moved from body to body, taking a moment to poke this one or that with his foot. He stopped and looked towards the western horizon, and then to the eastern horizon. He knelt down towards one body, covering his face with his arm, and reached down. She let out a gasp as the body reached up at Tyrian. The boy jerked back, knocking the hand away, but then the body lay still.

Tyrian rose and crossed back to his horse and remounted. He called out to the woman on the lead carriage horse, "Go!"

As they took up the steady march again, Tyrian stared coldly ahead. Serena pulled at his hair lightly, to get his attention.

"Dead? Dead? All?"

"Yes, Serena."

# # #

Tyrian suddenly felt a rush of fear. Although most people despised the Desert Pirates, few did them harm. Theobald had told him they were a vital part of the desert commerce, an unspoken function that kept the flow of the King's fortunes in motion. He wondered briefly if it was the same militia that was hunting down Heir Theobald. Was there a militia gone mad?

Tyrian snapped the reins hard and pushed his horse on faster. He took a quick look back and the carriage was not far behind.

Tyrian rode through most of the afternoon, driving the carriage horses harder than they were used to. The day was wearing on and he wanted to get to the desert trading post before sundown. As Tyrian rode on Serena fought off sleep again, afraid of her memories, trying to hold on to the present.

As they finally neared the Desert Trading Post, Tyrian pulled his horse to a stop.

The boy motioned all of the girls to get out of the carriage as he unhitched the two decrepit horses. The scared girls gathered in a tight circle. He drew his sword and brought it down in one broad stroke, splintering the short carriage railing into several strands of wood. Tyrian made a small pile of the bits of wood and splinters for kindling. He quickly found two long shreds and rubbed them together, sparking a flame, and then built a healthy fire, which created a warm orange glow against the fading daylight.

Tyrian took the older woman by the shoulder and whispered, "You stay here. Do you understand?"

"I will go with you," the woman replied.

Tyrian smiled as he realized she spoke his language. "We speak a common tongue. I am Tyrian."

"I am Margda," the woman replied.

Tyrian gave her a slight nod, then turned back to the horizon and said, "You must stay here and care for the girls."

"No. You will need my help. Serena can take care of the girls."

Without further discussion, Margda approached Serena and took her small face in her hands. Tyrian listened to the woman's voice soften as she gave direction in the girl's own pungent dialect; Tyrian was noticing that the languages of the central tribes sounded bizzare and sharp.

The girl nodded in understanding, and then looked to Tyrian. He pointed at the fire and nodded back.

"Stay here, Serena," he said gently. "We will return."

Serena quickly took charge, finding tasks for each of them.

Tyrian took the two old horses by the reins and began walking towards the Desert Trading Square, Margda at his side.

The walk into the trading encampment should have taken no time at all, but pulling the old, tired steeds along behind them made the journey considerably slower. When they finally reached the encampment, they found a tent with one old vendor behind a table. The thin, crouched man did not look up as Tyrian and Margda entered the tent. He was whittling a piece of wood, which was slowly taking the shape of a tiny horse that would soon be joining the team of model steeds that sat before him.

Tyrian cleared his throat and pointed to the live horses outside of the tent saying, "I've got two carriage horses here, friend. They won't be much help in the field, but they can pull a wagon."

The old man looked up from his work and squinted to get the horses into focus. "Those old beasts? You want to sell me those old jennies?"

Margda stepped forward and spoke softly to the old man, "They have plenty of life in them left. They just carried a pack of girls through the Bandelarian Sands. Look at them. They are still full of energy."

The merchant's gaze turned to the woman and then back to the horses. He lowered his head and rubbed his eyes.

"Old man," Tyrian said, "I need to feed these girls and get them passage across the sands."

Margda touched Tyrian's hand gently, stepping forward and leaning in close to the old artisan.

"Can't you help us, old merchant? These horses will serve you well."

"I can pay you ten coins for the horses."

"That's not enough, old man," Tyrian demanded.

"Surely there is something else you might need," Margda interrupted.

The old man looked Margda up and down and then looked Tyrian directly in the eye.

"I will pay you ten coins for the horses and twenty coins for the woman here."

"She is not for sale," Tyrian barked. "She is no slave."

"Everything in life is for sale, boy," the merchant laughed.

"She is not for sale!" he repeated.

"Then take your horses and leave me to my carving," the old man growled.

Margda led Tyrian out of the tent. They found privacy under the awning of the neighboring shop.

"It is meant to be. This is a part of the journey. Sacrifice is a prayer for the living and my lifeblood flows for others. You must let this come to pass, Tyrian."

"I did not save you to sell you off as a slave again, Margda," Tyrian pleaded.

"Sometimes the sacrifice of one for the many is our duty."

"He is not worthy of forcing this sacrifice, though. Hell has a special place for the likes of that dog," Tyrian exclaimed.

"Tyrian," Margda said, looking him deeply in the eyes, freezing him. "Those girls have seen too much for their young eyes. Right now they need passage across the desert. My life's path has already been laid out. And I trust that that old merchant is part of that path."

"It is not right. You fought for your freedom only to be betrothed through gold coins to a haggler such as him? I foresee a miserable life with him."

"One must look at one's life not as miserable or pleasurable, Tyrian, but as a life alone. There are pleasurable times and miserable times that balance out at the end. One must tend to the signposts along the way."

"How does one know a signpost from something different? How does one not get misdirected?"

Margda smiled and gently touched his face. His skin was warm. She could tell he was surprised by her touch. She wondered if he had ever felt such a soft touch on his face and smiled as he pressed his cheek ever so slightly into her palm. She was suddenly taken with his innocence, he was betraying his youth.

"Trust in the one who guides you. Whether that be the one god of Azjik, or the God-twin of the coastal tribes. Or the many gods of the northern people. Or, Tyrian, whether it be a simple trust in one's own voice. That is how you decipher a marker of life from a marker of death."

Margda reached into her cloak and pulled out a small package wrapped with a tattered cloth. She placed it in Tyrian's open palm, but as he started to unwrap it she quickly stopped him.

"No, Tyrian."

"But what is this gift?"

"This will be a reminder of this moment. And the lesson that our journey has many diversions and many paths. This is not a gift."

"If it is of value, how did you keep it from the Desert Pirates?"

"All beings have their superstitions."

"What is there to be superstitious about in this?"

She wrapped his palms over it and touched his face again gently, wiping the sweat from his brow. Tyrian closed his eyes tightly, comforted by her in a way that he had never been by the aunts who had raised him. His throat seized and he was taken aback.

Tyrian's voice cracked, "You could be of help on our journey, Margda."

"I will be. But not as you envision. Take this and lead those girls to safety."

"You want me to look the other way while this dirty bastard purchases your life?"

"For now, take this and put it away. You will understand on another day."

"I do not like this."

"Where will you take them?" Margda asked.

"I am going to Coteville. I will send them there ahead of me."

"Coteville is a good choice. They will find safety there."

Relucantly accepting Margda's sacrifice, Tyrian followed her back to the merchant's tent. She stood behind Tyrian as he approached the merchant.

"Old man, I will take thirty coins for the two horses and this woman as your wife, not as your slave."

"Splendid," the old man grinned widely. "I've no use for slaves. But a wife will do me wonderfully."

The old man's hand shook excitedly as he reached into a small chest and counted out thirty gold pieces. He stacked them on the table before him, between two small horse figurines. Just as quickly, Tyrian snatched them up. He turned and exited the tent, not looking back as the merchant led Margda away.

Before he left the Desert Trading Post, Tyrian purchased dried fruits and meats from one vendor. From another he bought some blankets.

The sun was beginning to set now and Tyrian was worried that the fire may have gone out at his little camp. He began to jog as left the encampment, the harsh warm air beginning to cool now.

When he reached the girls, he found them huddled close to a still healthy fire. The crackling flames partially shielded the girls from the cold night air. Serena sat serenely, singing to the girls. The youngest ones fought sleep to hear her sweet voice. Serena exchanged looks with Tyrian. They both seemed to acknowledge Margda's absence with subtle nods to each other.

Tyrian dropped his bag on the ground and dug out handfuls of dried fruits for the girls. He placed the blankets at their feet and found a spot to sit by the fire, stoking it absent-mindedly with a left-over shard of wood. The rising flames lit up the girls' faces, their eyes widening with excitement as the embers popped and crackled. He found Serena watching him and he smiled. She suddenly looked older to him than she had before.

When he was satisfied with the fire and had fed his horse, Tyrian sat down next to Serena and ate a few bites of the dried meat. The girls were still huddled together, most of them fast asleep.

"Sleep, Serena."

She smiled, not understanding Tyrian's words. Her fatigue agreed with his direction, though as she leaned against him, curling up to his warmth. He felt her breathing, and soon it was slow and steady. She was asleep. His let his head fall back and he found himself gazing up at the wide-open sky. It was still new to him, the vastness and the depth of the blackness, with the pinholes of light in so many different designs.

Tyrian closed his eyes and tried to meditate. But soon his mind wandered to the mysterious package Margda had given him. He pulled it out of his pocket and unwrapped the cloth, revealing a small silver key. He held it in his hand. The key absorbed the distant light of the moon and seemed to glow. It was long and thin and its tip had four teeth, each of a slightly different length. The handle had a wide, round medallion shape to it, with etchings that he did not recognize. He wrapped it back up and hid it away inside his cloak.

The fullness of the moon and the sound of Serena's breathing combined to serve as a meditation all its own and the night passed quickly.

As dawn approached, Tyrian woke Serena and had her ready the girls. He left the splintered remnants of the carriage in its crippled state as he led his horse, with Serena atop it, and the girls into the Desert Trading Square.

At the edge of the encampment they discovered a merchant who sold passage across the desert. A carriage was waiting, the first of the day. It was empty, but two men stood next to it, apparently dispatcher and driver.

"In which direction is Coteville?" Tyrian asked. The dispatcher, a tall, dark-haired man with a wiry beard, nodded his large head away from the sunrise. "Is that the quickest route?" Tyrian asked. "Will I get there directly?"

The merchant nodded. Tyrian dropped several coins on the counter before the dispatcher. Then he motioned Serena to start loading the girls into the carriage.

"These girls need passage to Coteville," Tyrian ordered.

The merchant smiled. "I can send them off, but it's dangerous out there, boy, and such a parcel may not last."

"I pray for your sake that they do not get lost."

"Why not take them yourself then, boy?"

Tyrian gripped the man's wrist in his hand, making him wince with pain. "My haste is not your consideration. Just know that I must arrive immediately, and these young girls will arrive safely after me. I will be waiting for them in Coteville, dog. If they do not arrive after one setting of the sun, I will be back here and have your head for it."

The merchant looked to the carriage-driver and gave him a look of pleading. The driver nodded back and then the merchant smiled again at Tyrian.

"They will arrive in Coteville not long after you, sire. That is my promise."

Tyrian turned towards his horse, but stopped at the rear of the carriage and took Serena's hand in his. "Take care, Serena. I will meet you across the desert in Coteville. The girls are under your watch now."

Serena gave him a helpless look of not understanding. He frowned, frustrated, and began to speak again.

She stopped him, taking his hand and pressing it to her lips and smiled. Tyrian gently pulled his hand away from her grip and mounted his horse. She watched as he urged his horse westward into the deep, gray void. Within moments he was no longer visible. She watched the spray of sand hanging in the air.

Serena was yanked out of her trance by the jolt of the carriage pulling away from the Desert Encampment, as it began its slow journey across the desert.

Chapter Ten

Roserie Argaune had many talents. Arguably one of his most useful gifts was his power of persuasion; it was the tool he used most often, since his motivations were always fluid and changing. To him all living beings were game pieces with which he played.

Argaune saw purpose in every living thing. His meditations taught him that there is no such thing as coincidence, that every moment was a marker on the road to one's final position, and that every living being you came into contact with moved you towards that end. These were the root principles of the religion that both Roserie Argaune and Heir Gabriel Theobald followed. But where Theobald's meditations led him to look inward and reveal his position in the world, Argaune's meditations did the opposite, leading him to look outward and reveal the position of others in relation to his own ambitions.

Argaune rode by night across the southeastern edge of the Sub-Bandelarian desert. He rode fast and hard, never stopping. By the break of dawn he had reached the coarse, straw-like grass that was the welcoming mat of the Vlyczcyys Steppes. There he found The Vilczyyz Tents, the loosely governed city-state that the Desert Pirates called home.

The tent-village stretched out across the sand like the remains of a long dead city, although it was actually quite alive. It sat along the grassy steppes that marked the end of the Bandelarian desert. The village wrapped around a large wooden cabin that to Argaune resembled a castle, albeit only in its architecture. It boasted no ornate markings or flags and no gilded trappings or intimidating bronze statues. The buildings were held together by rotted wood and iron fixtures; dirty cloths and grown-over moss hung in abundance. This was where the elders, the young, and the women lived.

A constant flow of Desert Pirates passed through to unload their stolen treasures. The elders kept a loose inventory and dispersed food, drink and clothes to the women and children.

Argaune arrived before the pirates sparked the first morning fire. He drove his horse around the western edge to an opening in the formation of tents and a flimsy rope that served as a gate. He dismounted and found a patch of sand to retire on, cooled from the hours of stark night air, and fell into an immediate meditative state. His mind became blank; he acknowledged only the feeling of a cool wind on his face and the absence of sound, careful to avoid any distractions that might intrude into that void.

Morning at The Tents came not with the first rays of sunlight, but with the first pirate to wake and ring the Fire Bell. Argaune waited to hear its tone, and was ready to spend hours in meditation if need be. As it happened, he was abruptly drawn from his trance by the sounds of small feet approaching. Without opening his eyes, Argaune could visualize the intruder and his mouth widened into a grin at the thought of the young desert vermin approaching him. The children of the Desert Pirates, deformed and dirty as they were, always brought cheer to the wizard's heart. They were innocent to their status in the world. They knew not the troubled life that lay before them, so they could laugh at a game of ball or smile at his tricks of small blasts and sparkles. The people of The Vilczyyz Tents adored Roserie Argaune.

Argaune straightened his mouth, feigning nescience as he felt the child draw closer and closer. Soon he could hear the child's breathing almost upon him, and he could smell the filth. Argaune reached out suddenly, grabbing the boy's ankle and yanking it, throwing the child to the sand. The boy screamed in his horrifying, nasal pitched howl, then burst into laughter. The wizard bellowed happily, matching the child's joy.

Argaune jumped to his feet and scooped the boy up in his arms, hoisting him over his shoulder, then marched through the pathetic gate into the tent compound. The boy laughed and barked out questions in his crude language. Argaune spoke it fluently, and made it sound nearly poetic.

"Where have you been, Wizard?" the boy asked.

"I've been hunting dragons in the dark caves of Awnetz, my boy," Argaune replied.

"Did you catch any?"

"I caught plenty. But they were of no use! Have you ever tasted dragon carcass?"

"No. Is it good?"

"Blagh! Horrible. But now, you must take me to your elders, boy. Win me an audience with your wise ones."

The boy wriggled and then jumped from the wizard's arms and ran towards the main compound. Despite his years, Argaune kept close behind him. Most men his age were bedridden, or crippled and needed a cane, but Argaune was as agile as a man half as old. Spending half of his life in meditation, he had learned long ago to exert only the energy one must for the task at hand.

The boy led him swiftly up the dirt road to the main house. There, Argaune stopped. He dropped to one knee, kneeling as a gesture of respect for the elders, something no other man of honor would ever do. Argaune knew his social station in life far exceeded theirs; his riches far surpassed theirs; his intelligent was far greater—but he also saw the value in honoring those who deserved it. So again he waited patiently. The boy knocked once and then sat on the stoop facing Argaune, not nearly as patient as the wizard; fidgeting and anxious.

After a short time the door opened and a hunched, decrepit being peered out. He wore a canvas mask that revealed only his sunken grey eyes and his pursed, chapped lips. His tattered and filthy robe reached barely to the height of Argaune's waist. He spoke through rotted and stained teeth. The creature was most likely a mutt of dwarf and human, Argaune guessed.

"Who's there at this hour?" the voice barked out to the morning.

"It is I, your friend Roserie Argaune of the Balles Hills," Argaune replied. The Elder swung the door open wide and bowed his head low—so low that Argaune feared he would topple over.

"Please, enter. Enter. Enter. Please warm our cold place with your light, oh wizard and wise man, Roserie Argaune." The elder swung his arm out wide, motioning an invitation. His voice was labored due to his deformed lungs and punctuated by raw coughs and gags.

"I apologize for my visit at such an hour, Enut, my friend. But I rode through the night."

"Nonsense, nonsense. You are welcome at any hour!" Enut replied, motioning the boy away as if he were a dog.

The child plopped himself at the foot of the steps, bored and anxious, waiting for the wizard to exit again.

Roserie entered the dark and cold receiving room of the Elders' Compound. It smelled of soured eggs and wood mold. He took a kerchief from his breast pocket and pretended to wipe sweat from his forehead before he covered his nose to breathe in.

"I've a flame here somewhere, wizard, forgive me," the creature fumbled to find a light.

"Not to worry," Argaune replied, as he reached over to a candle and pressed two fingers together, sparking a light on the wick. The wizard waved his hand in a graceful arc as the candles lit, one by one, across the room. Suddenly the room filled with the light of the flame and both the elder laughed and clapped his hands in delight.

"Wonderful! Wonderful, my friend!"

"My pleasure," Argaune replied.

"What is the reason for this honor, Roserie Argaune?" the dwarf mutt asked.

"I have come to ask you a favor, old friend. And to entice you with treasures to be won."

Enut cleared this throat and paused where he was. Under the flickering candlelight Argaune could see him stroking his unseen beard as his eyes closed in thought. Then the dwarf figure abruptly took a step back and motioned Argaune to enter the kitchen.

"Please, Roserie, let us have some cake."

Arguane entered the dining hall, a long, wide chamber with thick wooden tables and benches scattered in no apparent order. It was empty; even their whispers echoed in the vast unused space. The first shades of daylight were creeping in, and Argaune sensed movement in an adjacent room. Enut took up a bench in the center of the room and Argaune sat across from him.

As they settled into place, the figure from the other room emerged with a tray, which he or she placed between them. The figure appeared tall and lithe but was covered in rags and a head mask, so as to hide age and gender. The tray offered a cracked ceramic bowl with small cakes piled in it and a carafe of cold tea. These creatures certainly tried to be good hosts, Arguane thought, but they fell painfully short. Enut shoved three cakes into his mouth, one after the other, then poured himself a cup of cold tea.

"And what is your favor? And, more importantly, what is the treasure?" Enut asked between swallows.

Argaune watched Enut gurgle down his tea and kept an uncomfortable silence. He concentrated on the sounds beyond the room, waiting until all movement stopped. Enut shuffled in his seat, trying to force the quiet from the room. Finally, Argaune sat up and leaned in towards the small creature, unceremoniously pushing aside the bowl of cakes.

"In three days' time a party will be traveling the Road of Fathers towards the castle of King Azjik," the wizard began. "They will be carrying various gifts of spices and smokeables, items very much in demand in the desert markets. I can assure you that as the sun reaches its highest point on that day, they will approach the narrow cliffs known as the Iron Gates, just beyond the Witches' Bend, a perfect place for both surprise and for limiting their chance of escape."

"And you offer me this bit of information because you hope that they will be attacked by my brethren."

"My riddles are not so difficult to decipher, my friend. That is exactly my hope."

"Spices and smokeables can be found with any traveling party, my friend. What else will they carry?"

"They will have fine horses, gold and silver taxes for the king, as well as weapons and armor."

"Will they have women?"

"They will not have women."

Enut took a moment to think. His gaze shifted across the room, where the hanging dust flowed like a translucent river against the early sunlight, creating thick diagonal curtains. He watched small rodents waken and begin their busy day of scavenging.

"Who will lead this party?" Enut finally asked.

"The party will be leaving Coteville soon. It will be an official party."

Enut gasped and sat straight. "An official party, you say? I cannot send my brethren to attack an official party of the king. That is treasonous. Even for the likes of us refugees. We cannot attack an heir and his party, Mister Argaune."

"You will be under the guidance of my God-twin, my friend."

"It is a country of God-twins, wizard. They will all have God-twins. I cannot ask my hunters to make such a suicide bargain. I am sorry. Anything else you may ask of me, friend."

"But I ask nothing else. This is what I ask."

"It sickens me to deny your request, but I must."

"You will not deny my request, Enut," Argaune stated coldly. "You will go to your peers and together you will direct two platoons of your villainous Desert Pirates to be at the Iron Gates in two days, where they will find a traveling party. You may keep all of the spices, smokeables, horses, armor and weapons... but anything else you find must be brought back to me."

"Mister Argaune," Enut's voice grew shaky, quivering with fear. "You cannot possibly expect me to..."

"I do expect you to, my friend," Argaune corrected the deformed dwarf as he reached over, and placed his hand on top of Enut's. Argaune looked Enut directly in the eye. Enut could not hold the gaze and looked away, but soon he felt the warmth of Argaune's hand increase until it was burning his flesh. He tried to pull his arm back but Argaune's grip was too tight; he could not break free. His eyes watered and his face tightened in a grimace. He tried to scream out, but his clogged lungs only let out a gurgle. The wizard began to smell the sour odor of the dwarf's burning skin.

"It...burns!" Enut managed to yelp.

"Just as your hand burns now, little friend, this whole filthy village will burn if you do not honor my request."

Argaune's grip tightened and his eyes penetrated Enut's. Steam rose from their hands and the small creature whimpered.

"I will send some pirates, Argaune. I will. I promise. Please spare me. Spare our tents. I will sacrifice fifty of my men for this foolish mission."

Argaune finally let go and pulled his hand away. Enut's hand was red and scarring already. He yanked it back and cradled it in his lap. Argaune moved the carafe of cold tea towards him and then rose to his full height.

"Thank you, my friend. Your deeds will be rewarded, I can promise you that. You must remember, though, that treasures beyond what I listed must be brought to me. I've taken inventory on certain items that must stay intact."

"Yes, Mister Argaune," Enut whimpered, lowering his head as he poured the cold tea over his burned hand. He could not bear to watch the wizard exit. He kept his gaze down to his lap and waited to hear the heavy footsteps quiet.

As Argaune departed the building, he found the young child waiting for him on the steps. The boy grabbed hold of the wizard's hand and led him back down the road. Argaune kept his stride slow, taking smaller steps so that the child was able to keep up. As he walked, he reached into his cloak and pulled out a large bluish-colored marble. He held it out in front of the boy, who held out his hands. Argaune dropped the marble into the child's palm and then waved his own hand over it. In an instant it was no longer visible, although the boy still felt its weight.

The child looked up to the wizard with a wide grin and curious eyes. Argaune wrapped his hand around the boy's hand and curled it up in a fist around the invisible marble. He winked one eye and let out a small laugh, then opened the boy's hand to reveal two marbles, again visible. The boy laughed loudly as Argaune picked up his pace, leaving the boy behind.

Argaune soon came upon his horse and hoisted himself into the saddle. He waved at the child of the Steppes and pushed his steed towards the white ocean of desert ahead of him.

The boy stood watching until the wizard's image had vanished into the haze of the sand and heat. He then turned and walked back up the dirt road, smiling at his gift from the wizard, eager to show it off.

Chapter Eleven

Heir Gabriel Theobald's homecomings always engendered an exquisite feast in celebration. His return meant a banquet and music lasting well into the evening. Even unannounced, he could barely pass through the city gates before word had spread throughout the capital village, and a banquet was arranged.

The feasts almost always centered around his favorite stew of boar roast, vegetables and rice. The local bakers competed in preparing the perfect loaf of sweet bread to soak up the succulent broth. The evening's highlight, though, centered on the slicing of a rum-soaked Cote-berry pie, with hints of almonds and ginger, which was his wife, Océane's, specialty. Gabriel always insisted on enjoying it with his own reserve of sweet honey wine.

Océane Theobald was a beautiful woman. Slightly taller than her husband, she carried about her an air of confidence and effortless command. Her humble manner of constantly caring for others was never mistaken as servitude, for she could just as easily lash out when punishment was necessary. She wore her four decades like a crown atop her graying red hair, draping her shoulders like smooth silk. The first thing one saw when Océane approached was the kindness in her eyes; the second was the slight smile on her lips. She approached strangers and loved- ones in the same manner, with arms outstretched to clasp their hands and proffering a light kiss on the cheek. Despite her impressive height and broad shoulders, she seemed delicate and petite.

Océane had borne Gabriel four children, all but one of them girls, and cared for them as lovingly and as sharply as a she-wolf would her cubs. She was fastidious in handing out discipline during Gabriel's long absences. Her children loved her dearly, and on occasion she would find one or more of them gazing at her in adoration. She bathed in the glow of her children's love, warming her like the rays of afternoon sunlight.

As was the tradition in Coteville, Océane had been covenanted away at birth for marriage upon her fifteenth year. Along with her hand in marriage, her husband was promised a vast estate on the banks of the Silver Bay, in the Southern-most part of Coteville. The marriage also included part ownership of a lucrative boat-building operation. Augustain, as the eldest Theobald brother, was to have Océane as his bride when the time came. Sadly, though, Augustain was killed during a battle, while leading the Cote Militia to fend off Desert Pirates on the edges of Coteville. Upon Augustain's death Gabriel, the next oldest, inherited the young girl's promised hand.

And so, on Océane's fifteenth year and on Gabriel's seventeenth year, they were married. Within days of their wedding, Gabriel departed to train in Azjik's Regular Stand Army. Azjik was at war with barbarian hordes from the Sociun Islands, and so, for the first three years of marriage, Gabriel and Océane did not see each other.

When Gabriel finally returned to Coteville, several months after the barbarians' defeat and the capture of the islands, he was no longer a boy and Océane no longer a girl. His return was expected to be a routine homecoming of a soldier to his wife: a feast, then a long night of stories at the inn with his father and brothers, then home to lay with his wife. But as he crossed the threshold of their cottage and saw her waiting for him in the sitting room, it seemed as if they were laying eyes on each other for the first time. He did not recognize this woman, having left a teenage girl behind three years before, and she did not recognize him, now a full-grown, battle-scarred soldier. They stood speechless for long moments, drinking in the nectar of their newly born romance.

Soon they were in each other's arms, where they discovered a deep love and formed a bond that only grew stronger each day. At one time Gabriel had yearned for adventures beyond the walls of his beloved Coteville, but upon the birth of their first child, Anjelain, he wanted only to remain at home with his family. Unfortunately, as his family grew, so did his responsibilities. And, on his father's retirement, the position of Coteville heir was handed down to him; and once he had attained that honor it meant more time away from home. Both Gabriel and Océane understood the responsibility that came with that position and it changed them, not only individually, but as a pair. Now, during his absences, she became responsible for fulfilling the duties of an heir: settling disputes, meeting counselors, attending ceremonies. And the people of Coteville accepted her as a leader with open hearts. To many she was truly the embodiment of Coteville—beautiful and just.

# # #

Heir Gabriel Theobald's long ride from the Desert Trading Post had brought him once again to the beloved gates of Coteville. His heart jumped with joy. He had not been home in two seasons. But now lush green pastures and rows of brilliant marigolds welcomed him at the gates.

Gabriel pulled his horse to a stop and waited for the entry guards to greet him. He closed his eyes and breathed in deeply, taking in the mixture of damp sea air and the sweet fragrance of roses and other blossoms. He could not wait to see his dear wife and children. He looked down to see Wolf moaning hungrily. The poor dog had made the trek across the desert by his side. Gabriel marveled at the dog's strength and resilience. Were he a man, he would be among the fiercest of warriors in the King's First Stand.

As the two entry guards approached, they recognized their Heir and immediately dropped to one knee—each with the opposite knee, so as to form a spiritual barrier on either side of Gabriel—and bowed their heads, barely hiding the wide grins they wore.

Gabriel dismounted his horse and looked beyond the gates into the heart of the city. He reached out a hand to touch Wolf, who nuzzled up next to him. "Rise," he ordered the entry guards. As they rose, he realized he did not know them. They were boys, most likely just fresh from the academy.

"Take my horse and feed her," Gabriel said. They both stumbled over themselves to do his bidding, leading the tired horse away, as the second set of guards approached to relieve them.

Gabriel led Wolf onto the main pathway down into town, the hungry beast moving from patch of grass to patch of grass, trying to decipher each new scent. The heir moved with a distinct purpose. He heard the heavy crash of the gate closing as he descended the dirt path.

He was anxious to reach his beloved wife.

Gabriel and Wolf gradually made their way down into the main square. As if the slow breeze had announced their arrival, a growing crowd of citizens gathered at the fountain square. Children were hastily cutting and tying flowers to the trees. The boys and men dropped to one knee and bowed their heads as he passed. The women all curtsied graciously. He was careful to greet each one with a smile.

At the far end of the square stood his regal abode. It seemed, like a crouching father, watching over his brood with pride. The house had two levels and stretched across the width of the square. The front door opened onto a porch-like platform that ran along either side of the square, like arms welcoming all comers.

And, as Gabriel reached the square, he could see his radiant wife standing just outside the door, holding close to her bosom their son, Gabriel Theobald the Second. At the foot of the stairs posed their three daughters—Anjelain, Beatrice and Nicitania—all youthful variations of Océane. Gabriel had to steady his steps, restraining his instinct to run towards them. Instead he stroked the nape of Wolf's neck harder. The dog lapped up at his hand, calmed by the touch.

By the time Gabriel stepped onto his property, the entire town had gathered in the square, cheering and bowing at his return.

Without looking back he climbed the few steps to his porch, took each daughter in his hands one by one and kissed each on the forehead. Then he raised the youngest, his son, up into the air and embraced him tightly. And, as if well-rehearsed, the eldest daughter, Anjelain, took her brother from her father's arms, freeing Theobald to embrace his wife.

Gabriel kissed Océane fully on the lips and swung her around so that he was facing the crowded square and she was facing him. They smiled widely and gazed into each other's eyes, as reunited lovers do. Finally, Gabriel stepped forward and held his hand high up towards the sky, waving to his countrymen.

"Dear people of Coteville," he shouted, to thunderous applause. "It is good to be home! I am here for only a short rest, yet long enough still to enjoy the feast of welcome that Coteville always provides me. Let us eat and drink tonight!"

And with that, their heir disappeared into his home, his family behind him. Wolf followed at their heels, anxious to be away from the crowd.

Once inside, hidden from view from the townspeople, Gabriel collapsed into a heap in his sitting room, his soft leather chair cradling him like the nanny he'd had when he was a child. It was only now that he realized the extent of his exhaustion. All at once his limbs ached and his breathing grew heavy. Océane came to him with a small pot of tea and a plate of cheese. He sipped the warm drink but let the cheese sit untouched.

Wolf lay curled up at his feet and was soon fast asleep. That is, until Anjelain, Beatrice and Nicitania entered the room and discovered him. Within seconds they were on top of him, rubbing their faces against his soft fur and scratching his belly. Despite his fatigue, Wolf enjoyed the attention and lay back, a prisoner of their little hands.

Gabriel held out his hand to Océane and whispered to her, through his half-sleep, "My dear, please summon me a scout rider. Let me nap for a moment, then I will address him." Océane kissed his hand in response, then ushered the three girls out of the room.

When Gabriel awakened the sun had already vanished. His sleep had been broken by the chill that swept in from the open window, even though Océane had covered him with a blanket. He sat up and stretched his legs, kicking Wolf unconciously. Wolf, startled and groggy, poked his nose into the air, sniffing for an answer to his curious environment, forgetting for a moment where he was.

Océane suddenly entered the room, as if Gabriel's waking had silently summoned her. "My dear, your scout rider awaits you in the library," she said.

Gabriel ordered Wolf out to the patio, then made his way into a small receiving room off of the meeting chamber where he found the scout waiting patiently. The young rider jumped to his feet, then turned instinctively to the west, dropping his right knee so that his left knee stood out, symbolically protecting his heir from the north. Had they been south of Azjik's castle he would have taken the opposite pose. Such well-rehearsed pomp meant nothing to some heirs, but Gabriel found it important; it represented a tradition that bound the many different cultures of Azjik's rule together.

"Rise, boy," Gabriel in a quiet and measured tone, taking the boy's hand in his. "I need you to ride from here to King Azjik's borders and back along the Road of Fathers, and report to me the conditions of the pass. I will follow that route once you report its safety."

"Yes, your Honor. I will ride fast and report to you immediately upon my return," the boy replied, then bowed and retreated.

Gabriel turned to see Océane waiting for him, dressed elegantly; her tall frame was draped with a light blue gown, cinched tightly at the waist with a golden belt. She wore a tiara, fitted snugly in her red locks. Gabriel stopped short to take in her beauty. She smiled broadly. How she loved being adored by her husband.

"I must wash now and prepare for our feast," he said softly, as he kissed her on the cheek.

"I fear our citizens have not eaten today, in anticipation of your banquet. I pray you don't make them wait much longer," she replied with a coy smile.

Gabriel retreated to his private dressing room, where he washed and changed into dark blue trousers and long, leather riding boots. Over his black dress shirt and vest he wore a velvet cape that hung to his waist. He now looked the part of royalty as he carefully sheathed his Honor Blade and joined his wife.

Gabriel and Océane stepped out onto the portico and greeted the townspeople. As the crowd cheered Gabriel marveled at the display of tables and decorations, hastily yet carefully arranged.

Gabriel descended the few steps and guided Océane down. They crossed the short distance to their head table, where a servant stood ready with a carafe of wine. Before they sat the servant poured them each a glass and they raised them to each other and then up to the throng. Gabriel cleared his throat and then proclaimed, dramatically, "Citizens of Coteville, my brothers and sisters, my children, it pains my heart to ever leave our fair city. But my return is always a rejuvenating welcome, and my soul is filled with fire and life once again. To Coteville! To Coteville! To Coteville!"

And the townspeople returned his call, shaking the air with a thunderous cheer, "To Coteville! To Coteville! To Coteville!"

# # #

Several hours after the feast and all of the music and dance had concluded, Gabriel was drained and wanted nothing more than to sleep. He had stayed long enough to greet everyone who insisted on passing along their prayers to him. He calculated that he had a little more than a day for the scout rider to make the trip to Azjik's castle and back, and that would give him enough time to rest up.

Noticing his fatigue, Océane took his hand and led him away from the square. As he looked back he could see that the square was quickly emptying; it was late, and the moon was just now beginning her descent to make way for the breaking sun. Océane led him into the house, where she disappeared into their bedroom.

Gabriel made his way to his meditation chamber, a small round room in the center of the house. It contained no decorations. There was nothing in the room except candles laid out on the floor in no discernible patterns and a single pillow in the center, directly below a round hole in the ceiling with a retractable window; it looked directly out into the night sky.

The tired knight stepped into the cold air of the meditation chamber and knelt on the pillow. His head fell back and he stared into the blackness of the sky above him. Soon he forgot about the chill and fell into a trance.

Within moments his ghost-like God-twin knelt before him, like a mirror image. The God-twin rose, as if standing, and spread its arms wide and upward towards the opening above. And, as gracefully as a dancer, the spirit took flight up and out of the room, into the air above the house.

Gabriel felt a chill that moved up his spine and the rush of it made him momentarily dizzy.

One never truly got used to the separation of God-twin and self. He remembered the way it was first described to him as a child, when a priest told him it felt "...as if a bird was hatched from an egg in your stomach and was abruptly taking flight, and taking with it your heart."

Through the God-twin's eyes, Gabriel searched out his surroundings. He looked out at the desert night, north to south and east to west. He knew that human marauders ventured into the desert on occasion to thieve while campers slept. Desert Pirates roamed in large packs, but only during the day. Others killed just for sport. The Bandelarian Desert was unforgiving.

Towards the horizon he spotted a lone rider. And beyond the rider, farther off under the grasp of the cold night, a wagon clumsily clawed its way across the desert. Gabriel sent his spirit flying towards the figures to investigate. As it got closer, he soon realized that the lone rider was Tyrian Fellhawk, his young apprentice. He had found his way to Coteville. Even in the Heir's meditative state, Gabriel's lip curled into a smile, proud of the boy's persistence.

Gabriel pulled himself from his trance and rushed into his dressing room. There he quickly changed into his familiar leather trousers, riding boots, worn blue tunic and his cape, and gathered his favorite blade. He crept out of the house and took a horse from his modest stable behind the house. He led the horse across the town square and then climbed into the saddle and rode back up the dirt path that he had descended only hours before.

As he approached the sentinels at the gates, he slowed his pace and held his right hand—his blade hand—up in the air, palm forward to signal he meant no fight. Even so, the young boys raised their blades as he approached, until Gabriel slowly rode under the torchlight and they could see his face.

As before, they knelt and bowed their heads.

"Rise, boys," Gabriel ordered.

Gabriel looked them both over, then nodded to the youngest boy. "Go home, son. I will assume your post."

The older boy smiled, thrilled at the thought of standing guard with his heir. The younger one reluctantly gathered his things and rode back towards the city.

"What is the reason for this honor, My Lord?" the older boy asked him.

"I am expecting a friend this night, boy," Gabriel replied. "I want to be the first friendly face he sees as he enters Coteville."

"Then I will be the second friendly face he sees, My Lord."

Gabriel laughed and gripped the boy's shoulder tightly. "Yes, you shall be!"

Gabriel climbed the short ladder at the gate's edge and took up his post at watch. It was a long and quiet job to be night guard; it seemed so many seasons had passed since he was a boy and first took that position. But now he was able to take it by choice.

He peered into the blackness beyond and saw nothing. He heard nothing. There was no wind this night, just a still, penetrating chill that hung in the air.

Suddenly they heard a rustling behind them. The boy turned to Gabriel but the knight was already standing ready, sword drawn. The boy quickly drew his sword, stepping closer to his heir. They could see nothing, but heard footsteps and labored breathing. Gabriel noticed something odd about the breathing, as it got closer. It did not sound human. It was a heavy breathing mixed with sniffing. As it drew nearer, the sound became familiar to Gabriel. He pulled the torch out from its cradle and pointed it towards the sound. It was Wolf. The dog had followed Gabriel's scent to the gates.

"I'm afraid you will be the third friendly face he sees, boy," Gabriel told the young guard, as he descended the ladder back to the ground and knelt before Wolf. Wolf nuzzled against him and licked his face happily.

"Sir," the younger guard spoke, "a rider approaches."

Through the blackness they relied only on sound, and the horse's approach seemed to take a long time. But finally the horse slowed to an easy trot and then a complete stop. They could make out a figure on horseback, just below them and outside of the gate.

"Who approaches?" The young guard called out.

"My name is Tyrian Fellhawk and I am here to see Heir Gabriel Theobald."

Wolf immediately jumped to his feet and called out to Tyrian with a series of howls and barks.

"Wolf, is that you?" Tyrian's voice betrayed his excitement. To Gabriel's delight, the boy no longer sounded like a warrior. He sounded again like a child. Gabriel laughed loudly into the night, filling the boy's heart.

"Master Theobald! I am here. I made it! And I have the pouch!" Tyrian called out excitedly.

The young guard opened the gate and Tyrian led his horse inside the walls of Coteville. He knelt down and embraced Wolf tightly.

"Do you know who follows you?" Gabriel asked.

"I purchased passage for a group of young slave girls. I pray that they can find refuge in your state."

"My boy, they will be welcomed by my people. Come, let me bring you to Coteville. We will rest for a day before we return our treasure to King Azjik. I have sent a scout along the Road of Fathers to ensure an open passage."

Gabriel turned to the young guard who had opened the gate. "You will escort us into the square." The boy nodded and took the lead. Gabriel then turned to the other guard, "There will be a replacement sent up. Tie Tyrian's horse up until the end of your shift, then take him down to the stables for feeding and cleaning."

Tyrian turned to face the path that led down into the town square. The sun had just crept above the horizon and the sky was still bluish from the night; daylight was approaching. Wolf moved up close to him, nipping playfully at his hand. Tyrian had feared he would never see Gabriel again, and that his apprenticeship had finished before it could begin. But now he was confident his training had not ended. It was an unfamiliar comfort to him. He was happy to be in Coteville.

Chapter Twelve

Wolf led Tyrian toward the main square, nipping at the boy's hands, licking and biting playfully. He pressed into Tyrian, herding him towards a tree or a flower, showing him the beauty all around them.

Your Honor," Tyrian said, "the wagon I commissioned to transport the rescued girls should be arriving soon."

"My God-twin's eyes saw them some distance behind you. I will send out one of my scouts to escort them into our gates."

Gabriel turned to the young guard who escorted them down the path and motioned to the desert beyond the gates. "My boy, ride out towards the Trading Post compound until you find this wagon of girls. Escort them back here safely. Meditate first and let your God-twin find their position." The guard turned and ran to carry out his orders.

The expanding daylight was beginning to reveal the sea at the far end of Coteville. Tyrian could taste the salt in the air. He stopped for a moment, taking in the cyan blue expanse that was the Silver Bay. As he looked down from the crest of the path, Tyrian could see the town wrap its borders around the bustling cove, then sprawl out into the vast green and purple hills beyond. He had never seen anything like it.

"Tyrian, this is my beloved city. You will be welcomed as a son of Coteville."

They fell into silence, watching as the strange angled shadows of the city's unique architecture began to shift from the sunlight. Here and there Tyrian could hear the sounds of life, as people started their days. He found himself drawn to the large fountain at the center of the square. The water flowing up and over the beautiful concrete statue looked like a translucent flower in constant bloom. He crossed the short distance to the pool that surrounded it and sat at the edge. He reached across and felt the water, letting it splash halfway up his sleeve. It was cold and jolted him from his trance. He looked over to see Gabriel standing nearby, smiling.

"Come, Tyrian, we have much to do today and now we must eat."

Océane had awakened early and prepared breakfast. As Gabriel and Tyrian entered the house, the sweet aroma of herbs and spiced tea welcomed them. Tyrian's morning meals had always been bland and flavorless—boiled oats, or the occasional baked potato. The flavors and aromas of Coteville were promising to be more opulent than any riches he could ever have imagined.

They passed through a front room and made their way onto a veranda in the back. There was a small table at the edge of the patio, looking out over a small flower garden. Another table off to the side held a platter of morning cakes, a dish with an egg and vegetable pie, and a pot with steaming spiced tea. Tyrian watched as Gabriel filled his plate high with food and then poured some tea. He followed suit and sat down across from him, his own plate heaping.

"You must not have eaten in the desert," Theobald laughed, as the boy devoured large mouthfuls.

"I ate, your Honor, but nothing as sweet as this," Tyrian said as he handed a cake to Wolf, who lay at his feet.

After a few moments, Océane came out onto the veranda. Without thinking, Tyrian jumped to his feet and dropped his fork clumsily, bowing his head. Océane let out a slight laugh and then motioned him to sit down.

"Those formalities have no place in our home, young man. I am honored, but I would be more honored if you simply enjoyed my cooking."

"Tyrian," Gabriel said, "please meet my wife, Océane. Océane, this is Tyrian Fellhawk, from the Great River Forest. He found me injured after my battle with Heir Volkummen's army. He and his father brought me back to health. And you've already met his friend, Wolf, whom I should say I owe just as much debt to."

Wolf licked at the air, smiling as best he could with such a mischievous face.

"Most pleased to meet you, ma'am," Tyrian said softly.

"I won't interrupt your meal any further. I must wake up this household for the day," she said as she disappeared inside.

After she had gone, Gabriel took a few more bites and then pushed his plate aside. Tyrian felt he ought to do the same, but instead continued to eat. He had built up a great hunger from the desert ride. But more than that, he wanted take in all of the flavors of Gabriel's home, to be that much more connected with his mentor.

"Today I will take you to the academy, where we train young men to be soldiers."

Tyrian sat up and finally pushed his plate aside, excited at the thought of meeting other boys his age.

"Come, leave your plate where it is. You can rest while I meditate and then we'll go see what my students are up to today."

"Your Honor, may I meditate with you?"

"If you wish."

Gabriel led Tyrian to his meditation chamber, where he silently took up his spot in the center of the room. Wolf found a spot near the doorway to lay, ever watchful. Tyrian stood awkwardly for a moment, then took a pillow and sat off to the side, closed his eyes and slowed his breathing. Every few minutes he stole a look through squinted eyes to watch his mentor, trying to decipher the secrets to his meditation.

Finally he simply closed his eyes. He listened to his breathing. Soon, his mind went blank. He felt as if his body were straightening out, as if he was rising above the ground and lying out straight. He heard a low humming that was strangely sing-song; it was his own voice. He thought he could hear words in the song, words in his voice. He listened more closely, slowly leaning forward as if trying to penetrate an unseen fog. He began to make out the words and then realized it was only one word, repeated slowly yet hidden in the hum. He heard his voice in the shallow silence, whispering "trust" over and over. "Trust... trust... trust...." He was not sure what it meant. Who should he trust?

He was deeply engaged in this mystery when a cold breeze hit him and caused him to open his eyes, abruptly breaking the trance. He looked up to see Gabriel standing above him. He did not know how long he had been in meditation, but it had grown considerably brighter outside.

"Come, Tyrian, let us go watch your peers in training."

Tyrian rose to his feet and followed Gabriel out of the chamber, shaking off his grogginess.

They crossed the short distance to the training academy, on the far end of the square. At first glance, it looked like a chapel. Along the front entrance he saw a wide dirt field where the youngest boys practiced. He noticed two groupings: nearest the entrance of the academy Tyrian saw boys fighting with long wooden sticks, while farther off towards the square a group of younger boys practiced simple footwork.

The two wide entryway doors that stood open revealed the oldest boys inside, dressed in loose fighting gear and wielding sturdy blades. As Gabriel and Tyrian approached the entrance, Tyrian could see that the boys were gathered in a circle around two others, who were sparring.

A hush fell over the room as Gabriel entered. The sparring partners stopped to bow. Two older men, instructors, bowed as well.

"Please, continue. Let us see what you've learned," Gabriel urged as he leaned against the back wall, Tyrian at his side.

Tyrian watched the boys closely; they were no older than he. He watched their feet and remembered when he had first seen Gabriel fight in the Great River Forest. It seemed so long ago.

Now Tyrian observed how each boy led with his left foot and rose or lowered himself with his hips, always keeping his knees bent. The taller boy pivoted back and forth on his rear foot while the other boy used more linear, yet graceful, movements back and forth, always keeping his weight on the rear foot. It made for an interesting fight, with the taller boy moving in a circular motion and the younger boy simply moving forward and back; each tried to maneuver the other off-balance.

When the taller boy struck from the side with a sweeping arc, the shorter boy took two quick steps back—careful to stay in form—and then deflected the attack with a quick upward parry and then back down, forcing the sword from the other boy's hands.

The crowd of boys erupted into applause as Gabriel stepped forward, handing the defeated boy his sword back.

"Well done, Andoni, well done," the knight praised the shorter boy. Then he turned his attention to the crowd of students, holding onto Andoni's shoulder firmly. "Andoni's strength in this match was his patience. Corin is every bit as skilled, but he was anxious. He became reckless in his attack. One must be patient enough to find that moment of carelessness; that's where true battles are won, in the moments of carelessness. Patience is the virtue a knight must live by."

Gabriel ushered the defeated boy out of the circle and motioned to Tyrian to enter. "Andoni, let us see how someone from the Great River Forest does against a boy from Coteville. This is Tyrian Fellhawk."

Tyrian stepped into the circle, slowly and reluctantly. Gabriel handed him the defeated boy's sword, and Tyrian held it out from his chest, awkwardly, as if accepting a cursed talisman. Andoni held his blade out to the side and took his stance. Tyrian felt lost; he could not remember what Gabriel had taught him. He clumsily held the sword out in front of him and bent his knees, trying to mimic the other boy.

Gabriel stood aside and nodded to the two boys to begin. They touched swords and then each took a cautious step back, sizing the other up. For his part, Andoni did not know what to expect from Tyrian; he had heard the legends of the barbarians in the Great River Forest, how they were blood-thirsty and ate their victims. Tyrian towered over the smaller boy, his broad shoulders seeming like wings.

Tyrian was careful to be patient and not make a clumsy move and so he stood frozen, his guard up. Andoni was no better. He would step forward, without attacking, and then step back again. There was no interplay, no lunging, no blocking, just steps forward and backward.

Finally, Gabriel stepped between them and smiled. "Being cautious," he spoke out to the gathering of boys, "does not mean inaction. One must attack at some point. And one must also force attack from his opponent." Gabriel then stepped away, leaving the two boys alone in the circle. Tyrian had noticed that the smaller boys from outside had wandered in to see him fight. The crowd had grown, eager to witness the barbarian boy. The room was full now.

Andoni was the first to attack. He lunged forward, with his sword pointed directly at Tyrian's stomach, left foot first. Tyrian stumbled back, deflecting the attack. Andoni's hands stung with the vibration and he was shaken by the strength of the larger boy.

But, as he moved back, Tyrian's feet crossed awkwardly, and he stumbled to the ground. Gabriel was there to help him up. Once he was on his feet, regaining his full height, his brow lowered in frustration and Andoni took two steps back in fear. Tyrian's anger was rising, but Gabriel, noticing the change, stopped him.

"Trust, Tyrian," the mentor spoke. Tyrian remembered the word from his own voice in meditation. He looked at the teacher, and his anger softened and his eyes widened in confusion. Was it Gabriel's voice or his own that he had heard? "Listen to my counsel, Tyrian. Your anger is blocking your reason. Trust that your hands will lunge when needed, that your feet will guide you."

Gabriel stepped aside again and Tyrian readied himself. He could see that Andoni was hesitant. He lunged forward, drawing Andoni into a defensive parry; he circled back and then charged forward again in an instant, catching the smaller boy off-balance. Then Tyrian came back to his original position, leaving Andoni unsettled and unsure. Again he lunged forward, forcing Andoni to parry, and again, he pulled back, quickly attacked once more. Tyrian's speed was too much for Andoni to react to, and the strength of his lunges slowed Andoni's responses, wary as he was of the stinging vibration of contact.

Tyrian held back, catching his breath, and circled Andoni. He felt more in control now. He forgot about the crowd of boys and focused on Andoni, watching his feet and his blade. Andoni moved cautiously forward and back in his linear form, taunting Tyrian's blade with quick jabs. Tyrian tried to draw him into an attack, to no avail. He tried to get him off-balance with his stop-and-start motion, but Andoni simply moved straight back, leaving Tyrian exposed. Tyrian's anger was rising again: Andoni was smaller and weaker than he; it should be a quick and easy fight.

Tyrian swung his blade around in a wide arc. Then, the younger boy, seeing an opening, brought his blade forward, cutting off Tyrian's attack. Tyrian's sword bounced off of Andoni's blade, and the younger boy came right back with another lunge, this time hitting Tyrian in the stomach. The dull practice blade bent him over in pain and he let out a deep groan. He took two steps back to recover, but again his feet tangled and he fell to the ground. He lost his grip on his sword as he threw his arm out to catch himself, and as he hit the floor he could hear the laughter of the crowd of students echoing in the room. He sat for a moment, looking up at the smaller boy, then rose to his feet, towering over Andoni. His fists clenched and he envisioned tearing the sword from the boy's hand, but when he felt Gabriel's touch on his shoulder he pushed that thought aside. He closed his eyes and took a deep breath.

"In battle, size and strength matter less than skill, patience and focus," Gabriel told the group. "Tyrian is a fierce fighter. Do not let this display fool you. I've seen him in battle and I've fought next to him. He has a great heart and does not give in to his fears. Today he was distracted, which is a lesson for both fighters. Andoni stayed focused, so he won. *Size and strength matter less than skill, patience and focus.*" He repeated the words for emphasis, then turned to Tyrian, feeling the tension in his shoulder, and announced, "Now, you must excuse our leave; Tyrian and I must prepare for our journey to the castle of King Azjik."

Gabriel bowed, then led Tyrian out. Tyrian focused on the warm grassy ground as they crossed the well-kept lawn. They walked in silence.

"I could have crushed that boy, your Honor," Tyrian finally spoke, his deep, cracking voice betraying his anger. "I could have crushed any one of those boys." Gabriel laughed as he looked over at his protégé, but he did not speak.

As they approached Gabriel's residence, Tyrian glanced hesitantly at his mentor. "Your Honor, can one call on their God-twin during battle, when they are not meditating?"

"You cannot call upon your God-twin in battle, for you must be focused in the moment. Meditating with your God-twin takes all of your concentration. But you can call out to him beforehand, to guide you. It is what we call the Combat Communion. You call your God-twin to inhabit your own body. He does not move you; you are always in control of your free will. But with the lightest of touch, if you are conscious enough, he will guide your feet, your hands, your waist. It is a useful tool, and very exhausting. I rarely call upon my God-twin for such a thing."

Tyrian realized he still had much to learn.

They reached the porch of the Theobald mansion and rested on the steps.

"You knew I would lose to Andoni," Tyrian guessed.

"Yes," Gabriel declared, "I did."

"But why?"

"Boy, you have something Andoni does not have, anger and fire. And he has something you do not have, training. So you both learned something by the duel. It served an important purpose. You fight bravely and fearlessly, which serves you well, but you must have a certain amount of fear. And little Andoni, well, he lacks confidence. You helped him today much more than he helped you."

Tyrian fell silent again. Gabriel rose but noticed the boy did not move.

"Tyrian, won't you come in?"

"Your Honor...," Tyrian looked to the ground, ashamed to speak further.

"What is it, Tyrian?"

"Master Theobald, I'm worried that the carriage of girls has not yet arrived. I feel that they are my responsibility."

"I sent one of my finest scouts out to find them. They will arrive soon. Your responsibilities lie with greater things, boy. I promise you that. My other scout will return soon and give us news of the road to the king's castle, and then we must leave immediately. You must be rested and ready for our journey. The treasure we carry must not leave our hands. You can trust my scout to guide the girls here safely."

Tyrian nodded but did not move. Gabriel sat down next to him.

"What is it, Tyrian?"

"Your Honor, there was a woman with the girls who insisted I sell her off to be married. I was trying to free all of them, but I needed coins for the girls' safe passage."

"She insisted, you say?"

"Yes. I argued with her, but she did not listen. She said it was for the better of the entire group."

"She is a wise woman."

"Was there another option? Did I fail her?"

"No, Tyrian. You did very well."

"It is unfair that this woman should be freed only to be bound again for simple coins. Is her freedom not as valuable as the younger girls'? Or yours? Or mine?"

"In theory, yes. But this world does not recognize abstractions as does your mind. You are a contradiction, boy. You have the body of a warrior, but the mind of a philosopher. But this is the world we are given and we must make the most of it."

"There is no justice in *this world*. I only want justice."

"Justice is a luxury."

Tyrian nodded, refusing to look up.

"You help the ones you can," Gabriel continued. "The ones you cannot help, you trust that their God-twins will guide them the rest of the way."

Tyrian closed his eyes and took in Gabriel's words. He let the slight breeze wash over his face. It cooled and soothed him. Then he remembered the gift from Margda. He suddenly sat up; Gabriel leaned in, sensing his excitement. Tyrian pulled the cloth-wrapped package out of his cloak and held it before him. He looked up at Gabriel as he removed the cloth, revealing the key, its shine dulled from years of neglect and weathering. He offered it silently to Gabriel, who took it in his hand.

"Where did you get this?" Gabriel asked, his voice suddenly deeper, his words slower.

"The woman I sold gave it to me."

Gabriel was silent as he turned the key over in his hand, studying its shape and the designs on the head.

"This is an Elven Grave Key. These are rare, and they unlock great treasure."

"An Elven key? A grave key? Your Honor, does this come from Elves? My uncle told me that Elves do not exist."

"They certainly existed once. The land upon which King Azjik built his castle is an ancient Elven burial ground. Every Elven soldier, elder, dignitary and noble was buried in a tomb there, with all of their belongings. This is very strange."

"Could she have found it along the way? Or purchased it in the Desert Market?"

"It is doubtful. Even the filthy Desert Pirates have superstition enough to honor the Elven dead. Elven Grave Keys are handed down through honor and trust, not sold for gold coins. Tyrian, this woman is no simple slave," he said with deep concern, as he handed the key back. "Keep that safe."

Gabriel rose and entered the house with no more words and Tyrian followed.

Tyrian went into the house but moved straight through to the south portico, where he let the cool breeze rush over him.

As he found a spot of grass below the patio, he felt the exhaustion, weighing him down like a heavy blanket. He lay back against the soft grass and looked up at the white clouds that painted the nearly clear sky. He let his mind wander to the desert. To Margda and the Elven Grave Key; to Serena and the other girls, and then to the road ahead. He began to imagine the Road of Fathers and what King Azjik's castle would be like. Soon, though, he was fast asleep, and his thoughts became a jumble of voices in the blackness of his imagination.

When he woke, it was to the moist, warm tongue of Wolf on his face and a delicate voice whispering, "Tyrian..."

He opened his eyes and saw Océane's round green eyes hovering above him.

"Tyrian," she repeated. "Gabriel is meeting with his scout, who has just returned from the Road of Fathers. He requests you meet him. Come." She held out her hand and guided him inside.

Océane led Tyrian into the study, where he found Gabriel, the scout rider, and several other older men, all dressed in velvet capes and crisp blue trousers. The men all had shiny, ornamented swords at their side.

As he entered the study, the room quieted. Tyrian studied the stern faces. Their gazes gradually turned to him and then eventually back to their respective conversations. Gabriel stepped forward, his deep voice silencing the room with authority. "Welcome, Tyrian," the knight greeted him.

Gabriel paused as if he were about to make introductions, but then abruptly jumped into the discussion at hand. "Our faithful brother Leonce has returned from the Road of Fathers. There is a gathering of Desert Pirates just beyond the borders of Coteville."

"About a hundred Desert Pirates, sir," the scout added.

"But, your Honor," Tyrian spoke hesitantly, "It is good fortune that you know. You can bring more men with you now."

Tyrian looked around at the older men, suddenly conscious of his own voice.

"It is true, your Honor," one of the older generals, Nicodème, agreed. "We can simply approach it as an exercise and be ready with five hundred men if need be."

Gabriel crossed the room in silence, filling his glass with water from a carafe on a small table. All eyes followed him.

"So we know they are there, but the real question is why they are there. Desert Pirates are forbidden from traveling on that highway."

"Until we have that answered, why not just be ready for a battle?" Nicodème pressed. "Must we take the Road of Fathers?" another officer, Dechaume, spoke. "There is the road that approaches the East Gate of the city."

"That would lengthen the trip by weeks," another, Croucien, replied. "I could not bear burdening ourselves over the likes of those scoundrels."

Gabriel spoke up, cutting off the debate. "It is true that taking another route would cost us time, and I daresay I've wasted enough time in getting our treasure to the king. But more importantly..." his voice trailed off. The men exchanged uncertain looks, sensing that their heir had come to a conclusion.

"There is an unseen reason that they gather," Gabriel continued. "The reason will make itself known soon enough. We can prolong the confrontation, but that will gain us nothing. Sometimes it is better to walk directly into a trap to discover he who preys upon us."

Gabriel examined the faces of the quiet men. No one spoke. He offered his silence to the room for debate, but there was none. He grasped Dechaume's shoulder tightly, but warmly, and said, "It is decided then. At the break of dawn we will take the Road of Fathers to King Azjik's gates. Dechaume and Croucien, your men will lead the party. Déodat, Nicodème, Placide and Theirn, we will take your men as well. That should be enough to push back against that vermin. Your men are strong enough to face any ghost armies that appear. I will ride at the front with my protégé, Tyrian, as well as our scout, Leonce." There was a low growl from the back of the room and Tyrian looked over to see Wolf, his hair standing on end and his body crouched low to the ground. He motioned for the dog to quiet, but Gabriel chuckled. "I'm sorry, Wolf, but you will have to stay in the comfort of Coteville during this mission. You can protect my house: that will be your mission!"

The men began shuffling out, leaving Tyrian, Wolf and Gabriel alone. Gabriel took a book from a table and sat beside the fire. Tyrian hesitated briefly, and then moved closer to Gabriel.

"Your Honor," Tyrian said, "I look forward to riding with you again. I want to thank you for welcoming me into your home and letting me continue with you on your journey."

"Tyrian, this is as much your journey now as it is mine."

"Has your rider returned from the desert yet, my lord?"

"No, he has not."

"Perhaps I can ride out there tonight, before morning break."

"Tyrian, you feel a responsibility towards those girls as much as I feel a responsibility towards my rider. But we must trust their fate to their destinies. For now, you must rest."

"Sir..." Tyrian spoke again, but stopped when Gabriel sat forward, uncrossing his legs.

"Tyrian, you honor your word. That is a great quality and one that reinforces my instincts in asking you to join me. It is rare, even for some of the knights in Azjik's Regular Stand. You must never lose that. But for now, you cannot. There is a greater task at hand. We must leave their fate up to their God-twins. And you must trust in your own."

"Yes, your Honor," Tyrian bowed and then exited, Wolf close behind.

Tyrian found his way to a guest room, where a bed had been made for him. He undressed and climbed under the covers, his gaze drawn out towards the moon whose brightness filled the small chamber. His eyes refused to close as his mind raced. He wondered where the carriage of girls was and why it was taking so long for them to arrive. They must have been attacked. He again tried to close his eyes to meditate, but they sprang open at the smallest sound outside the window.

He rose and walked to the window, staring out at the empty night. Wolf jumped to his feet and nuzzled up next to the boy, afraid to let him leave his sight again.

Justice. The boy kept thinking about the cruelty of the world he was seeing. He had been orphaned by violence and guilt. Coteville seemed like a utopian refuge, but beyond these borders all he saw was cruelty. Perhaps, if he were to find the girls, bring them back to safety before the light of dawn, Gabriel would reward him. Maybe the King himself would honor him with a place in his army; perhaps even his First Stand Army.

Then, almost as if drawn by something outside of himself, he quickly dressed and climbed out the open window, scaling the jagged, tiled edges along the frame of the house. It was only two stories down from his sleeping chamber and he dropped the short distance onto the cool grass below. He looked up at Wolf who growled from the window. He hushed him best he could.

Tyrian quietly crept to the back stable housing his horse and untied it from its place of rest. As he was leading the steed around the side of the house he heard something behind him. He stopped, reached for his blade and crouched low, holding it with two hands before him. Then he heard the familiar growl of Wolf.

"Shh. Quiet," the boy whispered. The dog quieted but rushed up to him, sniffing and licking his hand.

"Very well, you can come, but stay close by," Tyrian said. He walked the horse out beyond the town square until he reached the dirt road that led to the city's gates. Then he climbed onto his horse and rode off into the cold, black desert, Wolf following right behind.

Chapter Thirteen

Tyrian was still sleepy and struggled to see through the darkness. The carriage carrying the girls could not be too far out. Below him he could hear the panting of Wolf, running at his side. He could see flashes of light now and then but could not tell if they originated from the sky or from the ground.

He let his eyes fall closed, as they were of no use in this darkness anyway. He became enthralled at how his steed moved with such precise gracefulness; there was a rhythm to its gait, and Tyrian was able to let his mind clear slightly. He did not try to block out the sounds around him; he tried to focus on them. Wolf's panting. The horse's hooves. As if he were a shepherd, herding sounds, his mind slowly gathered them into a single melody. With his eyes closed, he swore he could see the desert landscape as clearly as if the sun had suddenly risen. He thought he heard voices off in the distance. The voices were a mix of child-like cries and barking orders. He opened his eyes and saw a stream of fire blazing across the horizon.

Tyrian sat up in the saddle and tightened his thighs against the horse, taking charge once again. "Wolf," he called out, "we must move faster!" He whipped the reins against the neck of the horse, pushing him towards the fire.

The moving river of light seemed to be fixed on the horizon. Gradually he was gaining on whatever was the source of the migrating blaze. He could now make out figures on horseback. The riders at the front and the rear of the pack held torches high in the air. He could not count the number of riders, but it seemed the size of a small militia.

The sky ahead was just now starting to break with a sliver of sunlight, along the edge of the horizon. Morning was approaching. Tyrian slowed the horse, holding back a safe distance. He came to a full stop, letting Wolf catch his breath. He could hear the riders call back and forth to each other as they rode and he could feel the thunderous wave beneath him, the stampede shaking the earth. Tyrian could see that they rode in a direction just east of Coteville, towards King Azjik's castle.

As the lid of the night sky gradually lifted, patches of the desert floor were becoming visible. A short distance ahead of the stream of riders he could see a huddle of figures. He squinted his eyes, peeling back the darkness as he rode in their direction.

Finally he could fully make out the shapes: a carriage turned over on its side, two horses lying prone on the desert floor and two standing nervously nearby; nine young girls; two corpses, and next to them a tall figure on one knee, with his sword drawn.

Tyrian's horse sped up on its own, as if reading his mind. The boy quickly recognized the tall figure as Heir Theobald. Wolf let out a yelp, catching sight of him.

Tyrian pulled the horse to a halt, then dropped to the ground and sprinted to the wagon. When he reached the group he recognized Serena instantly. Her eyes widened as she saw him approach. Looking around, he identified one of the corpses as the poor driver of the coach; the other one was the scout rider whom Gabriel had sent sent out.

"Tyrian, what are you doing here?" Gabriel demanded.

"Your Honor," Tyrian replied, "I feared for the girls. I thought I could find them and return to ride with you before the sun came up."

"The sun is just now coming up. You would not have been there to ride with us. I told you to stay where you were and you disobeyed me."

"Forgive me, Master."

"Your recklessness will get you into trouble, Tyrian. Now be quiet, you and that beast of a dog. We are no match for those riders, if they see us."

"What happened?" Tyrian asked cautiously. "Your scout rider has been killed!"

"He was cut down by whoever attacked this wagon."

"Why did they not take the girls?"

"Because I fear it was not Desert Pirates who attacked."

"Who, then?" Tyrian asked, in a quieter voice.

"I am not sure. They are riding towards the Road of Fathers. I have a feeling they are off to join our our mystery riders in the Witches' Bend. There is more to this than meets the eye, boy."

Gabriel looked at Tyrian and noticed the sorrow in his face, exaggerated now by the yellow tint of the quickly rising sun. "I was worried about my scout rider. And I wanted to put your mind at ease before we rode the distance to King Azjik. I came upon the girls' wagon and the rider as they are now. They were attacked but something drew those foreign agents away."

They all sat in silence, watching the riders disappear into the distance towards the Road of Fathers. Serena clutched Tyrian's arm and leaned against him. While he felt he was becoming her protector, he also felt a sense of safety being with her.

Tyrian looked at Gabriel, and as the growing daylight helped bring figures back into focus, he studied the knight's face. He had not yet seen this look of concern on Gabriel.

When Gabriel was confident that the charging mercenaries had passed, he rose to his feet. He surveyed the desert, examining the entire horizon. Several strides away sat a deep depression in the landscape, into which the riders had disappeared. Certain they were now alone, Gabriel sprang into action.

"Girls," Gabriel barked out, "gather your things from the wagon as best as you can! We must hurry."

"Your Honor," Tyrian pleaded, "do we have time to get them back on foot before our party leaves?"

"We have very little time, Tyrian. We must pack up the girls on these old horses, as best we can. I'm afraid there is a growing army of mercenaries that awaits us. The Desert Pirates are not ones to plan out attacks—especially on militias. There is something devious behind all of this. But we must get going now."

Tyrian helped Serena onto the horse. As he gripped her waist to help her up, she squealed. At first, he thought he had grabbed her too forcefully, but when he looked into her eyes he could see the real reason. Fear!

Tyrian turned quickly to see what had frightened her. On the ledge that rose above the deep basin stood a rider, still and sinister. He sat up high in the saddle and Tyrian could barely see the quiver and bow strapped to his back. He wore a battle helmet which had ivory ram horns on each side, twisting forward like antenae. Tyrian remembered the figure from the patio of Gorka Osa's estate. The rider seemed almost serene as he watched Gabriel, Tyrian and the girls.

"Your Honor," Tyrian whispered to Gabriel, but then he noticed that once again the Heir was in his fighting stance, ready for battle. Tyrian drew his own blade and stepped forward, next to Gabriel.

Behind the rider, in a cloud of dust a second appeared, charging forward, a single upturned horn protruding from the front of his helmet. Tyrian remembered this rider from that night as well. The figure charged quickly, sword held out before him.

Gabriel recognized the two riders as Babbel and Dò bbeldam, from their attack on him in the back alley at the desert trading post.

As Babbel passed Dò bbeldam the first rider took up the charge, pulling out his bow and drawing an arrow.

Gabriel motioned to Tyrian to move off to the side. He wanted to draw the riders away from the girls and the horses. As the attackers approached, Tyrian could see a third figure appear just above the edge of the basin.

Silhouetted against the rising sun, this was the third figure in Gorka Osa's yard that night; he was perfectly still and his presence commanded authority. He stopped at the same spot where Dò bbeldam had moments before. He did not join in the attack but instead held his position and observed.

Tyrian stole a quick glance at Gabriel, then moved a few steps forward. Babbel was riding towards Tyrian, but then suddenly veered off towards Gabriel. Dò bbeldam pulled back on his bow and released an arrow. In an instant, Tyrian heard a scream and looked over to see one of the girls fall victim to the shot—the arrow had cleanly cut through the throat, and protruded from the back of her neck.

"Serena, get down!" Tyrian yelled.

Babbel angled his horse away from Gabriel at the last moment, sweeping the knight's leg with a short staff and knocking him to the dirt.

Gabriel quickly regained his footing and turned to face Dò bbeldam, who was coming upon him quickly. Tyrian charged Dò bbeldam, leaping into the air and sweeping his blade in a wide arc at the assassin. Tyrian's sword caught Dò bbeldam's helmet, knocking him off his horse. Tyrian glanced up at the rider far off on the basin ledge. The figure was as still as death.

The mysterious figure removed his helmet and held it at his side. Tyrian now recognized the long reddish-brown hair of Gorka Osa, who seemed to nod slyly at the boy. Tyrian was jolted from his trance by the impact of Dò bbeldam, who had regained his feet and tackled him, dagger drawn. Tyrian found himself on his back, fighting off the full weight of the older, helmeted mercenary. Tyrian's forearm jutted out, blocking the arm wielding the shiny dagger now dangled over his face like the frozen tongue of a serpent.

Tyrian struggled to steady himself, bracing his forearm against Dò bbeldam's wrists so that the dagger kept its distance. He managed to pull his right knee up and wedge it against Dò bbeldam's chest. Tyrian stretched out his free hand against the ground for balance and in one quick move, rolled himself backwards, straightening his legs and throwing Dò bbeldam into the air.

No sooner had Dò bbeldam hit the ground than Wolf was on him. The beast locked his fangs around Dò bbeldam's forearm, forcing him to release his dagger. The mercenary screamed out in agony, his cries falling flat against the endless desert. Tyrian grabbed the dropped dagger and pounced on top of the older man. Dò bbeldam swung his free arm up to strike Tyrian but was stopped by the bite of his own blade. Tyrian drove the dagger clean through his attacker's forearm. Wolf held on tight to the other arm, blood now dripping into the dog's mouth.

Suddenly Tyrian brought the dagger down again, this time into Dò bbeldam's chest, driving it as deep as he could. Tyrian was enveloped with rage and could not hear the screams of the girls nearby, or Gabriel shouting, "Leave him, Tyrian, he is no longer a danger!"

No, he could hear nothing but the gasping of his own breath. Again he brought the dagger down into Dò bbeldam's chest. And again. Sweat poured from his face and mixed with the tears of anger that flowed.

Even after Dò bbeldam was still, his body already separated from his spirit, Tyrian gave a few more useless blows that did not satisfy his anger. Only when Wolf had let go his grip and nudged the boy with his snout did Tyrian realize that his victim had fallen. Tossing the dagger to the side, he stood up, looking first at the girls, cowering together, then to Gabriel, watching him with shock, then over to Gorka Osa, who casually replaced his helmet on his head and turned his horse towards the Road of Fathers. Gorka Osa soon was gone, down from the ledge and into the desert valley below.

Not far off, Babbel had made the decision to abandon this fight. He had watched in horror as his friend was killed at the hands of this mad child, and then in despair at Gorka Osa's casual retreat. He whipped his horse into a sprint and raced to catch up with Gorka Osa.

Tyrian counted eight girls left. Obviously several had not survived the desert passage, and now one had fallen victim to the arrow of Dò bbeldam. He noticed that Serena had taken on the role of caretaker of the younger ones. Now she moved with the confidence of survival.

Tyrian decided that the dead girls were better off than the ones who had to continue crossing this harsh desert. His anger grew. He thought briefly of cutting down the survivors. He imagined forcing his blade into Serena's young body, saving her from the life ahead of her. His eyes teared up. He could not bear it. Again, he felt helpless. He wanted freedom and happiness for her.

Gabriel quickly gathered the remaining two carriage horses together with Dò bbeldam's horse. Tyrian gently lifted Serena atop Dò bbeldam's white steed. He put the reins in her tiny, white hands and helped her grip them tightly. Then he placed a younger girl behind her, wrapping her small arms around Serena's waist, nodding at her to hold tightly. Serena grabbed his hand before he could walk away. He looked up at her and smiled, the only comfort he could offer at the moment.

"...guhd bay?" she struggled to say.

"I will meet you in Coteville. I promise," he replied.

Gabriel had placed the other girls on the carriage horses and straddled his own horse, sword at his side.

"Tyrian, Wolf must lead these horses back to Coteville. We cannot spend the time escorting them. They are close enough and daylight is here. They'll get there safely. My militia has already left—we must catch up with them."

Tyrian nodded and then knelt beside Wolf. "Wolf, lead these horses directly back to Coteville, do you understand?" He pointed in the direction of the town and then pointed at the girls. "Do you understand?" The dog barked at him and then licked his face. "Wolf, do not stop for anything. Do not let these horses stray! Go!" With that Wolf jumped behind one horse, then another, nipping at their legs, pushing them into a sprint. Tyrian watched as Wolf ran with them, circling them like a shepherd dog.

Tyrian walked over to Gabriel and tried to hand the pouch to him.

"No," Theobald said firmly. "This is not an honor that I have given you, it is a responsibility. I have considered taking it from you, more so now, after this display of recklessness. But I need you. Do you understand that? If I were not in an hour of desperation, I would take it from you and give it to someone else, someone who can control their rage. But you are the one I need to fulfill this duty. You must control yourself. You put not only yourself and me in danger, but more men than you know."

Tyrian lowered his head. He put the pouch back inside his cloak. He looked his mentor in the eye, and his voice quivered as he replied, "I am sorry. I am able to fulfill your wish. I will try to control myself..."

"No!" Gabriel interrupted him. "You will not try! You will control yourself!"

"Yes, sir."

"Hold it close inside your cloak. When we are attacked, they will look for it on me. If there are too many of them and we find ourselves fighting in chaos, you must slip away and take that to King Azjik. Do you understand? If anything happens to me, do not try and save me. The most important thing is to get this pouch back to our king."

"I understand, your Honor," Tyrian replied, then quietly mounted his horse.

"Your Honor," Tyrian said, after he settled himself into the saddle, "that rider that watched us in battle—I know him. His name is Gorka Osa."

"How do you know him?" Gabriel asked him sharply.

"He helped me escape from a slave owner who had purchased me. He gave me room and fed me. Gave me this horse and supplies. He is a kind man."

"He is not as kind as you think," Gabriel stated. "He is dangerous. Gorka Osa is one of the Three Riders, Tyrian. He is a mercenary and an insurgent against King Azjik. They attacked me at the Desert Trading Post. Together with Babbel, our second attacker, and the poor fellow you killed. Gorka Osa is a danger to us, boy."

Tyrian did not respond, and after a long moment of silence Gabriel said, "Your anger troubles me. What you did to Dò bbeldam was beyond necessary. His death was imminent; you did not need to make it a cruel death. Even the most villainous devil should be given the opportunity to face his death in dignity. You took that from him."

"I am sorry."

"In addition, you were blinded. If there were more of them, and you were alone, you could easily have been killed. You become blind to your surroundings when you enter a rage like that.

"We are about to face an unknown army," Gabriel continued. "You will be fighting alongside the best militiamen that King Azjik has to offer. But we do not know the skills of the men we will fight. I must have faith that you will fight wisely. You are as strong as any of Azjik's generals, but that strength is worth nothing if you are foolish. You carry an important treasure and I need to be assured that it will reach its destination."

"It will, Heir Theobald. I promise."

"I suppose you will prove yourself one way or another in time. For now, let us go. We must catch up to our brothers."

Gabriel pushed his horse into a gallop. Tyrian's attention was suddenly drawn upward and he looked into the sky, where he saw a hawk circling high up near the clouds. He looked ahead at Gabriel, who was quickly moving across the desert, and whipped his own horse to catch up.

The sun had finally crested over the horizon and was beginning its grueling climb up through the sky as the two riders swiftly made their way towards the Road of Fathers and, eventually, the castle of King Azjik.

Chapter Fourteen

Heir Volkummen steadied his horse. His militia waited restlessly in a gully alongside the Road of Fathers. Volkummen examined his troops down the column, man by man, glaring into each soldier's eyes, saying nothing. Occasionally a soldier barked out a battle cry and the others called back, fiercely. Volkummen was following Roserie Argaune's advice and holding his troops just off of the main highway.

Greit Schultheis moved to the frontline, approaching Volkummen from his place in the rear. He dismounted and knelt respectfully, head bowed.

"Your Honor, our scouts have returned. The Desert Pirates have assembled as expected, just beyond the Witches' Bend on the Road of Fathers," Greit reported, and looked up at his heir.

"Scum," was all Volkummen could muster, flinging back his matted red hair in disgust.

"Our northern scout reports mercenaries from the desert, near the Garthan Dunes... heading just south of the Witches' Bend," Greit continued.

"Could this be Gorka Osa's meddling?" Volkummen growled.

"Your Honor?"

"Never mind. I've heard no word from the wizard, we must wait until he has everything in order. I will scout the road myself. Keep the troops busy and angry."

Volkummen snapped the reins on his horse, pushing him past the columns of soldiers and up the gully wall. Greit remounted his horse and took up Volkummen's place at the lead.

Volkummen rode out of the gully and onto the desert floor, suddenly out of sight of his men. He looked in the direction of the Road of Fathers, where the Desert Pirates were gathered.

Heir Volkummen's Militia was at the southernmost edge of the desert. The air was thinner and colder here. The ragged rocks of the mountain range rose up on all sides of the gulley. The Witches' Bend was a deep passage cut into the mountain that allowed the only access through the mountain range, and down towards the plateau that led to safety and the open highway to Azjik's gates. It had taken the King's men two generations to cut through, and create the shortest route through the mountains, although it could be dangerous at times, due its isolation and no outlets, save the north and south openings.

At either side of the entrance to the passage loomed two giant stones, cut like spears pointing into the sky, known as the Iron Gates. They served as crude sentinels, warning of the darkness beyond.

Volkummen scanned the high desert floor, empty of soldier, pirate or mercenary. His eyes were drawn to the peaks that seemed to engulf the horizon, crawling up the skyline like a dragon army. He had heard stories of inhabitants who spent their entire lifetimes in the mountain depths.

It was foolish for the Desert Pirates to wait inside the canyon, Volkummen thought. They sat inside the narrow passage, and were sure to be pinned in by the Cotes. How Argaune had convinced them to do this he would never know. He understood little of the wizard's workings.

Volkummen pulled a reed of Uhln birch from a pouch on his belt. He dug his teeth into its hard bark surface and bit off a mouthful to chew on. Soaked in plum brandy and then smoked in exotic island leaves, it soothed his mouth and calmed him. He spat the black liquid remnants onto the desert floor and turned northward, to search the sky for signs of Argaune's God-twin. There he saw the giant hawk, which made a wide circular formation across the blue sky.

Volkummen turned his horse and descended back into the gully, to wait with his militia.

# # #

The young riders that followed Gorka Osa looked identical, thought Babbel, with their brown face paint and shaved heads. They had the stormy eyes and wild stares of orphaned youths and they wore longbows on their backs and swords at their sides. He counted about fifteen riders, none of them aligned to a flag. Their race was hidden under paint and feathers, and Babbel did not recognize their manner of dress or style of riding.

Babbel had for years admired Gorka Osa's ability to find young soldiers and to ignite in them a passion to his cause, whichever cause it was at the moment.

Gorka Osa had raced ahead and Babbel pushed his steed to catch up to his general and his small band of mercenaries.

Breathing hard, Babbel caught up to Gorka Osa. Without thinking, Babbel demanded quietly, "Did you not see what became of Dò bbeldam?"

At first Gorka Osa did not answer. He turned to look at Babbel, who had removed his one-horned battle helmet and attached it to the side of his saddle. The stocky warrior sat forward in his saddle and looked back at the younger riders.

After several moments of silence, Babbel asked, "Do these boys know where they are riding to?"

"They are riding into glory, Babbel."

"Whose glory?"

"Dò bbeldam was weak," Gorka Osa stated suddenly. "He was sick. He had a hundred opportunities to leave us and secure a safe pasture. But his choice was the same as our choice will be when that day comes: to die on the battlefield. Neither you nor I could have helped him against that boy. You know that as well as I do."

"You have gathered an army of orphaned mercenaries, ready to die at your command, and yet you ordered Dò bbeldam to fight. Why did you send him to his death, instead of any one of these boys?"

Gorka Osa did not respond. He turned his gaze to the desert ahead. Babbel did the same.

Overhead the hawk circled once, then twice, and then disappeared.

"The survivors of this fight will be the first chosen for the new king's personal guard. The survivors of this fight will find a greater glory than has ever been known. My friend, I hope you stay with me to see that day."

Gorka Osa pushed his horse ahead, taking note of the hawk's path and following it. The pack of riders picked up the pace as well, and Babbel let himself fall behind to take up the rear.

# # #

Tyrian and Gabriel followed close behind the freed slave girls for some time. Wolf worked hard at keeping the girls' wagon at a good pace; sprinting freely ahead of them, then falling back to push them harder, circling them all, then again returning to the lead.

"Tyrian, we leave them here," Gabriel called out. "They are at a safe distance from our borders now. We must meet up with our brothers. Come!"

Tyrian followed Gabriel's lead, but turned back every few seconds to watch as the girls disappeared from sight.

As they raced towards the Road of Fathers, Gabriel rode with an intensity that Tyrian had not yet seen. His face was like stone and his eyes were like steel, staring intently at the road ahead. Tyrian pushed his horse harder to keep up with Gabriel. They spent the better part of the morning riding in search of the Coteville militia.

Finally, in the distance, Tyrian could see a veil of dust, as if storm clouds were vaporizing from the ground itself. As they drew closer, he could make out horses. He thought that this must be the militia.

Gabriel whipped his horse into a sprint, finding a new reserve of energy. Tyrian pushed his own steed faster.

The landscape ahead appeared much the same as they'd seen all day. Blue-gray skies. Brown, dry and cracked ground beneath them. Surrounding them, nothing but open space: no trees, no mountains, nothing to hide them from what lay ahead. Tyrian, still not used to these open spaces, suddenly felt vulnerable, as if an enemy could attack at any moment.

Gabriel swiftly closed the distance between himself and his militia. He leaned forward, thighs tight against the horse's sides.

When Gabriel and Tyrian were just about to reach the militia, one of the soldiers in the rear turned back, hearing their approach. He cried out to the others, "Brothers of Cote, our Heir has arrived!"

As if on cue, all heads turned back to see Gabriel for themselves. The men slowed their horses just slightly, to let him take the lead. Their faces greeted him with smiles. They waved and bowed their heads as he rode by.

"Tyrian," Gabriel calleded out, "you take up the rear position."

Tyrian found himself riding next to a lanky older man, who nodded and then turned his grim expression forward.

The battalion was about two hundred men strong. They all wore the crimson and gold colors of Coteville. Along the edges of the formation rode young boys with the Cote flag held high. There was no other pageantry. The rest of the men wore crimson capes over their armor and had the same steely gaze as Gabriel.

Tyrian marveled at how easily Gabriel slipped into his role of leader and commander. With no formalities, he immediately began issuing orders to his men, all of which were followed without question.

They rode for several more hours at this pace, until dusk approached. Tyrian had seen coarse rocky ridges gradually rise from the horizon; as the Cote Militia moved further south, the scaly formations seemed to wrap around them.

Tyrian saw the columns of horses all slow, then come to a stop. As if trained, the horses formed a circle around Gabriel, the scout, Leonce, and another soldier. Tyrian wedged his horse into the gathering. He saw Gabriel's horse anxiously move about in a circle.

After several moments, Gabriel spoke. "We will camp here tonight. I want four guard shifts of three men; we will all need our rest tonight."

Tyrian watched as every man fell into his duty. The Cotes were well-trained and well-disciplined. Leonce escaped the circle and rode southward to scout the immediate area. Gabriel, meanwhile, dismounted and convened privately with several of his generals. Tyrian sat atop his horse for some time, watching as each of the men found a place to rest.

"You can pitch your tent here next to mine," a boy's voice called out. Tyrian recognized it as that of the boy who had defeated him in the duel. Andoni had found a patch of sand and was laying out the poles for his tent. Tyrian dismounted and laid out his own tent next to Andoni's.

"You are a great fighter, Tyrian," Andoni said. "All of the boys were afraid to duel with you. We've heard grand stories of the barbarians from the Great River Forest."

"It was a pleasure being bested by you," Tyrian replied.

"I will be honored to join you in battle, Tyrian. Stay close to me and together we will dispose of the entire band of desert scum between the two of us!"

"Yes," Tyrian agreed, "you and I will dispose of all of them."

In the center of the circle food was already being cooked, and the smells brought back to Tyrian the memory of Coteville.

"Have you ever been to King Azjik's castle?" Tyrian asked.

"Yes, only once, two seasons ago."

"What is it like?"

"It is brilliant. It has towers that reach to the heavens. It has streets of gold and silver and everything shines. I am excited to go back. I hope someday to serve in the King's First Stand Army."

"Then we will fight shoulder-to-shoulder someday."

The sun was already setting and torches were set on lances at the edges of the camp. Gabriel knew that a militia camping along the Road of Fathers was enough to ward off most desert wanderers; no civilized being would attack one of Azjik's militia. They were safest if they were seen and heard.

As they were finishing their meals and the moon had begun to appear out of the blackness of the night sky, Leonce returned. His horse came to a halt just outside the circle of tents. He was greeted with a plate of meat and bread and a schooner of lager. He chewed down a hefty bite and washed it down with the beer as Gabriel approached, flanked by his generals.

"The road was empty, your Honor," Leonce reported. "There were no signs of the thieves who were there just one day ago."

"Maybe they were hunting and they are now gone," suggested Ethune, one of the generals.

"Not on the Road of Fathers," Gabriel replied. "It is forbidden. I have seen armies riding across the desert, and I saw Gorka Osa and one of his Three Riders leading a group of mercenaries—all towards this spot. My feeling is that the Desert Pirates have hidden themselves, and they still lie in wait for us. We must reach the gates of King Azjik's castle, and there are obstacles that await us." Gabriel turned again to Leonce, "How far did you go, boy?"

"Just in sight of the Witches' Bend and the Iron Gates."

"Then that is where we must be ready for battle. For now, let us rest."

Gabriel retreated silently to his tent. All of his men followed suit without question. From the outside one could see the glow of candlelight illuminating the interior of Gabriel's tent. A vague outline of the heir could be seen, low to the ground, as he sat in meditation. After a short time a second figure appeared, his God-twin. The ghost-figure rose above its physical twin, through the opening of the tent and up into the cold desert sky. With its arms outspread it floated beyond the Cote encampment and towards the Witches' Bend and the Iron Gates and beyond.

There the God-twin glided through the opening between the narrow rock walls, unseen by the sleeping pirate army. Back in his tent, Gabriel saw the images in his head of the Desert Pirates sitting, lying, standing asleep; awaiting the coming morning and their battle with the Cote Militia. The specter flew the length of the Witches' Bend passage and back, sending his visions back to Gabriel of the sleeping pirate band. Soon the God-twin was back in the tent, sitting cross-legged before Gabriel. Gabriel knew, now, what awaited them. But the picture still felt incomplete, and his God-twin counseled him, in his meditation, to remember the attack in the desert, the wandering armies. There was more to the battle ahead than what his vision had given him.

# # #

The band of Desert Pirates huddled together in their crude camp. Some pitched tents, some slept on the canyon floor, some did not sleep at all. They had lit intermittent fires where they cooked; others begged for food or went hungry. About fifty of them had crammed themselves tight into the canyon. They had no discernable leader. Most of them did not know the reason they had come. They were like animals, packed together with no order in their ranks.

At the edge of the canyon two pirates stood off by themselves. They kept silent, staring off northward into the desert. One of them, the taller one, had his sword drawn and held it in a tight grip. The other paced back and forth nervously.

Suddenly, a hawk appeared out of the darkness. It became visible only at the last instant and both creatures jumped back, shrieking. The taller one raised his sword, but the other pirate gripped his arm, recognizing the bird.

"It is the wizard," whispered the shorter one. "Enut said to look'fr a talk-bird."

"How does a bird talk?"

"Shhh!" the hawk chided them. It found a jutted edge on the rock wall next to them, taking a position from which it stared down at them. Both pirates stood back in awe, forgetting to breathe momentarily.

"Enut serves you well," the hawk spoke in a whisper, forcing the two figures to step closer.

"You bring us news?" asked the shorter one.

"Yes, indeed. The intruders are camped out just north of here. They will rest for the night, as should your... men. At first sunlight they will enter this canyon, ignorant of your position. I will fly above them; you can look for my flight, which will be your signal."

"Is it true it is one of Azjik's militias?"

"It is of no matter who they are. There are two armies that follow from different directions to aid you, should you need it. You must just hold the canyon."

"When will the—," the taller one began to ask, but the hawk spread its wings and let out a screech that echoed ominously through the canyon. Just as quickly as it had appeared, it was gone, leaving the pair alone. The fear they both felt remained unspoken, and thus unacknowledged. They returned to the others in the canyon.

# # #

Volkummen stood alone at the top of the gully. His men slept. His horse stood quietly, resting. Greit waited patiently at the bottom of the gully for him to return. Volkummen kept his eyes on the sky, watching for Argaune's hawk. He studied the darkness for any sign of movement. He observed the path of the moon, to calculate the passage of time. He recalled the gods' architecture of the canyon, mapping it out in his mind, based on the many times he had passed through it.

Volkummen hated inaction. This plan of Arguane's was taking years to put into place; every step brought them closer, but they still remained far from their goal. If he had his way he would storm Azjik's castle with his men and lay waste to the lot of them. But instead he put his faith in Argaune's grand design.

For now, Heir Volkummen could only wait.

Chapter Fifteen

Tyrian lay in his tent, fixated by the silence. He had barely slept through the night, and now he was beginning to hear movement in the tent next to his, Andoni's.

Through a small opening in the tent, Tyrian could see the bluish-black of the night sky, decorated with scatterings of pinhole-like stars. As he tried to meditate and steady his mind, he watched the dark hue of the sky steadily lighten until it gradually appeared translucent, as if a veil had been pulled back.

In the last moments before morning light he heard the far-off cries of the Desert Pirates, a sound somewhere between a sweet melody and horrific screams of pain. He knew not what the voices meant to convey, but he had heard them every morning in the Great Desert. They could be morning prayers, he thought. They could be war cries. They could be torturous in-fighting between fellow pirates. Whatever they were, to Tyrian they sounded like ghosts calling from the grave.

Now, though, Tyrian began to hear more activity in the circle of tents: the clanking of cooking pots; hacking and groans of the older soldiers as they awakened; the snorts of the horses, active once again.

He sat up, put on his trousers and tunic and then waited. Finally, he heard Andoni call, "Tyrian? Are you awake, Tyrian?"

"Yes," he replied.

"We should rise. They will be feeding us soon, and then we will ride into the canyon."

Tyrian quickly rolled up his sleeping pad and tent. Within moments the circular camp had vanished and, in its place, stood an army ready for battle. The older men in the militia huddled around Heir Theobald, while the younger boys circled around the struggling fire, devouring their breakfast sausages and tea. Tyrian and Andoni sat off to the side, not speaking and barely touching their food, just watching the elders.

After what seemed like a long time, the older men finally dispersed and made way for Heir Theobald, who stepped up onto a large boulder. Leonce, the scout, called out, "Gather round, brothers of Coteville. Your Heir speaks!"

Tyrian and Andoni jumped to their feet and hurried to the front of the crowd, within reach of Gabriel. Andoni knelt on one knee, and then Tyrian did the same. The group of soldiers formed a semi-circle around their Heir, silent and respectful.

"My dear countrymen," Gabriel began, as he looked out at the assembly. "I have chosen you to ride with me because you are the finest in our land. Coteville raises men of the highest honor and soldiers most brave! No battle is inconsequential, as no man is indispensable. My life rests in your hands as much as yours rests in mine. Today, we ride to King Azjik, a journey made a thousand times with no fear. But today, just beyond the Witches' Bend, an army of Desert Pirates awaits us in the canyon. We will engage them. But they are not the real enemy today. We must be ready for others. Do not waste your energy on the dirty desert vermin. Dispose of them as you will, but beware other adversaries that await us."

There was silence. None of the soldiers knew of whom Gabriel spoke, but they now were mindful of what lay ahead. Gabriel let the silence permeate the desert air for a long moment. Then he pulled his sword from his side and thrust it into the air.

"For Coteville!" Gabriel called out.

"We ride!" the battalion called back.

"For Coteville!" he called again.

"We'll die!" the call came back.

"Then let us ride!" Gabriel sheathed his sword in his horse's saddle, then mounted. As if in a choreographed dance, everyone moved to follow his lead.

Shortly, the entire platoon had found their steeds and were mounted and in perfect columns. Gabriel waited. He looked through the throng of soldiers and found Tyrian, at the rear.

"Tyrian Fellhawk, come forward," the heir-general called out in a most formal voice unfamiliar to the boy: it was not as warm and intimate as he had known, but rather a deep, direct tone, barking out an order rather than gently passing wisdom.

Tyrian maneuvered his brown horse through the columns of soldiers and approached the heir.

"Yes, your Honor," Tyrian bowed his head.

"Come closer still," Gabriel motioned to him. As Tyrian drew his horse alongside Gabriel's, the heir leaned in towards the boy, and whispered cautiously.

"You and I alone know what you carry in your cloak. You must promise me that you will take it to the King, no matter what happens today. Do not engage in fighting unless it is to defend yourself. When we reach the mouth of the canyon, you will ride along the exterior, with a small group led by Andoni. You must not get trapped. Do you understand?"

"Yes, your Honor."

"You must deliver that pouch to the King without fail."

"I will."

"Then our fate is in good hands. Go back to the rear, Tyrian, and stay close to Andoni."

Tyrian took up his place again next to Andoni.

"Tyrian, I will ride close by you," Andoni said. "I have received my orders and I will follow them, seeing you through to the gates of Azjik's Castle. Together we will enter his kingdom."

Tyrian nodded in response.

"We will not be in the fight," Andoni finally said, reading Tyrian's silence.

"Andoni, I have had more adventure in the past few suns than I have had in my sixteen years."

Andoni laughed.

"I want to be counted on," Tyrian continued. "I want to fight next to Heir Theobald and my new countrymen. But so be it. I have another path to ride. And I will ride next to you. We will keep each other safe."

Andoni's face became still. He reached out his hand and gripped Tyrian's arm tightly.

"Tyrian, you can trust me. I will get you to the gates."

Tyrian smiled and nodded. Their horses shifted impatiently.

There seemed to be an unease that lingered over the throng as Gabriel and his officers conferred. Then, finally, Gabriel turned his horse and began to cross the short distance to the Iron Gates. The others picked up the pace behind him, riding slightly slower than a sprint.

Both Tyrian and Andoni rode silently at the rear of the platoon. They nervously scanned the desert, listening intently for any sign of movement. There was none. The desert seemed eerily aware of the battle to come. It was as if every critter, every grain of sand and tumbleweed were afraid to move, for fear of attracting the anger of either army.

The militia rode a short while until it reached the Witches' Bend, a wide, rocky stretch of road that seemed to darken as it approached the base of the mountainous canyon walls that made up the narrow passage beyond. There was no sign of Desert Pirates, only the rugged dry rocks on either side of the most dangerous stretch of the Road of Fathers.

Gabriel slowed his horse to a stop and soon the entire militia was standing still, waiting. Gabriel said nothing. He looked back at his men. He then looked up at the rocky walls and out at the desert they had just come from. He signaled Andoni to proceed, then nodded to his generals before pressing his horse on again.

Andoni, in turn, nodded to Tyrian and they separated from the rest of the army, a few other boys with them. Their horses hugged the rigid edge of the giant rock formation, along a crude dirt and rock pathway. Soon, their trail had bended gradually so that their countrymen were no longer in view behind them.

Tyrian found himself on a very narrow, rocky route on the outer wall of the mountain. It was a route that had been cut into the stone generations before. He kept his horse as close as he could to the side of the rock. The horse nervously twitched at the sudden edge of the passageway. Andoni took note of his friend's anxiety and smiled warmly, "Just go slow, Tyrian." Tyrian turned to look at the boys behind him and they rode with the same confidence as Andoni. He sat back in his saddle and relaxed, letting his horse lead the way.

# # #

As Heir Theobald and his troops entered the canyon, a cold darkness descended. The walls of the canyon, narrow with crooked, sharp edges, ascended abruptly. There was still no sign of an attack. The silence hung on the jagged rocks.

Gabriel pulled his horse to a stop. He sat up in his saddle; the sound of a few falling rocks caught his attention. It was the slightest of noises. In unison, the other riders also stopped. Gabriel swung a leg over his horse and dismounted, drawing his sword slowly from the saddle sheath. He nodded to his generals, who did the same. They formed a line of five commanders on foot, slowly entering the depths of the canyon.

Another rock hit the ground, and then another. Gabriel looked up and discovered several Desert Pirates clinging to the rocky sides of the canyon walls above them. The Pirates had been camouflaged by rock and dirt. They immediately dropped to the ground upon discovery, and it looked as if the walls themselves were collapsing. Gabriel and his commanders stopped in their tracks, assuming defensive positions, swords held out before them.

The Desert Pirates, not used to being on the offense in battle, approached hesitantly. The Cote Militia quickly dismounted and a few of the younger boys led the horses to the rear, away from the two armies.

Gabriel looked to his two generals, Dechaume and Croucien, who stood on either side of him. The Desert Pirates approached slowly but still did not attack. Suddenly Gabriel seized the moment, nodded to Dechaume and Croucien then charged into the front line of pirates. The desert creatures seemed frozen in fear. From the rear a small group of pirates, apparently eager for engagement, stumbled over the others to get to the front. The three Militia commanders quickly cut down the first line of pirates, leaving them bloodied and writhing on the ground, only to be trampled by the Cotes who charged forward.

Gabriel was wary at how easily the pirates were falling. They were certainly not as well-trained and strong as his Cote brothers, but he felt they must have been hardened from the scavenger's life they led. They lunged with what seemed like half-hearted attempts and cowered below dented and chipped shields. Few of them had armor or helmets.

"Dechaume! Croucien!" Gabriel called out. "Steady the assault. We must be ready for a stronger attack behind these scoundrels."

"Agreed," Croucien called back. "This is much too easy!"

Gabriel fought his way along the canyon wall, opening up a hole for his soldiers to rush forward. Dechaume and Croucien did the same, moving along the opposite canyon wall. Within moments the soldiers of the Coteville Militia were pushing back the Desert Pirates, cutting them down by twos and forcing their way through the canyon.

Gabriel sheathed his sword and scaled the canyon wall. He climbed above the battle, out of reach of the pirates, and moved higher to get a view of the road ahead. He found a small ledge that he propped himself upon and looked down along the roadway. He saw about fifty Desert Pirates charging against his men. Leonce had counted over one hundred when he'd scouted, so Theobald guessed a second assault would come from the north end of the canyon in an attempt to trap them.

Gabriel called out to a third general, "Wimund! Take your regiment back to the mouth of the canyon at the Witches' Bend. We cannot get ourselves trapped in here."

Wimund shouted back acknowledgment of his orders and retreated with twenty of his own sons and nephews, charging back towards the mouth of the canyon.

Gabriel stayed on his ledge, directing his soldiers on, warning them of dangers and pointing to openings in the battlefield. He drew his sword again and would lean down to strike a pirate who came within reach. His soldiers continued their rapid advancement.

"Push forward," Gabriel yelled. "Do not waste your energies. Push forward!"

Soon, the pirates were falling backwards over each other, each column collapsing on another. Some of the Cote soldiers even re-sheathed their swords and began pushing them back with their bare hands.

Screams of horror filled the canyon as scores of Desert Pirates were trampled and suffocated.

Gabriel watched his militia advance with ease. Then, suddenly, he heard a human scream, as one of his men dropped to the canyon floor. Then he noted the same occurence with another soldier.

Gabriel's eyes swept over the canyon floor in search of the ghost attackers but saw nothing. Another soldier fell to an unseen attack. This time, though, Gabriel noticed the position of the soldier as he fell, chest out, head back and arms flailing, before he disappeared beneath the crowd of fighters. He looked up in the direction of the impact and scoped archers positioned and hidden by the rocks, just as the Desert Pirates had been earlier.

Another soldier went down. Then another.

"Dechaume! Croucien!" Theobald called out, pointing up along the walls.

Dechaume and Croucien pulled their round metal shields from their backs and held them up high, directing their soldiers to do the same. The Desert Pirates, realizing that their foes had shifted their focus, found a new confidence and began pushing forward.

"Archers, forward! Make way!" Gabriel called out. Immediately the soldiers opened up a small circle in the middle of their columns for the rear guard archers to move up and take position. Several of the younger soldiers crowded around the Cote archers, using their shields to protect them as they began firing arrows up along the canyon walls. Gabriel watched as several of the attackers fell to their deaths in the canyon.

Gabriel started to climb higher to get a better view of the enemy archers when he felt a sharp pain in his thigh, then a burning. His leg gave way and he found himself falling from the canyon wall. He hit the ground sharply, coiling up in pain. His leg was pierced by an arrow, blood spilling from the wound. He leaned against the wall as Dechaume rushed to his side, fending off attacks while the heir tended to his wound. The arrow had struck him on the very edge of his thigh, the tip coming out the other side. Gabriel carefully grasped the arrowhead and pulled the shaft the rest of the way out of his leg. He then touched his tongue to the edge of the arrow tip, testing for poison. It tasted only of blood. And then he noticed the blood coming from both sides of his leg. He sheathed his sword and gripped his thigh tightly.

"My Lord, how bad is it?" Dechaume shouted.

"It is not serious. I am lucky that it passed all the way through, and hit only the muscle," he replied. Refocusing on the scene, he called out, "We must move our archers up further. We will not get through this canyon with those assailants up there. I fear we are being held back as they wait for further reenforcements, Dechaume. We need to get through! Leave me and get those archers up."

"Yes, my lord," Dechaume said, as he returned to the heart of the battle. Dechaume's unit formed a wedge, cutting through the line of Desert Pirates and opening up for the Cote archers to move forward. Once better positioned, they began cutting down the enemy archers from the canyon walls. The soldiers at the front pushed forward again.

Gabriel edged his way behind a protrusion in the canyon wall for protection. He pulled the cloth back from the tear in his trousers and exposed the wound. He then took a small vial from his cloak and poured a few drops into the wound, his muscles tightening at the sting that followed. From his belt he untied a pouch given him by Tyrian's father, Cabatic. It held a gray paste, which he rubbed around the outside of the wound and inside both openings. Finally, he wrapped a clean cloth around his whole thigh, tightly.

Gabriel sat for a moment, catching his breath and watching the battle ensue, trying to focus on the attacking archers. They wore dark attire, making them hard to see against the rock. He rose to his feet slowly, hugging the dusty wall, and craned his neck so that he could count them. At first he noted eight, but then saw movement in the darkness of the wall and knew there were more.

"Archers against archers will not suffice. We must get them down from that canyon wall," Gabriel called out Dechaume.

"But how?" Dechaume asked.

"We must force them down," Gabriel concluded.

Chapter Sixteen

Argaune's hawk had made its way to the skies over Tyrian and Andoni. It drew wide circles above them, effortlessly staying directly overhead.

Tyrian noticed this as he and Andoni ascended the rocky path. As the roadway narrowed, Tyrian grew nervous about the closeness of the edge and drew his horse away, trying to keep track of the hawk above. The horse knocked up against the rock, then bucked back, scaring the boy even more.

"Let your horse go," the boy behind him called. Tyrian turned to see a lanky youth of about twelve years nodding to him. "Your horse will follow Andoni's, if you let it."

Tyrian focused on the path ahead, not looking straight down. He tried closing his eyes to concentrate but became dizzy. He listened for any sign of a battle in the canyon, but they were far enough along the trail along the rock's outer path that he heard only the whistling wind. He let his mind drift to Coteville, to the fountain in the town square. He pictured Serena washing her feet in the pool at the base of the fountain. He pictured her sitting with Océane on the patio, drinking tea. He found himself yearning to be with her.

He fixed his gaze down at the near-perfect mane on his horse's neck. Suddenly the horse reared, front hooves kicking, almost throwing Tyrian off.

Andoni's horse reacted nervously to Tyrian's, kicking its hind legs in anxious spasms.

"Hold steady," Tyrian called to the boys behind him. They gently coaxed their steeds to a halt, giving Tyrian and Andoni space. Tyrian tried to relax his own horse, grabbing the reins tightly. His horse bucked again, and he lost his hold on the reins and fell to the ground. He quickly crawled out of the way, for fear of getting kicked by the frightened horse.

Tyrian caught himself before he fell over the edge, and rushed to calm his horse. He grabbed the reins and pulled the horse's head towards him, rubbing its nose. He saw Andoni's horse flailing about.

"Andoni, calm your horse!" Tyrian called out.

"I am trying!" Andoni called back.

Tyrian stroked his horse's head, trying to soothe him when he heard Andoni scream. He looked over and saw the boy falling from his horse onto the ground, rolling across the pathway and then, in front of Tyrian's horrified eyes, over the edge.

Andoni flung out his hand as he fell over the side, grabbing hold of the threshold. His horse continued its frenzied tantrum. Tyrian yelled at the other boys, "Stop! Move no further!" The boys struggled with their now panicked horses.

Finally, Tyrian saw the source of the terror: the road ahead was covered with snakes of all shapes and sizes. The path underneath could not be seen, it was so thoroughly covered with the creatures.

Tyrian turned back to Andoni, who was holding on with a weakening grip.

"Hold on, Andoni! Hold on!" Tyrian yelled to him. Andoni looked up at the barbarian boy, his eyes describing his terror.

Tyrian swiftly moved to his saddle and pulled out a rope; he wrapped it around his waist twice and then threw the end onto the road, motioning to the other boys to grab it.

"Quickly!" he yelled, as they stumbled over each other, eyes wide open with fear. Andoni's horse still bucked and whinnied, dangerously close to the edge.

"Hold this line tight or I go down with Andoni," Tyrian shouted as he leaned forward, over the edge and reached his hand out for Andoni. Tyrian gripped Andoni's wrist tightly with two hands, but the boy did not let go of the lip of the cliff.

"Let go, Andoni. You must let go."

"You can't hold me, Tyrian. I'll drop."

"I can hold you. You must let go!"

Andoni's horse gasped, stepping backwards erratically, as several serpents reached its hooves, wrapping themselves around its ankles and slithering upwards. The terrified beast kicked its front legs out in panicked, jerky motions as it stumbled backwards, slipping on the loose rock at the edge and tumbling over the side. Andoni looked down, watching his horse tumbling to its death.

"Get those horses back or they'll all go down," Tyrian snapped at the boys. Once again they forced their horses back. Tyrian's steed was now starting to buck again, as the snakes were getting closer.

Tyrian gripped Andoni's wrist tighter and pulled at it, using his other hand to try to pry his fingers from the ledge. Realizing he wouldn't have strength to hold on much longer, Andoni finally put his faith in Tyrian and let go.

Tyrian braced his feet, digging them into the rock and dirt below him. The boys holding the line winced at the combined weight of both of them, but they held strong. Tyrian pulled with the full strength of his bulging arms, digging his feet into the ground as he slowly stepped back, pulling Andoni up. Andoni felt himself starting to rise above the lip of the road. He kept his gaze on Tyrian, refusing to look downward. Tyrian's face was red and straining as he gradually pulled Andoni up over the edge and onto the road again.

Tyrian helped Andoni up onto his feet, steadying him with his firm grip. Andoni grabbed Tyrian by the shoulders tightly. "Thank you, Tyrian! You saved my life."

"We must get rid of these serpents!" Tyrian cried, as he drew his sword and started cutting away at the moving carpet of snakes.

One of the boys rushed to Tyrian's side and Tyrian asked, "Can you see where they are coming from?"

Andoni, still catching his breath, looked across the sea of snakes for their source. Tyrian was busy trying to clear the road when another of the boys came to his side with his shield held low, then another and another joined them. They began scooping the creatures over the edge in slithering bundles.

As Andoni drew his sword to help clear the roadway, he noticed the source. From a hole in the mountainside the size of a small window, the snakes were pouring out like flowing water. The distance was that of a few steeds ahead of them. Andoni pointed to the opening, "They come from the side of the mountain! From that hole!"

Tyrian looked down at the road with despair. There were now five boys cutting away at them but the snakes still came, completely covering the rocky surface of the road.

"This is futile!" Andoni cried. "They just keep coming. We'll wear ourselves down."

Tyrian looked up at the sky, as if seeking a clue to a path out of there. He saw nothing but blue sky and the circling hawk.

He turned his attention back to the road and continued cutting down the flowing serpents. Then he remembered the hawk that had seemed so out of place in the Great River Forest, when he had first attempted meditation alongside Gabriel. It circled him in the desert, and now followed him along the mountain path. This was no ordinary hawk.

Tyrian noticed that the hawk stayed in view of the snakes, and specifically the hole from where the snakes descended. He guessed there was some dark magic between them.

Tyrian quickly sheathed his sword and pulled his curved iron and hammered copper shield from his still-nervous horse. He urgently shined the smooth metal surface with a cloth hanging from his belt.

He held the shield above his head, facing the sun, which sat directly above them now. "Tyrian, what are you doing?" Andoni yelled.

"Keep those snakes away from the horses, Andoni," the boy replied. Andoni continued his assault on the snakes, while Tyrian maneuvered the shield, trying to find the glare of the sun. He kept an eye on the slowly circling hawk as the shield finally caught the sun's rays. Turning it slightly, he bounced the sun's glare up onto the hawk. At first there was no reaction, but as Tyrian adjusted again, he aimed the glare directly into the bird's eyes, blinding it.

He thought he saw the hawk falter in its flight, but then he looked at the snakes and there was no change in their movement. He struggled to keep the glare in its eyes, then saw it jerk back and forth, and then up and then down. The snakes started to slow and change direction, not altogether but individually. There was no more uniformity.

Tyrian held the sun's glare on the hawk. Andoni smiled at Tyrian, needing no words to say what he thought. Then the hawk was falling downward, its wings flapping uselessly as Andoni and the other boys continued chopping at the serpents and brushing them over the side. The hawk fell out of sight and Tyrian tossed the shield aside to help the boys. The hole in the rock wall was still spewing snakes, albeit more slowly.

"Andoni," Tyrian called out, "we've got to close that hole! Can you clear a path for me and I'll cover it with this shield?"

"Yes!" Andoni replied and moved forward, swinging his. Tyrian followed Andoni's lead, kicking at the snakes that moved around his feet. The other boys were making progress clearing the road and they were beginning to see the rocky surface again.

Tyrian reached the opening and scooped up the snakes that were seeping out of it, pushing them back inside and trying to cover the hole with his shield. He held the shield tight against the wall with all of his strength, surprised at the force of the snakes trying to come out. Tyrian glanced away and saw that the serpents on the road were starting to follow each other over the edge of the mountain. Andoni and the other boys were bent over and brushing them in large groups towards the edge, helping them along their path to death.

Suddenly, Tyrian heard a wild screech and looked up to see the hawk hurtling towards him, long talons outstretched. The hawk was larger than he had thought. Its yellow eyes were open wide, the pupils glowing red. Tyrian flung his arm up to protect his face. The hawk clawed into his forearm, grabbing hold tightly. The bird lifted him off the rocky floor just enough to set him off balance and then let go, causing him to fall to the surface of the, stony path.

Tyrian quickly regained his feet and reached for his sword, but the hawk had already returned, reaching its long wings out and thrashing him in the eyes, momentarily blinding him and knocking him back to the ground. Tyrian tumbled over a few times, losing grip of his sword. He jumped to his feet once more but the hawk attacked again, talons piercing the leather of his tunic. The boy fell backwards, knocked unconscious as his head hit the surface of the pathway.

When he came to, moments later, Tyrian found himself a short distance away, on his back with the screaming hawk tearing at his clothes ferociously. His threw his arms were over his face and neck, trying to protect himself and fight at the same time.

The hawk eased its attack and crouched in front of him. It was glaring at him, as if pausing to catch its breath, blood dripping from its beak. "Andoni!" he yelled. He looked around frantically and saw no one. He heard their voices but could not see his fellow soldiers. He raised his head slightly, and realized he had been lifted above the passageway and was perched on a narrow ledge in the rock wall. He arched his neck, looking over the side, and could see Andoni and the other boys a good distance down the mountain, on the trail, which was nearly cleared by now. Andoni seemed to be looking for him.

The vicious raptor began prodding at his chest, gentler than before, apparently searching for something.

Tyrian instinctively grabbed the front of his tunic, which covered the small pouch he carried. The hawk raised its head, looking him in the eye, and for a moment it seemed that Tyrian was staring into another man's face. The eyes that stared back seemed to acknowledge him and the bird's head nodded ever so slightly, but then the hawk began its attack on his chest again. Tyrian held on to the pouch under his tunic tightly with one hand and with the other suddenly reached out toward the hawk's throat. He caught hold of it and squeezed tightly, shaking it back and forth, trying to set it off balance.

The hawk shrieked loudly, its cries echoing across the rock wall. Andoni and the boys looked up, finally seeing Tyrian. The giant bird wrestled to break free of the boy's grip, but it could not. Tyrian held on tightly, squeezing with all of his strength. He could feel the fight waning in the bird. He let go of the pouch and took hold of the hawk with both hands now, squeezing the last breaths from the bird.

The bird became limp, and he flung it over the ledge, sitting up slowly to watch it crash against the road, where Andoni was now gathering the horses back together.

"Andoni!" Tyrian called down. "Take my horse and continue along the road. I will find you up ahead."

"No!" Andoni objected. "I cannot let you continue alone, Tyrian!"

"Only to find a safer path down to you, my friend. Just continue on. I'll find you around the bend coming up."

"Tyrian—" Andoni started again, but Tyrian was already scaling the rock. The barbarian boy did not look back; he moved swiftly, but cautiously, along the rock wall.

"Be careful!" Andoni yelled up reluctantly, his warning echoing back to him. The young Cote officer mounted Tyrian's brown horse and led the other boys forward along the mostly cleared pathway. The remaining snakes had retreated back into the cold damp inside the mountainside.

# # #

Far, far away, in a small makeshift tent at the edge of the desert, Roserie Argaune was pulled from his trance, like a drowning man pulled from the water. His head fell back as he fought for air. He looked around his tent, confused at first, trying to find anything recognizable as a clue to the reality that surrounded him. He had spent so many hours looking through the eyes of the hawk, his God-twin vessel, that he felt lost in his own skin. He breathed in the desert air that blew in through the opening in his tent, the dry and stale desert air.

He rose to his full height and stepped out into the desolate void. It had taken him so long to immerse himself into the hawk's being and train it; he was exhausted at the thought of finding another beast. But for now, his plans were set into motion.

Argaune walked into the desert, feeling the hot grains between his toes, scratching and massaging like the best gypsy masseuses of the Reschtain plains. But he was not relaxed. He swore he could feel the pains of the hawk's strangulation in his own throat.

After taking in the arid breeze, the ghost pain in his throat subsided and he returned to his tent, sat down again on his meditation mat and closed his eyes. His dead hawk could still be of use, for just a bit longer.

# # #

Tyrian pulled himself up higher, his footing along the crooked mounstainside unsteady at times. He moved along the wall, hoping to find a clear path down towards the passageway. Andoni and the other boys rode along slowly, waiting for him to descend, but Tyrian eventually lost sight of them.

The surface of the rock was brittle and Tyrian was careful. He kept his movements deliberate and direct. He focused his eyes on the placement of his feet and hands. His movements were so slow, in fact, that he knew he was making almost no progress towards meeting up with the rest of his party.

Concentrating on the positioning of his hands, Tyrian suddenly felt his foot meet empty space. He looked down as his foot frantically felt nothing but air. A cold, damp breeze tickled his shin, the source of which was a gaping hole in the mountainside. He moved his body closer, hugged up against the opening and peered into it; there was nothing but darkness, save a sliver of light revealing a dirt floor. He swung his body forward the short distance, landing just inside the opening.

As he regained his footing, Tyrian looked into the darkness of a tunnel. The air felt cold and damp. He noticed a glow from further down the tunnel that could mean an opening on the other side. He knew Andoni and the other boys were progressing along the outside of the rock formation. And he knew he should try to rejoin them. But he was so high above the path. And his instinct told him to follow the light. He heard the word "trust" again, echoing in his head. "Trust." He decided he would trust his instincts and walk towards the glow, deep in the heart of the rock.

As he moved deeper into the tunnel, he heard the distant sounds of water. The glow was gradually getting brighter as he crept further in.

Tyrian moved through the tunnel carefully, methodically. He probed lightly with his toes along the surface before planting them—each step an investigation of what might lie below him. His hands reached out into the cold damp air, feeling the emptiness for clues. Every now and then he heard a pebble fall, or the clacking of rock against rock, and he would stop and seek the source of the sound, his eyes straining to pierce the darkness, only to find nothing.

He suddenly realized that the heart of the glowing light and the sound of water both originated from the same spot. The stillness of the air and the near silence sent a chill up his spine.

Tyrian finally reached the source, which turned out to be a small pool with a fountain set in the center. The fountain was crudely carved in stone, and the water dribbled out, betraying a grandiosity that had long since waned. He stood in awe for a few moments, wondering who had built this chamber and how old it was. He sat down at the edge of the pool and washed his wounds in the cool water. He realized that the stale stench of the air had sweetened. And then looking up he found a wide opening in the rock ceiling. The inner edges of the opening looked smooth. Could they have been cut by man? Elf? Another being?

The soft, rippling sound of the fountain filled the otherwise quiet chamber.

He cupped the water with his hands and drank it down. Hunger pangs suddenly wrenched his stomach and he wanted nothing more than to sit peacefully on the patio with Heir Theobald, as they had on a morning that now seemed many days ago.

His rest was interrupted by a strange sound of scraping. He opened his eyes and looked back towards the tunnel, struggling to see through the darkness. He could find nothing, but the sound grew closer. It sounded as if something was being dragged towards him.

Tyrian stood up and drew his sword. His calves shook with fatigue and the sword felt heavy in his hands.

Then he saw, entering the fountain chamber, the very hawk he had just killed. It moved along the floor as if being pulled, but there was no other figure beside it. Its wings seemed to act as legs, slowly shifting the bird forward. It was the strangest thing, Tyrian thought. It was as dead as the moment he'd killed it, and yet it moved. It progressed lifelessly, drawn along by some unseen energy.

When the bird reached the edge of the pool of light, it rose and floated just off the ground, so that it was suspended upright in the air before him. Tyrian looked to and fro, then up and around, trying to find the source of the hawk's reanimation. But there were no signs.

Then a voice, echoing in the wide circular chamber, declared: "You are Gabriel Theobald's apprentice..."

Tyrian could still see no other beings around, so he moved closer to the suspended hawk. Again the voice spoke, low, in almost a whisper. "Yes, your eyes and ears do not fail you. I know who you are, boy."

"Is it a hawk who speaks?" Tyrian asked cautiously.

The reply was a hearty laughter that lingered too long for the boy's comfort, and then there was a pause. "You can lower your sword, boy. You have killed the vessel of my God-twin. It is only useful now for me to speak to you; it can no longer harm you. Come closer."

"Who are you?"

"I finally know who Gabriel Theobald's apprentice is. Such a grand specimen. The Heir of Coteville is a wonderful judge of character and I'm sure you mean to serve him well."

The hovering carcass circled around the boy. Tyrian stepped back, afraid to touch the feathers of the dead raptor.

"Yessss," Arguane's voice echoed in the chamber. "I know the type of boy you are. I recognize the anger. The despair. I was once as lost as you are now. Orphaned. Constantly searching for someone to teach you how to be a man."

"I have a father!"

"You must be careful where you stake your flag of allegiance. With the wisdom of age you'll learn lessons that may conflict with the teachings of your mentor. In every man's life, he will have experiences that contradict what others have told him. You must remember, boy, to make choices based on your own principles, borne of your own hardships."

"You are a witch. You are a dark wizard. Only the devil speaks through the carcass of a dead bird."

"Be that as it may, you are now my audience and I can speak freely to you. I am Roserie Argaune, excommunicated Priest of Coteville. Exiled advisor of King Azjik, and Disciple of the Balles Mountain Twelve. And you are the barbarian boy of the Great River Forest."

"My name is Tyrian Fellhawk."

"My boy, there are only four men alive who know the power that exists in what you hold in your cloak. You have no idea the danger that you are in."

"I will kill any man who tries to take it from me."

"What you have in your possession will move armies of thousands against each other. It will awaken long forgotten tribes, thought to be dead all these years. What you have in your possession will send thousands to their graves. Your life will mean nothing compared to the thousand lives that follow yours. You must be careful. You must be very careful." Tyrian tightened his grip on the hilt of his sword and lifted it again, high and even with his chest, ready to strike.

"Do not waste your energy cutting down a dead bird, boy. I mean you no harm... in this form."

"This is a nightmare. I must be asleep. I'll wake up in my bed at the Fellhawk Compound no doubt at any moment."

"This is no dream. Just know that Gabriel Theobald cannot protect you. If you choose to follow him, there are dangers to you that not even he is aware of."

"Is this the message you came to tell me, wizard?"

"Yes," Argaune held the bird's gaze on the boy's eyes, letting the silence control the cold chamber. And then, "The message is simple, the warning is not. You must trust your God-twin, not the words of a would-be heir to a dying throne. You have the free will to hand that pouch over to Heir Volkummen. That is the easiest course of action for you."

"I will take my chances with Heir Theobald. And whatever form you come to me in, I will strike you down."

A cold laugh came from inside the beak of the hawk's corpse. "So be it," the voice finished. "Be warned that what you hold close will be taken from you."

The suspended hawk suddenly went limp and fell to the ground with a thud. It was still, as still as the cold air that hung in the fountain chamber. Tyrian paused a moment, then stepped forward, poking at the corpse with his boot.

# # #

In his desert tent Roserie Argaune sat back, exhausted and tense. Even for a man of his spiritual strength and gifts, it was almost too much for him to inhabit a dead being and levitate it. For now, he lay back in the shelter of his tent to sleep. There was nothing more he could do while the battle in the canyon raged. He would rest for several days and then return to the outskirts of King Azjik's castle. He was content to know the identity of the one holding the teeth of the Green Kaditz Dragon.

# # #

Tyrian sheathed his sword. His eyes were drawn to the brightness of the exposed sky above. Through the wide opening in the ceiling he saw white clouds painted against a canvas blue sky. Hanging over the edge of the perimeter he suddenly noticed an aged and tattered rope that dangled above him.

He crossed over to it and pulled at it, testing its strength. Satisfied that it would hold his weight, he climbed the short distance to the surface above him.

When he pulled himself out of the cave, into the bright sunlight, he felt the sudden burn of the sun on his skin. He found himself on a wide dirt and grass field that served as the roof to the cave he had just come from. He heard the distant sounds of a battle. He was close to the canyon.

Tyrian rushed to the edge of the field and crouched down low at the top of the canyon wall. He could see, far off below him, the scattered images of two battling armies. He moved along the canyon's edge to get a better view. He found a spot closer to the battle where he could make out the two sides, the Cotes and the Desert Pirates. He had expected to see the Cotes forging past the Desert Pirates, but found them at a stand-still.

Then he saw the reason: arrows flying from the canyon walls on both sides. He lay down against the rock and peered over the edge. Below him he saw the archers, with their brown body paint and feathers, perched on small ledges cut into the rock wall. They were not of the Desert Pirates, yet they fought with them. They stood scattered on ledges all along the canyon walls on both sides.

Tyrian moved quietly away from the rim. He found a boulder and carried it along the edge of the canyon wall, positioning himself over one of the archers. He held the boulder out and then let it drop, hitting the archer squarely and splitting his head open, sending him from his perch and down into the canyon below.

Tyrian ran along the edge of the cliff and found himself above another archer. He pulled the dagger sheathed on his belt and jumped over the side, dropping to the ledge below.

Chapter Seventeen

Heir Theobald heard a thud and turned to see the limp body of an enemy archer sprawled on the canyon floor below. At first Gabriel thought it was a casualty from one of his own archers, but then he noticed a struggle up above and another archer go over the side.

"Tyrian!" Gabriel yelled across the canyon. He could see the boy turn and wave back.

Tyrian picked up the fallen boy's bow and his discarded quiver. He set an arrow in place and turned it on another archer on a nearby ledge. The arrow hit the boy in the chest, sending him over the side as well.

Tyrian quickly leapt down to the next ledge, just behind another archer. Grabbing the stunned boy from behind and pinning both of his arms, Tyrian swung the archer around just in time for the boy to catch an arrow in the stomach, as the other archers tried to stop Tyrian. The boy convulsed in pain as he tried to break free, but Tyrian did not let go. He could hear the whooshing sounds of arrows flying past him, and he instinctively swung his makeshift shield back around, this time from the other side. He did this several times, until the boy's lifeless body became too heavy to hold, then he tossed him over the ledge. He crouched low and moved towards another ledge.

Gabriel felt both incensed that Tyrian had disobeyed him by entering the battle and grateful that he had come to their aid at this moment. He had to admit to himself that his militia had been at a stalemate with their attackers and Tyrian's surprise attack had tipped the balance. Rare for him, Gabriel stood frozen as he watched the boy move from ledge to ledge, dispatching the archers with seemingly little effort.

Moving his attention back to his troops, Gabriel urged Croucien to take advantage of Tyrian's attack. Croucien quickly led his men back into the heart of the battle with the Desert Pirates. They pushed their way up to the front, opening up a hole for their own archers to fill. Within moments the Cote archers had lined up again, their backs against the western wall, with Tyrian's victims falling one by one at their feet.

The enemy archers on the eastern wall were slow to adjust but soon were facing their new attackers head on, realizing they had no cover and were suddenly on the defensive.

"These filthy beasts smell better dead than they do alive," Croucien growled, as he charged before his men, taking on two of the pirates himself. Unlike most generals, he led from the front of his men during battle. His men fought nearer to him than other units did to their captains; together they formed a tight semi-circle that forced a wedge into their aggressors. Now they pushed into the Desert Pirates, forcing them back against each other and into the opposite wall.

Croucien held a short sword in his right hand and his left hand gripped a dagger. He jabbed with the dagger, keeping his attackers off balance and on the defensive. He wielded the sword only for open lunges, once he had forced them back far enough. His soldiers fought more carefully, holding only one blade and a shield. Croucien's philosophy was that if he kept his attacker on the defensive, he needed no defense, but it was a strategy that worked for him and him alone. Gabriel had argued against his style over the years, but Croucien was surly and stubborn.

The Desert Pirates proved no match for him. He fought two at a time. He shoved them together and then forced them back; moving to the left or right, whichever way he wanted them to go. His thick legs held a wide stance as he bent low, pushing up now and then with a lunge or jab.

A short distance away Croucien noticed a fallen pirate who was struggling to get back to his feet. The general angled himself in that direction, pushing two pirates backwards. They bumped into each other as they backpedaled, directly into the fallen pirate, who was almost to his feet by now. They both stumbled over him and the three collapsed into a pile.

Croucien made quick victims of them all, then moved back to his semi-circle of soldiers.

Gabriel was now scaling the wall behind Croucien's men, working his way up the cut-in ledges towards Tyrian. Arrows still flew at him, but less often and less precisely, as the archers were now scrambling and wary of Tyrian. Gabriel clung close to the rock as he climbed upwards, directing his attention to the archer on the ledge closest to him. Even though his legs were tired, and his thigh still burned from the arrow shot, he made quick progress up the rock.

Gabriel reached a ledge where the archer seemed frozen, watching Tyrian, who now appeared to be in a rage. The archer had dropped his bow, his useless hands hanging at his side. Gabriel gripped the archer's ankle and yanked him over the edge, then pulled himself up. He retrieved the boy's bow and took aim at a boy Tyrian struggled with. His clean shot struck the archer's thigh; the boy jerked back, wincing in pain, then tore the arrow from his leg and continued his fight. Gabriel let fly two more, one after the other, piercing him first in the lower back and then in the back of the neck. The boy's body stiffened as he let go of Tyrian and fell lifelessly to the canyon floor below.

"Thank you, your Honor," Tyrian gasped.

Tyrian dropped to the ledge directly below him, slowly working his way down the cliffside, looking for more archers to dispense of.

Gabriel spotted a fallen quiver of arrows and quickly turned his bow on the archers on the opposite wall. He cut down two of them instantly. They seemed to sense the tide of battle turning and knew they would soon be outnumbered. They saw the Desert Pirates retreating. Some of the archers on the eastern wall began climbing down, while others disappeared into gaps inside the rock wall.

Gabriel crouched and fired at the archers who were higher up. Three remained there and they were at quite a distance from him, but his bow was strong and he pulled the arrow back as far as he could. He sent the first arrow soaring directly across the chasm into the wall beyond. It hit just next to one of the three archers and the boy looked up, noticing Gabriel; he aimed his own arrow at the knight.

Gabriel jerked to his right, almost tumbling off the ledge but avoiding the shot. He immediately reloaded his bow and sent off another arrow, this time striking the boy in the stomach. The boy dropped his bow and clutched his abdomen, falling forward and over the ledge.

On the ledge below, Tyrian was struggling with the last of the archers on the western wall. He had the large boy pinned down to the rocky floor of the ledge. He pressed down on the archer's wrist and tried to control the boy's other arm, which swung wildly at him. Every now and then Tyrian would catch a fist in his jaw or eye and his head woud swing back. This archer had incredible strength. After the third such blow Tyrian's head was starting to throb. His fatigue, the heat, and the impact of the boy's punches were all taking their toll.

The archer managed to leverage himself onto his side and then flip over, switching positions with Tyrian. Suddenly Tyrian found himself on his back, his throat closing under the iron grip of this giant boy. He kicked his leg, trying to gain some leverage, but he could not. The boy brought down another crushing fist to his face, knocking his head back against the rock. Tyrian could feel his breath getting slower; his vision grew cloudy. The other boy's eyes glared from his brown face. Tyrian turned his head to the left, as much as he could under the grip of the giant boy's hand. On the opposite side of the canyon, on the rim above the canyon, he could see Gorka Osa atop his black horse, watching. Then he began to lose consciousness.

Gabriel looked down to the ledge below and saw Tyrian's limp body underneath the bulk of the foreign mercenary. He fired an arrow, catching the giant boy in his side. The boy pulled it from his side and tossed it away, seemingly unfazed, and kept his tight grip on Tyrian's throat.

Gabriel was out of arrows. He threw the empty quiver aside, then pulled a dagger from his belt and dropped to the ledge below. The boy looked up, surprised, and released Tyrian from his grip. Gabriel grabbed the aggressor's shoulder and brought the dagger down to the back of his neck, but the boy reached up, seizing Gabriel's wrist. Gabriel jerked his arm back to force release, but the boy was too strong.

Gabriel released the dagger and clenched the boy's wrist, digging his thumb into the space between his thumb and forefinger, pressing forcefully on the nerve. Then Gabriel thrust his head foreword, butting him directly in the nose. The boy relaxed his grip and Gabriel forced him down, picking up the dagger again. He pounced on the boy, bringing his dagger down into his throat with all of his force.

The crimson spray from the boy's throat blinded Gabriel. He closed his eyes and turned away as he stabbed again and again until he was sure there was no fight left in the archer. Wiping the blood from his face, Gabriel turned to Tyrian, lying unconscious next to him. He put his hand on the side of the boy's throat, feeling for a pulse—it was faint, but still there. He was breathing.

Gabriel reached into Tyrian's tunic and found the pouch, still intact. He opened it and examined the contents quickly. Then he returned them and re-tied the pouch snugly, pushing it back inside the blouse. He slapped Tyrian on the cheek a few times.

"Tyrian! Tyrian!" he called.

"Your Honor...," Tyrian said, as he slowly came to. He looked up and grabbed Gabriel by the arm. "What happened? Have Andoni and the others arrived?"

"They have not."

"They were ahead of me. I am sorry, your Honor. We were on the trail, as you directed. We were stopped by a swarm of serpents and when we cleared the road of that, there was a strange hawk—a hawk that had the eyes of a human. It carried me up onto the mountain and attacked me. It was searching for something on me, in my tunic, and I think it was searching for your pouch. I fought the bird off, but it had enormous strength. After I had killed it, its corpse spoke to me."

"What was the voice like?"

"It was old and distant, like a ghost. It spoke with the accent that you carry. It said its name was Roserie Argaune."

"Just as I thought, boy. We are being followed by the wizard Argaune. Tyrian, you must be careful. He is extremely powerful and dangerous."

"He warned me about you, your Honor."

Gabriel did not respond. He looked down at the canyon below. The Desert Pirates were now in full retreat. The archers from the eastern wall had all dispersed and vanished. A handful of Heir Theobald's men still fought the Desert Pirates, but the bulk of the militia were tending to wounded comrades or repacking their horses, which had been brought back from their holding place at the entrance to the canyon.

Gabriel turned back to Tyrian, saying, "We must get down below, and continue through the canyon. We are not finished yet, and there's no telling what awaits us on the other end. Can you make it down?"

"Yes, your Honor."

They made their way slowly back down the canyon side and rejoined the rest of the militia. Croucien was helping his men clear the canyon road of bodies when Gabriel called him to mount his horse.

"Dechaume! Croucien! We must get through the canyon before any reinforcements come," Gabriel yelled.

Tyrian mounted a spare horse and rode up next to Gabriel. "Stay close to me, Tyrian," Gabriel directed. "We know not what lies at the opening of the canyon. We must be prepared for anything, and you must stay unharmed."

Tyrian nodded to him and then noticed Dechaume and Croucien riding up close to them. They both looked at Tyrian and then at Gabriel and nodded silently.

Gabriel turned to the mounted soldiers behind him, calling out, "For the dead, may their God-twins guide them to their heaven. For the living, let us be brave and continue to Azjik!"

Dechaume and Croucien took up the lead, followed by the men from each of their units. The rest of the militia securely enveloped Gabriel and Tyrian.

The Cotes had lost roughly a quarter of their men to the archers, but still numbered strong. They rode through the remainder of the canyon. At one point the path grew so narrow that it seemed they were in a pitch-black tunnel, with the walls so close that the horses could only ride in single file. The pathway became as dark as a grave and deathly silent.

Tyrian instinctively lowered his head, although it was too dark to see any dangers. He felt his horse slowing a bit and he gave up control to the steed, which closely followed the horse in front of him.

The tunnel seemed to go on forever and he wondered if there was an end. But the Cote horses had made this journey many times and their hooves knew the path. They rode as if they could see.

Then, as abruptly as it had become dark it became light, as their horses filed out of the tunnel and emerged on the other side of the mountain. They found themselves in a large, wide opening of lush, green grass, surrounded by shrubbery and short, leafy green trees.

Suddenly the troops encountered the remaining Desert Pirates, waiting just inside the surrounding trees, looking tired and forlorn, but swords drawn just the same. Behind the haggard pirates stood the young, foreign archers who'd survived the battle. Now, though, they brandished long broadswords. And off to the side, no longer on horseback, Gorka Osa and Babbel, waited, helmets at their side.

Dechaume and Croucien brought their horses to a halt in the middle of the field. Suddenly two armies faced off at a very close distance.

Gabriel motioned to Tyrian to stay put while he dismounted and stepped forward.

"This is the King's road and, by his law, I order you to make way for the Militia of Coteville." All were silent. The Desert Pirates emitted fatigued grunts in their vulgar gurgling language. But the rest of the foreign soldiers remained hushed, deferring to their leader, Gorka Osa, who stepped forward, slowly approaching Gabriel Theobald.

"What a pleasure to make the acquaintance of an heir to the king. Where are you in line, your Honor? Must two hundred men pass for you to assume the throne?" Gorka Osa asked, sneering.

"It is an honor in itself to be an heir," Gabriel replied. "I seek not the throne, but the protection of he who sits on it. Now, in the name of King Azjik, make way for the Coteville Militia."

"We will make way once we retrieve what we have come for."

"There will be no bargaining, Gorka Osa."

Gorka Osa's eyes sifted through the crowd of soldiers until they landed on Tyrian, tucked away within the pack of riders.

"Heir Gabriel Theobald, with all due respect, you are in possession of something that I want," Gorka Osa hissed, "and I will not make way until I have retrieved it."

"Thieves and mercenaries have no place on this road. It is under the protection of the militias of Azjik."

"I am neither a thief nor a mercenary," Gorka Osa barked, his anger rising. "I refuse to pledge my allegiance to a foolish, immature figure who comes to his decisions based on the advice of a hundred self-serving agents. His epoch is finished, *your Honor*! This kingdom is crumbling from within, and you would be wise to take heed of this."

Gabriel drew his sword and took a few steps forward. He approached Gorka Osa slowly and deliberately.

"You will now move aside and your men will retreat. The Road of Fathers is not for the likes of you."

Babbel unsheathed his sword and held it out before him. The young mercenaries did the same. One by one, Gabriel's soldiers drew their swords. Dechaume and Croucien moved closer to Tyrian. Gorka Osa took notice of this.

"I will not retreat. I think you know what I am seeking."

"Whatever you seek is not here. My patience has run out, mercenary."

Tyrian nervously covered his chest with his hand and pulled his horse back a few steps.

"There is my would-be apprentice, Tyrian Fellhawk," Gorka Osa said, as he slowly moved his horse towards the boy.

"Gorka Osa…" was all that Tyrian could say.

Gorka Osa moved a few steps towards Tyrian and Gabriel stepped forward. Just as Gorka Osa reached for his sword, they heard a thunderous sound of hooves. Gorka Osa turned around and looked out into the brush beyond the road. His mercenary troops turned to look as well.

It seemed the entirety of both armies stood frozen until the sound revealed itself as the militia of Heir Volkummen, which appeared quickly through the brush, outnumbering the mercenary army. Volkummen's soldiers pulled their horses to a standstill just beyond the circle of enemy riders.

"Heir Volkummen," Gabriel called out.

"Brother Heir, I received word of illegals on the Road of Fathers and came to help clear the way."

Tyrian sat up in his saddle, recognizing Heir Volkummen from the battle in the Great River Forest from what seemed so long ago. He remembered the red flowing hair and beard. He remembered the majestic brown horse.

Gorka Osa turned to Heir Volkummen, saying, "Why, I have the pleasure of meeting two royal heirs this day. You can certainly clear these desert scum from the road, but there will be no need to confront my men and me. We will leave of our own accord, once we have retrieved what we have come for." Gorka Osa looked directly at Tyrian. Volkummen took note of their silent exchange.

"A welcome sight to be sure, Heir Volkummen," Gabriel said, "but there will be no need for further bloodshed this day. We will proceed to the audience of Azjik as scheduled."

"Then I will escort you back to the kingdom myself," Volkummen replied.

"We need no escort, but thank you."

During this exchange Gorka Osa had turned towards Babbel, who stood off to one side, gripping his sword tightly. Babbel sensed a slight nod and quietly took a few steps backwards towards the brush. He watched Gorka Osa move ever so slightly closer to Tyrian.

Gabriel's eyes darted from Heir Volkummen to Gorka Osa to Tyrian. He stood tense with nervous energy.

Babbel could sense that Heir Volkummen was distracted by the multiple armies, and he inched his way towards the red-haired heir. He pulled a small dagger from his belt and sidled up close behind Volkummen's horse.

"I would gladly help you dispose of these desert vermin if it pleased you, your Honors," Gorka Osa said, in a loud, booming voice, demanding the attention of both heirs. Gabriel sneered at the renegade while Volkummen chuckled at the offer.

Abruptly, Babbel plunged his dagger deep into the hind leg of Volkummen's horse, sending it screaming and bucking into the center of the open field and causing panic among the other horses. Volkummen was thrown back as his horse bucked.

Volkummen quickly pulled his feet from the stirrups and let himself fall to the soft grassy floor. He instantly sprang to his feet, sword drawn and lunging towards Babbel. His blade found its way into Babbel's gut, curling the mercenary over in pain.

Suddenly, the field was as chaotic as a giant hornet's nest, with horses charging in every direction, their riders helplessly carried along.

In the confusion Gorka Osa had reached Tyrian's horse and hoisted himself up. He pinned the boy's arms behind him and kicking the horse into a sprint in one quick motion. From a pouch in his cloak he took a damp leaf, the size of his hand, and held it over the boy's face, filling Tyrian's breath with a strange scent that soon left him unconscious. His limp body lurched forward, restrained only by Gorka Osa's arms, which now held the reins of the horse as well.

Gabriel quickly leaped onto his horse and sprinted after Gorka Osa and Tyrian. Behind Gabriel charged Dechaume and Croucien.

Gabriel followed Tyrian's horse onto the open road. He pushed his steed hard, still just out of reach of Tyrian's horse. He could feel Dechaume and Croucien on his heels but he focused only on Tyrian and Gorka Osa.

Gorka Osa rode into the open again. He steered Tyrian's horse towards a large man-made formation of rocks which could be seen in the distance.

Gabriel was closing the gap between himself and his captive protege. He knew the arrangement of stones to be a maze of boulders and stone walls, some man-made, some natural. One could hide in there.

"Hy-ah!" Gabriel cried out, kicking his horse harder. As he began to close the gap, he could see Tyrian's body slumped over. He looked back to see Dechaume and Croucien right behind him, and further back, Heir Volkummen.

Gorka Osa pulled the horse into a sharp turn, disappearing into the labyrinth of rocks. He brought his horse to a slow walk, going around a few turns and then stopping in a circular opening, seemingly alone.

Gorka Osa dropped to the ground, just in time to catch Tyrian's limp body as it lurched over the side. He guided the boy's large form to the ground and laid him out. He immediately began his search, through every part of Tyrian's tunic, belt and pouches.

Tyrian suddenly came to and swung wildly, hitting Gorka Osa square in the jaw. He kicked Gorka Osa in the stomach, then sprang to his feet and pushed Gorka Osa back a few steps.

"Tyrian," Gorka Osa said slowly, "I believe that you have what I am looking for."

"Gorka Osa," Tyrian said, still groggy. He could feel the ground beneath him tremble as Theobald, Dechaume, Croucien and Volkummen drew closer.

"The Mountain Pirates stole it from the ones who unearthed it. Heir Theobald stole it from the Mountain Pirates. And now I am stealing it back."

"I will not release the pouch to you. My mission is to bring it to King Azjik and that is what I will do. You will only get yourself killed by attempting to take it from me."

"You are brave, boy. My offer still stands to mentor you."

Tyrian was silent.

Horses could be heard pulling into the rock maze; the breathing, the clopping of the horse's feet. Gorka Osa looked away for a second and then back to Tyrian.

"Tyrian, you must learn the ways of anarchy. Anarchy is survival, boy. Man's true nature is that of the animals—bestial, barbaric—it's where our hunger and passion lie. Order and the rule of one man are unnatural to us. Think hard of what you want. It lies there in the wild."

"NOOOO!!!" Tyrian screamed.

There was a sudden rush of horse hooves as the pursuers charged to his call.

"The Heir of Coteville cannot help you. You are alone in your journey."

"I will kill you first," Tyrian said, leaning in towards the mercenary. Gorka Osa leaned back, chilled by the young boy's directness.

Gabriel suddenly appeared around a wall of rock formations. He swung his leg around and came to the ground, feet spread out and sword drawn. Right behind him were Dechaume and Croucien, both mimicking their heir's perfect dismount. The five of them formed a crooked, conflicted circle: Tyrian, Gorka Osa, Heir Theobald, Dechaume and Croucien.

"You will put down your weapon and let this boy go," Gabriel coldly.

Before Gorka Osa could respond, Heir Volkummen brought his horse to a stop just beyond the circle. All eyes turned to him as he slowly, methodically dismounted and approached them.

"Gorka Osa," Heir Volkummen began, "you have already defied the will of our king once this day. You would be ill-advised to proceed any further."

"Your Honors, two heirs of distinction, I beg your pardon, but this is between the boy and me."

Another set of horse hooves unsettled the ground beneath them as Andoni and the other boys approached. Tyrian reached into his tunic and gripped the pouch tightly in his fist, as if to reassure himself that he still held it. Gabriel took notice of this and nodded to him.

Heir Volkummen moved forward, putting himself between Tyrian and Gorka Osa. He reached out his hand toward the boy and used the gentlest voice he could muster. "My boy, why don't you give me what you hold, and I will get it to King Azjik."

Tyrian's eyes darted to Gabriel as he took a few steps back.

"No," was all he could say.

"I will ensure that your prize gets to our dear king. And that your bravery is duly noted. Give me the pouch."

Tyrian could hear in his voice that Heir Volkummen had only so much patience for the charade of gentleness he was playing.

"Do you see how this works?" Gorka Osa sneered. "The devils of Azjik's order will tempt you. Only I can offer you the freedom that you seek."

"Give me the pouch," Heir Volkummen ordered.

Tyrian stepped back again, drawing his sword against the red-haired knight. There was suddenly a hush of awe in the small crowd.

"No!" Tyrian repeated.

"Tyrian," Gabriel cautioned, "do not draw your sword against an heir. By Azjik's law that is an instant death sentence."

"Listen to your mentor," Volkummen said, stepping closer, "and lower your sword. I will relieve you of the burden you carry."

"No," the boy said again, as he half-heartedly lowered his sword.

"I can either cut you down now, or leave you as an example for the king. Either way, it is useless for you to fight me."

"Tyrian, lower your sword, get on your horse and ride towards King Azjik. Now." Gabriel slowly drew his own sword and moved closer.

Volkummen took note of this, finally drawing his own. Tyrian exchanged looks with Gabriel, then looked to Gorka Osa and then to Andoni, who held the reins to his beautiful brown horse. He took one last look at Volkummen and then sheathed his sword and moved towards Andoni and his horse.

Volkummen lunged at the boy, but Gabriel was there to answer the attack, forcing space for Tyrian to proceed. The boy quickly mounted his horse and disappeard from the rockery nook and out of the maze. Andoni rode at his horse's heels.

The two swords of the heirs clanged against each other, echoing in the open air.

"You dare draw your sword against me," Volkummen roared.

"Leave the boy," Gabriel warned.

"No man shall draw his sword against an heir, not even another heir. That is the King's law."

"Then I have broken his law. But you will let that boy go."

Gorka Osa moved toward his horse, but found himself cornered by Dechaume and Croucien, pinning him down with their swords.

"Let all the witnesses here proclaim that you drew first," Volkummen said to the ones gathered.

"So be it," Gabriel answered as he brought his blade up, deflecting a powerful blow from Volkummen.

Tyrian smacked the reins against his horse, pushing it out into the open and onto the Road of Fathers. He looked back and saw Andoni right on his tail.

Tyrian focused on the road ahead and pushed his horse faster. He could see a speck on the horizon. He hoped it was the castle entrance of King Azjik's kingdom.

"Keep going, Tyrian. I'm right behind you!" Andoni yelled.

Tyrian did not answer. He looked straight ahead. His mind raced. He was afraid for Gabriel's fate.

Chapter Eighteen

As they drew closer to Azjik's castle, Tyrian felt a cool headwind that slowed his pace ever so slightly, yet calmed him at the same time. Andoni had pulled up beside him. The boys exchanged anxious looks, and somber smiles.

The castle gates were now coming into view and Tyrian's excitement at reaching Azjik's castle was tempered by his worry.

"The gates are not far," Andoni finally spoke.

Tyrian could now make out the giant iron arches atop the main gates, spun and hammered with shining silver and gold inlay.

Andoni pulled slightly ahead of Tyrian.

"When do you think Heir Theobald will join us?" Tyrian asked.

Andoni turned to Tyrian, looked back at the road they had just traveled, then again towards the gates they were quickly approaching. His thoughts did not need to be voiced, for they were the same as Tyrian's—*may Heir Theobald's God-twin guide him out of harm's way.*

The entrance was now in full view; human figures were intricately sculpted into the pillars that framed the gates. A small army of guards stood at the foot of the portal.

Tyrian watched the guards move into battle position, lances held forward, swords drawn. Beyond the sentries he could see more soldiers moving busily, seemingly unaware of anyone approaching. On the guard towers and upper levels, more guards watched curiously. There must have been a hundred soldiers stationed around the entrance.

Andoni pulled his horse to a stop before the Lead Guard and Tyrian came up just behind him. Andoni dropped to the ground, motioning Tyrian to dismount as well. Andoni bowed his head and looked to Tyrian, who followed his lead.

"You wear the crest of Coteville; do you come with Heir Theobald's blessing?" the Lead Guard asked.

"Yes, sir," Andoni replied. "My heir follows behind us. We engaged some Desert Pirates on the King's Road. Heir Theobald dispatched us ahead of him, as my friend here carries with him a treasure for the King."

The Lead Guard moved to Tyrian and motioned him to rise. He looked him up and down, not recognizing his foreign features.

"Your companion wears no markings. Is he your prisoner?"

"No, sir," Andoni replied. "He is a friend of Heir Theobald. He carries with him a gift for King Azjik's eyes only."

"Let me see this prize."

"I have been instructed to bring it to the King and the King alone," Tyrian replied.

"I must see it before I let you pass through these gates," the Guard repeated, as he reached toward's Tyrian's shirt. Tyrian stepped back, reaching for his sword.

"Tyrian, no!" Andoni pleaded.

The Lead Guard pulled a dagger from his belt and took a step backward. "Release your grip on that sword, boy," he ordered.

"You will take me to the king, so that I may deliver Heir Theobald's gift."

"As a Guard of the Gates of Azjik, I command you. You will surrender your delivery!"

"I will not!"

Seeing the stalemate a second, more mature, Guard stepped up and said, "We will take you as a prisoner until your Heir arrives to negotiate with our King. You must surrender your blade."

Andoni nodded. Reluctantly, Tyrian released the grip on his sword and let it fall to the ground. The two guards stepped back and lowered their own weapons. Satisfied that the tension had been eased, Andoni placed his own sword on the ground next to Tyrian's and dropped to one knee, holding out his wrists for binding. Tyrian followed his lead.

"I request that you take me prisoner as well, as I brought the boy here," Andoni said.

The walkway to the main castle compound was short. As Tyrian and Andoni were escorted away, they could see their horses being led off towards some stables.

Tyrian and Andoni were brought to a drab, unadorned cabin a short distance from the main road that led up into the main castle.

Once inside, Tyrian realized it was a jail of sorts. It was sparsely furnished, with only four beds, a table and chair. There were no windows. The only light came through slits in the wall and ceiling.

"You have the independence of your barbarian brethren for sure," Andoni said with a sigh of resignation, after a few moments.

"I have not come this far, Andoni, to hand this pouch over to some foolish guard at a gate."

"Yes, but sometimes these things need to be handled more delicately."

"We have no time for pleasantries."

"Well, now we have ample time for discussion about pleasantries, thanks to you."

Tyrian peered through the darkness to read Andoni's face. Andoni's tone seemed terse. There was a moment of silence until both boys burst out laughing.

"Yes, I suppose we have time for that now, do we not?" Tyrian said, his laughter tapering off.

Tyrian collapsed on one of the beds, falling quickly into a light slumber, his mind sifting through strange sounds seeping in through the walls.

Several hours later the doors to the cabin opened, revealing the full darkness of night outside. A chill filled the room as a Guard entered.

"Follow me," the guard growled.

Tyrian and Andoni stepped out into the street, where two more Royal Guards waited.

"Has Heir Theobald arrived?" Tyrian asked.

There was no answer. The royal guards exchanged looks among themselves, then urged the boys on.

"Where is Heir Theobald of Coteville?" Tyrian asked again.

"Quiet, boy," the Lead Guard finally replied.

"Tyrian, we will find out soon enough," Andoni whispered.

They hiked up a small dirt path to a side entrance of the main castle itself. Even the dignity of being led through the main entrance was eluding Tyrian. The door was unmarked and, once inside, he saw no adornments or markings. The entryway and halls were simple, stone and cold. Tyrian and Andoni were whisked into a narrow, well-lit hallway and up some wide wooden stairs.

After the guards walked them through a long maze of hallways and antechambers, they found themselves in a wide circular chamber with a long table and several doors. The table had a purple velvet covering, with a bowl of fruit, and carafes of water and wine. It looked like a meeting room of sorts. Chairs placed adjacent the table were wooden, intricately carved, with tall backs.

Tyrian saw several more Royal Guards standing next to each of the closed doors that bordered the meeting table. Tyrian and Andoni were separated and each was led into a different room.

When Tyrian was ushered into his room he found a narrow, but colorfully covered, bed and a wide brass washbasin. The Guard motioned him to step away from the door.

"Where have you taken Andoni?" Tyrian asked the guard.

"Wash up," the Guard answered. "You will find a clean robe against the wall. I will be back for you soon."

"Have you received word of Heir Theobald's arrival?" Tyrian pleaded.

"I have not," the Guard replied softly, acknowledging the boy's concern.

"Will we meet with the King to present our gift then?"

"You will meet with the King after tomorrow's sunrise. Meanwhile, I will retrieve you under the night's covering, for the nightly call to The One Disciple." And with that he closed the door, leaving Tyrian alone.

Tyrian sat on the bed, a soft comfortable sleeping platform. He lay back, but was no longer tired. His mind worked on intricate puzzles of what would come next. He came to no conclusions.

He rose and used the basin to wash up, then changed into the long crimson robe. It was simple and heavy and had Azjik's crest on the right breast.

He sat back on the bed and waited.

Tyrian suddenly realized that he did not miss the Fellhawk Compound. It was as if the sun had risen for the first time and he did not want it to set. The Great River Forest was a dark cave compared to the vast desert lands, the beauty of Coteville, and the shining promise of Azjik's kingdom. But his family, he was sure, missed him. He wondered if his father had led a search party, or if they mourned his loss at the hands of a neighboring barbarian clan. And his young cousin, Djuri, oh that adventurous little boy! He had probably wandered into the forest to find his father, Cabatic, impatient with Tyrian's absence. Tyrian did miss their games.

As the glare from the moon outside began to light up his room, the door opened and he was led back out into the circular meeting chamber. There he found Andoni, dressed in the same style of crimson robe as he. They nodded to each other, but did not speak. Something about the room forced silence on the boys. Only when they were led back down the stairs and down another hallway did they feel free to speak.

"Where are they taking us?" Tyrian whispered to Andoni.

"To the King's temple, to call to The One Disciple. The King decrees that all must pray to his god's prophet, nightly under the cover of darkness."

Tyrian said nothing else. His gaze wandered to the simple decorations protruding from the walls and ceilings; tiny sculptures placed in odd arrangements. Here there was a horrific head, seemingly in anguish. Several steps away and closer to the ground was a sculpture of a beautiful woman playing a stringed instrument.

The flat silence of the passageway soon gave way to a torrent of murmurs and echoing chants, as they approached the entrance to the main temple.

The temple itself was a vast tower, attached but set off from the main castle. The center of the room featured a deep pit, where a healthy fire roared. Wrapped around the pit stood a series of altars where several hooded men sat, heads bowed and chanting. Stone benches were cut into the walls along the perimeter. The spiral of stone benches rose to halfway up the length of the tower. The temple was already filled with worshippers, all anonymous in their identical crimson robes.

Tyrian and Andoni were led to an empty bench with Royal Guards posted on either side. No worshippers sat close to them; no one acknowledged them.

After a moment he observed the hooded figures at the altars rise to their feet and raise their hands, palms out. The crowd of worshippers did the same. Tyrian marveled at the display of hundreds of crimson robes rising at once, like a strange, red waterfall-fountain of limbs. Across the temple he could see a small procession enter and ascend a ramp to a secluded balcony. This must be King Azjik. He stood taller than his entourage and was dressed the same, except for the long golden medallion at his breast and the shining crown on his head.

King Azjik appeared younger than Tyrian had expected. He looked slightly older than Gabriel and had short, close-cropped hair. He wore no whiskers, and his face seemed kind. He smiled as he took his seat. Tyrian could tell that he truly enjoyed the majesty of this event.

The tower became hushed as everyone followed King Azjik's lead and took their seats. Sitting next to him was a frail, older man with a long, flowing white beard. Atop his white head he wore a long black hat, similar to the style the Desert Merchants wore, except for its blackness. Tyrian decided this elderly man must be Farafah Fruz, King Azjik's closest advisor; he saw him lean in now and again, whispering in Azjik's ear. Whenever he did this, the young King gripped the older man's forearm and listened intently, nodding or furrowing his brow in answer.

The hooded men around the pit took their respective places at the altars and began reciting passages in a melodic, dreamy dialect. The chant was hypnotizing and could have been played by stringed instruments, had Tyrian not seen them singing it. It was truly beautiful, and passed along the circle as each man sang his verse and then another continued the words, one after another.

Tyrian felt someone's eyes on him and looked down a few rows where he discovered, to his surprise, Heir Theobald, sitting and wearing the same red robe. Gabriel smiled and nodded at him, then turned back to the ceremony. Tyrian leaned over to Andoni to speak, but Andoni whispered quietly, "I knew he would be safe."

Then, just as he felt comforted by seeing Gabriel, Tyrian also noticed Heir Volkummen across the pit, eyes closed and head bowed. His palms suddenly sweated and he wiped them on the lap of his robe. His eyes darted this way and that. He felt Volkummen's energy directed at him, although the red-haired heir continued looking down.

The service seemed to last for hours. Tyrian was drowsy and fighting sleep as his head did a dance of nodding forward and back. But then he straightened up, alerted to a shuffling within the entire temple. The priests all took their seats again, heads bowed. Instinctively, Tyrian looked up to the royal balcony and saw Farafah Fruz slip a small piece of paper to Azjik. Azjik rose and stepped forward, holding the paper before him.

"My countrymen, tonight we praise our One God through his One and Only Augur. Remember his words, 'The god speaks to the One Disciple and the Disciple becomes the god.' He is the one who will guide us to the mountain kingdom and glorious rapture. He is the one who looks over the lesser gods of the mountain regions, the desert, the plains, the valleys and the forest. Our One Disciple is just and advises me directly on the judgment I place upon my good people. He is the one who presents us with The Three Books of Hjara, the one and only set of laws given to man. Our One Disciple alone advises me how to enforce his laws; we are simply the Children of his Will. We must remember that any judgment from my lips to you, however harsh it may seem, comes not from me, but from the One Disciple who reveals his secrets to me. There is judgment coming. But beyond the valley of judgment lie the wonderful, fertile fields of a thousand years of peace promised to us."

With that, the King smiled, bowed his head and sat again. He seemed to sneak a look at Farafah Fruz, who closed his eyes and nodded.

The Royal Guards began ushering the rows of worshippers out of the temple and into the hallways that threaded their way back into the main castle.

In the hallway, Tyrian pushed his way past his guards to find Gabriel.

"Your Honor!" Tyrian called out. Gabriel stopped and turned to the boy.

"Tyrian, I am proud of you. I knew I could trust you to bring the pouch to the king. Tomorrow morning he will see us and you can present it to him."

"I was afraid you would—" Tyrian began, but Gabriel gripped his arm to quiet him.

"Tyrian, you mustn't speak. I may yet pay a horrible price for my choice. But you must focus on giving that pouch to the king. Forget about the rest. Andoni will stay by your side as long as you need him. Now go with your Guards. Sleep for the night, and tomorrow we will face our future."

The Guards caught up with Tyrian and pulled him away. Gabriel smiled and soon was lost in the crowd. Tyrian and Andoni were again led back through the same maze of hallways as before, away from the masses and back to their sleeping chambers.

Once again in the seclusion of his bedchamber, Tyrian sat on the floor, cross-legged, to meditate. He closed his eyes and tried to conjure the spirit of his God-twin. He opened his palms and laid them face up in his lap. He let his head fall back as his mind became clear and silent. He let the sounds outside his door become rhythms in his consciousness and the cool air held him still. He sat for what seemed an eternity, holding steady in his trance. Then, off in the distance of his subconscious, he heard a noise, a voice almost, a song. It sounded far away and his head moved forward as if to lean closer to it. Then he could make out the words—softly, but in his own voice, "Trust... fear... trust... pain... trust... trust."

Tyrian could feel himself begin to pull out of his trance, wondering where the voice came from, but then he dropped back into his mediation. He heard the words again, now clearer: "Trust... your fear... trust... trust your pain...." That was all. He sat still for some time longer, but he heard no more words and no more sounds.

Finally, exhausted, he disrobed and climbed into the bed. Under the thick covers, with a cool breeze coming in through the open window, he surrendered to his fatigue and lay back, quickly falling asleep.

Chapter Nineteen

Tyrian was awakened several hours later by his escort-guard. The pain in his head and the fatigue in his muscles had allowed him just a few hours of sleep. The religious ceremony honoring Azjik's god had lasted well into the early morning hours.

Tyrian found a silken tunic and trousers folded and laid out on the floor. He subconsciously gripped the pouch that had not left the twine around his neck, like a tangled necklace. Then he quickly dressed in the royal garb provided for him.

Tyrian followed the guard back to the circular conference chamber once again. This time, though, he found the room completely filled. Along the table sat several elderly men, deep in discussion. They hushed as Tyrian was led in. Andoni rushed to him from the other end of the room.

"Good morning, friend," Andoni greeted him.

"Good morning," Tyrian replied. "Who are all of these people?"

"They are advisors to the king. When King Azjik enters, remember to bow your head and do not speak until he addresses you."

Tyrian saw Gabriel enter with Dechaume, Croucien, and several Cote Guards. Suddenly the room became frantic, with everyone finding a place to sit or stand.

A Royal Guard entered, more intricately adorned than the rest, wearing a shining silver helmet with a plume of red feathers pulled back from the brim, and wearing a long crimson robe beneath a bronzed cuirass. The Guard acknowledged the gathering with a slight nod and then took a step back and bowed. Tyrian looked directly at his feet and closed his eyes.

King Azjik's footsteps were slow and deliberate, and he wore heavy boots that struck the tiled floor like violent reins on a horse's nape. They stopped, and a wave of whispers washed across the room. Then there was silence.

"Heir Gabriel Theobald of Coteville!" King Azjik finally spoke, his voice eloquent and measured.

Tyrian saw the old man, Farafah Fruz, standing close to Azjik. It was curious, the boy thought, that he was never far from the King's arm.

"Yes, your Highness," Gabriel responded, taking a few steps forward.

"You are one of my bravest and most honored of knights. Long ago I sent you on a mission to retrieve the sacred teeth of the long-dead Green Kaditz Dragon. I pray that on this wonderful day you have returned with them."

"Your Highness, I bring them to you today with the aid of my friend and protégé from the Great River Forest, Tyrian Fellhawk."

"Tyrian Fellhawk!" Azjik spoke his name as both a question and an announcement.

Tyrian took a step forward and then looked up, suddenly frozen at the sight of the King. He blushed under the gaze of Farafah Fruz, who was studying him closely.

"Yes, your Highness. I am Tyrian Fellhawk."

"Come forward, boy," the King ordered. Tyrian stepped towards the king but stopped midway. He felt the King's eyes examine him fully.

The King again addressed Tyrian. "The Great River Forest, an untamed land to be sure, full of barbarians and nomads. I have no militia there, but it still falls under my rule."

"My grandfather fought under the Great River Militia for the order of your house at one time," the boy offered.

"Splendid. Now you may present me my prize."

The room became hushed once again as Tyrian reached into his blouse and pulled out the small pouch. He stepped forward and held it out to the king, his head once again lowered. Azjik took the pouch and motioned him away.

Tyrian stepped back. He looked up slightly and watched the King examine the dragon's teeth in his palm. The King stole a look at Farafah Fruz, whose lips were pursed tight, his gaze fixed on the aura of the now glowing teeth.

"Well done, boy," the King declared. "And your escort, Andoni Oedan, as well." He moved the teeth around in his hand, holding them up before his eyes, as if they were jewels. "Such a simple matter. Such a simple matter," he mumbled to himself. He abruptly hid them away again in the pouch and handed them to one of his advisors.

"I thank you for your service to the kingdom, Tyrian and Andoni. Heir Gabriel tells me that you both wish to train for my First Stand Army."

"It would be an honor, Your Highness. I will train hard and sacrifice all," Tyrian said.

"As will I," Andoni said.

"Well, then, it shall be," he declared, stepping forward and placing his hand on Tyrian's lowered head.

King Azjik took a step back and then turned to Gabriel, sternly taking him in. "But now," the King stated, "I am afraid we have some unpleasant business to attend to. Heir Gabriel, it has come to my attention that during your return journey you engaged in some unlawful business on the Road of Fathers."

"It is true, your Highness. I trusted only this boy to return your prize to you."

Azjik turned to one of his advisors and nodded. The man turned and disappeared behind a door, returning after a moment with Heir Volkummen and several of his men. They entered the room and stood against the wall opposite of Gabriel. Another advisor placed two chairs behind the King. Azjik looked around among his small congress of elders and then to Farafah Fruz, who stood next to him. He helped the old man into one of the chairs, then seated himself in the other. Both men leaned in close and conferred once more before Azjik spoke.

"Heir Volkummen, tell me your version of the events."

Heir Volkummen, in feigned piety, stepped forward and bowed.

"Your Most Graciousness," he began. "Upon word of intruders on your royal highway, I led my militia to investigate. What I found was my brother, Heir Theobald, engaged in battle with a band of Desert Pirates who were aided by some mercenaries. Knowing that he had entrusted this barbarian boy with a sacred treasure for you, I offered to bring it to you personally. But the boy resisted."

"Did the boy raise his sword against you?" Azjik asked, stroking his chin.

"No. He gripped the hilt of his sword and would have raised it if were it not for the interference of Heir Theobald. I ordered the boy to hand over the pouch to me, but he refused. Heir Theobald bade him to leave. Again, I instructed the boy to stay and hand me the pouch. At that point Heir Theobald drew his own sword against me and the boy fled."

The room erupted into gasps and whispers.

"So the boy did not threaten you directly?" Azjik asked. Volkummen nodded. The King's gaze turned to Tyrian briefly. "Such a brave boy, who brought me such a grand gift…. But one must be careful in this world, who one stands bravely against. Pride gets the better of the best man, young Tyrian. You will make a great soldier if you learn to let go of your own identity and become a simple tool of Azjik."

Tyrian looked down, sneaking a glance at Andoni, who looked down in fear. Farafah Fruz leaned in and whispered to Azjik; then the King spoke again.

"Is this account true, good Heir Gabriel?"

Gabriel's head lowered as he answered, "Your Highness, Heir Volkummen speaks the truth. Against your law I drew my sword aggressively against another heir. I did it with full knowledge and reason, and I did so out of fear that your treasure may not reach you. I accept whatever punishment you place upon me. I only ask that this boy be spared any tarnish from my transgression. He refused Volkummen's request at my orders."

"It pains me, Gabriel. You are one of my most trusted knights. There must be no trial if you admit to your failure. But let us recess while I consider your punishment."

Abruptly Azjik rose and exited the room, followed by his flock of advisors. Tyrian felt a collective breath of release as each group of men convened amongst themselves. Volkummen's men surrounded him. The guards gathered around the table to pick fruit from the bowl.

Tyrian ran to Gabriel.

"Your Honor, I am sorry."

"No, do not be sorry, Tyrian. You did as you were told."

"What will your punishment be?"

"We will find out soon enough. There is no use in trying to see the future. What comes of his word will be. We will not look back."

"But I have much to learn from you," Tyrian whispered urgently.

"And you may still. Life has a long tail, Tyrian. Worry not. But also remember you have much to learn from others, as well. Now go back to your place, they will be back soon."

Tyrian crossed the room, returning to Andoni's side. The room could sense Azjik's return and they all fell back into their positions, heads bowed.

Azjik took his seat again, Farafah Fruz at his side.

Tyrian's eyes were glued on Gabriel. He could not believe what was happening. He felt responsible. Could he have done something different?

"For your insolence, Heir Theobald, I will strip you of your seat in the Chamber of Heirs. You will no longer lead the militia of Coteville. That honor will now go to your countryman and trusted general, Dechaume."

"No!" Tyrian screamed. The entire room turned to him. Andoni motioned him to quiet.

But Azjik turned to him, "Oh, yes, barbarian boy. This kingdom is built upon order. I have a duty to the order of this kingdom to punish any man who breaks my laws. Especially an heir. There is a sacred covenant between an heir and his king. Gabriel Theobald broke that covenant." Then he turned once again to Gabriel, "In addition, Gabriel, you are banished from the kingdom and from your home of Coteville."

"And what of my wife and children?" Gabriel asked.

"They must move out of their home. They are welcome to stay in your state, but they must vacate for Heir Dechaume and his brood. You are now condemned to exile. You committed the deepest of crimes."

"Yes, your Highness. I understand."

"Your Highness," Heir Volkummen stepped forward and motioned to Tyrian with a smile, "I will gladly take the barbarian boy into my militia under my own personal tutelage. I will train him well for a place in your First Stand Army. Give him two years with me and he will be the strongest soldier you have."

"Thank you, Heir Volkummen. You are a hardened warrior and he will learn well from you. Agreed, then. Tyrian Fellhawk, you shall join Heir Volkummen's militia for two years, and then you will be welcomed into my personal army."

Tears ran down Tyrian's face as he found himself weighing his greatest ambition against his greatest fear. He was to be a soldier in the King's army, but only after years under a tyrant.

Azjik rose to his feet and his courtiers pulled the chair away, dispensing of it in the corner. The King announced, "Gabriel, you must leave at once. You may ride the Road of Fathers only into exile. Good day!" He turned and exited. The room was quiet for several moments. No one seemed to know what to do next.

Slowly, Gabriel crossed over to his friend Dechaume and knelt at his feet, taking his hand. "Even in exile I will pledge my honor to Coteville and her brave heir. May your God-twin guide you well."

"Gabriel, my heart is with you always," Dechaume replied, choking back tears.

Gabriel embraced Croucien and the rest of his Cote officers and then quietly exited the room, without looking back.

Tyrian watched him disappear into the hallway like a figure in a dream being lost to wakefulness. He could still feel his mentor's presence hanging in the chamber. Tyrian wondered if it was Gabriel's God-twin, lingering, watching, saying its own goodbye.

Tyrian was frozen, unable to move, refusing to let Gabriel's absence become real.

# # #

Tyrian stood in the shadows of the main exit of the castle atrium. With the stillness of a cat, he appeared serene. The calm on his face and the softness in his eyes did not betray his anxiety. His anger heated his insides, as much as before, but his skin felt cold to the touch. His eyes scanned the plaza beyond, back and forth, sweeping the warm Ocuvian tiles serenely. He would wait as long as it took.

Finally, he heard some men approaching and ducked further into the dark corner. He could see three men descending the wide staircase and coming towards him. There were two guards, one on either side of Gabriel. His mentor walked proudly upright and looked straight ahead. They passed the boy and exited out onto the main yard. Tyrian ducked out of his hiding place and followed quietly.

He could see the guards stop and motion Gabriel on. They watched him walk solemnly towards the Road of Fathers. The guards eventually turned and entered the castle again, not seeing Tyrian, who crouched behind a large planter.

When he was confident they were gone he ran towards Gabriel, catching up with him. Even as his feet touched the soft, deep brown surface of the King's highway, he cursed it. The Road of Fathers had brought him nothing but disappointment and cruelty.

"Your Honor!" Tyrian called out.

Gabriel stopped and turned back. Speaking quietly but urgently he asked, "Tyrian, what are you doing?"

Tyrian looked down. Tears welled up. He was afraid to speak, for fear of letting go of his emotions.

Gabriel reached out and gripped Tyrian's arm tightly. He felt the boy's biceps suddenly relax, and his shoulders drop ever so slightly. Tyrian breathed out, comforted by Gabriel's gaze.

"You must go back," the Heir stated firmly.

"Heir Volkummen is the devil," Tyrian whispered. "I can see it in his eyes."

"He may well possess as much evil as a mortal man can possess, but he is, ultimately, only a mortal."

"He means to destroy me," Tyrian declared. "He will not forget our moments in the desert. Your Honor, he will try and break my soul!"

"He does not have the ability to break your soul. Only you have the ability to put out that fire," Gabriel stated forcefully. "He may well try, in his ignorance. But if you set your mind to it, you will win that battle."

"I am going with you," Tyrian suddenly said.

"No! You are not. You cannot. Your path has been laid out for you."

Tyrian did not move or speak. He wanted to stay in Gabriel's grasp longer.

At last, Tyrian gathered himself, straighted up and made his intentions clear, "I will train in the cruel, cold winds of Fulldalr. I will sustain a thousand lashes from my new heir. I will carry his firewood and feed his horses. I will sharpen his blade and shine his helmet. I will bow to my new heir, your Honor, knowing that one day, I will strike him down."

"I would counsel you another way, my boy, but I know it would do no good. If that motivates your survival, then you must care for that fire each and every day. But do not let that overshadow your own growth and reason."

"It will enrich me. And I will find justice, your Honor. If it is my own justice, unconnected to the false order granted by our king, so be it. But I will find justice in this land."

"You have learned much in a short time."

Gabriel finally released his grip. Tyrian straightened up again and his jaw tightened. Their eyes locked on each other.

"There are dark days ahead," Gabriel said gravely. "Who knows what armies lurk on the horizon? Who knows what this new superior army will be entrusted with? We must be cautious and alert. Our union has not been severed, Tyrian."

"I still have much to learn from you," Tyrian reiterated. "I will see you again. Take care of yourself, master."

With no more courtesies, Tyrian turned and walked back into the ever darkening shadows of the castle's oppressive walls.

Gabriel watched the boy's figure disappear, then turned and proceeded slowly into exile.

Chapter Twenty

Tyrian Fellhawk woke up cold. He rose from his bed to close the window, but it was not open. There was no breeze coming in. As he pulled back the heavy velvet curtains to check his surroundings, the glare of the low sun blinded him. He let the curtain fall back into place. Once again in darkness, he pulled on his trousers and blouse.

And still he felt a chill.

He sat on the bed, staring at the closed door before him. One night ago it had seemed like a majestic gateway to his future. But now he only saw the threshold to his sorrow.

He could not move. His paralysis was not actually physical, and it was not out of fear. He simply felt that his legs had nowhere to take him. His arms had nothing to reach for. Tyrian was not in despair, though. He was merely waiting.

Eventually he stirred and covered himself with his worn and dirty cloak, but still he felt a chill. The winter of Fulldalr seemed to be reaching through great distances to grip him.

There was a knock at the door, then an anxious voice on the other side said, "Tyrian, it is Andoni. May I enter?"

"Yes, come in, Andoni."

After his friend had entered, Tyrian asked, "Are there no guards keeping watch on my door?"

"They have all gone," Andoni replied. "There is no one to guard any longer. We are not prisoners. Heir Gabriel has gone into exile. All of the militias are preparing to leave. You must join the Fulldalr party soon."

"Yes. I suppose so."

Tyrian rose and began gathering his things while Andoni watched him.

"I will be sorry to see you leave, Tyrian. You have become a friend."

"I would have it another way if the choice were mine. But these are the roads laid before us."

"The world is so different today," Andoni exclaimed. "All I have known is Gabriel Theobald as my heir and general. And what will become of beautiful Océane?"

"You will see Gabriel Theobald again one day. Just as you will see me again, one day. I hold fast to my belief that you and I are not meant to be casual acquaintances. We may well fight side-by-side again one day. But, most assuredly, we will sit and share wine and tell stories of our adventures."

Andoni grabbed Tyrian's arm clumsily.

"Go," Tyrian said quietly. "Join your militia. And I will join mine."

Andoni smiled, and then exited.

# # #

Tyrian found the Fulldalr Militia assembled in the main plaza; forty horses and wagons were packed and dressed for a long journey. Heir Volkummen and his lead general and trusted confidant, Greit Schultheis, stood off to one side, smoking pipes of tobacco and conversing. Tyrian watched them from the castle entrance. The chill hit him again. He wrapped his cloak tighter around his shoulders.

He breathed in, closing his eyes.

Sounds danced along the edges of his consciousness: horseshoes on tile, wind whistling through hallways and doorways, muffled conversation outside. He fell into a deep meditation, reaching out for his God-twin. Slowly, he was able to raise the ceiling of his consciousness, pushing the sounds further out, until one faint voice crept in, stealing in from the cracks of his silence. "Tend... tend... tend... fire... tend... fire... fire...." The words took shape slowly: "Tend... to... your... fire... Tend to your fire."

# # #

Satisfied with his God-twin's words, Tyrian marched out into the main castle plaza. He stepped into the circle of horses and approached Heir Volkummen closely. The red-haired heir stepped back, unused to such direct contact.

"Throw your belongings in that wagon over there, boy."

"I will keep my belongings with me."

Volkummen looked the boy up and down and then leaned in to lock eyes with him.

"You will soon lose that tone of voice, Tyrian Fellhawk. You are now under my command. I am now your master."

"I am from the Great River Forest and I have no master. I will ride with you and fight for you. You will demonstrate what you know, and I will take what I choose from it. But you will never be my master," Tyrian stated plainly yet firmly.

"Your anger will not help you with me, boy," Volkummen hissed. "When I am done with you, you will know no allegiance but to me. I will take that anger from you as if I was chewing meat from a bone."

"Heir Volkummen, you need not worry. My anger is in a safe place that you will never find. For now, I submit to your leadership. For now."

With that, Tyrian moved away. He was pointed to a horse and saddled it, looking northward upon the Road of Fathers and imagining Gabriel's lonely journey. The voices around him dissipated. He waited for the militia to begin its journey. It would take weeks to reach his new home of Fulldalr.

But, for the moment, Tyrian waited, patiently.

More from this author

Steven R. Barron is an author and filmmaker. Films include the award-winning shorts: *SKIN*, ***History is Tradition*** and the feature, ***Investigations of a Dog***. Steven is currently in post production with his newest feature length drama, Shadows & Forms.

Mr. Barron is currently working on the second novel in Tyrian's journey, titled ***The Road to Anarchy.***

Look for the short story, ***The Princess and the Anarchist***, soon, which shows the further adventures of the mercenary, Gorka Osa.

Get a free copy of Tyrian's journeys and follow Steven R. Barron on his official blog:

http://tyrianfellhawk.wix.com/srb-blog